Cherry Whip
Twentieth Anniversary Edition

Michael Antman

Donovan Street Press Inc.

DONOVAN STREET PRESS

Library and Archives Canada Cataloguing in Publication

Title: Cherry Whip / Michael Antman.

Names: Antman, Michael, author.

Description: Twentieth anniversary edition. I Previously published: ENC Press, 2004.

Identifiers: Canadiana (print) 20250211335 I Canadiana (ebook) 20250211475 I ISBN 9781069096586

(hardcover) I ISBN 9781069096579 (softcover) I ISBN 9781069096562 (EPUB)

Subjects: LCGFT: Novels.

Classification: LCC PS3601.N755 C44 2025 I DDC 813/.6—dc23

COVER DESIGN:

Andrew Rogers, Joslin Lake Design

donovanstreetpress.com

To Irina

Foreword

Cherry Whip, presented here in its 20th Anniversary edition, is a novel about the mystery of human character in all of its wild and unfathomable diversity.

I cannot overstate the innovativeness of Cherry Whip in its tremendously convincing focus on the mental processes of character, not often enough encountered in recent literary fiction, especially when that focus is trained on a character with a background entirely different than that of the author. (Though this act of "imaginative sympathy" is, I believe, central to the art of writing fiction, it is nonetheless sometimes regarded as off limits by many figures in contemporary culture.)

Any doubts the reader may have about the author's habitation of a character very much unlike him will be dispelled by the brio of the novel's opening section, in which Michael Antman atomizes the Japanese protagonist Hiroshi's perceptions of a world that is not only unfamiliar, but utterly overwhelming to him in its sensory assault. That world, New York City, functions almost as a second major character in the book, and at times as a kind of antagonist to the sensitive, artistic, but utterly oblivious Hiroshi.

The novel also takes place in Hiroshi's dreamlike memories of the small town in Japan where he grew up. In its depiction of an eerie "Forbidden Pathway" outside that town, and in the fey imaginings of the main character's disturbed older sister, it is difficult to avoid comparing Cherry Whip to some of the novels of the great Japanese novelist Haruki Murakami. However, whereas Murakami is largely concerned with the mystery of existence, Cherry Whip is about the mystery of character.

Michael Antman brings to his novel a wealth of enthusiasms, for food, music, language, and an unrelenting attentiveness to the sensory experience. For other novelists, these are sometimes portrayed as distractions from the true core of life. For the author, they constitute the very essence of that life — a personhood that is only fully realized, however, when we confront, and understand, what motivates us, as Hiroshi finally manages to do by the book's conclusion. The ending gave me chills, as I believe it will to any reader who follows Hiroshi's arduous, often comical journey to self discovery.

Christopher Guerin

Christopher Guerin is the author of the short story collections Loverless Love *and* The Story of My Universe and Other Stories, *and* My Human Disguise, *a collection of 625 sonnets.*

Part One

1

From the moment he'd hit American ground, the ground had been hitting back.

Hiroshi's command of English was as close to flawless as that of any Japanese person he'd ever known who hadn't actually lived anywhere further west than Fukuoka. His vocabulary was quite large. It was, he thought in English and in an atypically un-Japanese and un-Hiroshi way, something to be *reckoned*.

Or was that reckoned *with*? He made a mental note, again in English, to check the phrase in his precious, though currently un-pocketed, pocket dictionary of idioms.

Hiroshi was just as proud of his English pronunciation, of the way his tongue and palate could pick their way light-footedly through, for example, "particularly," a word even many native English speakers had difficulty with, unconsciously substituting "especially" whenever they could.

And he was proud, as well, of the way he'd handled this crucial trip, his first ever to America, where he was, in some very small circles in Manhattan at least, well-regarded and eagerly anticipated.

His flight over had been trouble-free, and, once he was on the ground, his heavy backpack and duffel bag had leapt puppy-like off the carousel to greet him. Well, alright, actually he'd yanked them off with one hand, and in fact with some difficulty, having to hold on at every moment with his other hand to the old-fashioned baguette-shaped case containing his $4,000 clarinet, a father's gift.

But at least both of the bags were there, and he'd managed with trembling arm (trembling, he'd hastened to assure himself at the time, with weight, not nerves) to maneuver them through a fluttery opening in a troupe of eleven-or twelve-year-old girls in olive-green uniforms who'd flown with him from Narita – Girl Scouts, he was fairly sure.

But was it, in fact, a "troupe," as one would call a group of itinerant actors, or a "troop"? That was the question that, along with the "reckoned with" issue, troubled the surface of Hiroshi's mind as he wavered on the jute mat in front of a hardware store on Lexington Avenue, three blocks west of Central Park and two long blocks south of the Academy, in Manhattan, New York, U.S.A.

Hiroshi wavered in a figurative sense, wanting very much to go into the store but knowing that if he lingered he might arrive at the Academy late for his first and only Master Class, and in a literal sense, because the jute mat was so stiff, with such large and distinct jutes – *jutes?* – that it was almost impossible to stand still without rocking from side to side.

Maybe this was due to the fact that he wasn't heavy enough to compress the stiff fibers – Hiroshi weighed only 126 pounds – and perhaps such rugged foot mats, designed to vigorously scrub any soles that entered the store, were a good thing in a country where people strolled with their shoes still on right off streets where dogs had been walking, into not just hardware stores but homes.

Still, below the surface of his mind, where he pondered

vocabulary questions and savored the memory of the incredibly delicious hot pastrami sandwich he'd had the moment he'd dropped his bags — though not his clarinet — at the hotel, even below a deeper level of his mind, where he contemplated the fact that he was expected by a group, a troupe, of jazz prodigies and protégés barely younger than he, there dwelt a tactile awareness that something was not quite right.

This awareness had begun not with the subtle swaying he was currently experiencing, but a half hour before, as he'd walked to his current location from the delicatessen where he'd triumphantly ordered his first-ever hot pastrami sandwich. His instructions had been to take a taxi directly from his hotel in Gramercy Park to the Academy, which was on 72nd and Lex, but he'd jumped out of the cab when it reached 59th Street, fearful he wouldn't find a real New York deli near Central Park. He was a great walker. But the whole distance from 59th to 70th, he'd scraped and scuffed the soles of his shoes on the New York sidewalks again and again, as if there were waves in the neat squares of asphalt. He'd stumbled once, and banged his sneaker-clad big toe against a sidewalk crack twice.

Could it be, he wondered at some level he wasn't quite aware of, that the sidewalks in New York were slightly higher than those in Tokyo? But that was absurd, he sensed without thinking it through, because if the sidewalks were a bit higher, he would be higher, too.

Or could it be the first symptoms of a neurological disorder such as amyotrophic lateral sclerosis (a medical term even he did not know in English, but the general idea of which he was familiar with), which would eventually render him, his recording career just beginning to pick up steam (a head of steam?), unable even to grasp his clarinet?

Of course, it was likely nothing other than jet lag – he'd

had some concert dates in Europe last year, but had never flown as far as this before. So, without being truly aware that he was testing the theory, Hiroshi decided to walk the three blocks to Central Park — even though that would leave him at the bare minimum five blocks from the Academy — just to see if he would stumble on the uneven ground or display other symptoms of an acute neurological crisis.

First, though, he walked into the hardware store, where he stumbled almost immediately over a warp in the old-fashioned wooden floor. He became rather desperately worried.

But this was fascinating – not merely hardware, which he'd always loved, but *American* hardware, different in clever and surprising ways. The excitement, accordingly, began to crowd out the corporeal concern. It would be impossible, he reflected, to describe to a homebody like his girlfriend just how stimulating it was to be in a place like this where everything was slightly different – it was like jumping back into his consciousness as a four-year-old, except that he had little intention, as much as he might want to, of jumping up and down excitedly.

For no reason in particular, he had an erection.

It was his first erection ever in America. It seemed to be his first of any sort in quite a while, whatever that might mean. It seemed to mean something quite important. He thought again, fleetingly, of his girlfriend and their last night together, then sent the image packing to another country.

Exceeding his initial expectations, this hardware store actually appeared to be some sort of antiquated general-purpose store, with racks of neat square packets with idealized illustrations of flowers on them — containing seeds no doubt — and a small section for toys, and another small section with greeting cards and candies and woven baskets for Easter. It was April in New York.

Hiroshi had seen Easter paraphernalia before, of course –

the Japanese celebrate, or at least sell gifts that are designed to take advantage of, virtually every Western holiday except for Groundhog Day. But much of what he saw now was fascinatingly strange. A small package, shaped like half of an egg, called "Cherry Whip." *That* was interesting. It wasn't even whip-shaped, like that detestable licorice stuff. Obviously, it was some kind of sweet, and, as the beef and mustard taste in his mouth was beginning to turn to mud, he bought the candy, intending to eat it.

But then he remembered the entire embryonic sack that was at this moment curled up in one corner of the overstuffed duffel bag he had pulled off the carousel earlier today, waiting to be filled as full as its brother for the return trip – though not, as the original bag would be, with dirty laundry and American magazines, but with souvenirs. There were a few items here that would make appropriate o-miyage, and the candy egg, he reflected, would be nice for his little half-brother, Manabu, five this month.

So he bought the egg, as well as a pretty packet of marigold seeds and a small flat plastic case containing miniature tools of various configurations, and, paper bag in one hand and clarinet case in the other, headed back into the street.

He arrived at Central Park at one o'clock, just the moment his Master Class was scheduled to begin. He cared, on one level, but on another and very unfamiliar one, did not.

The breeze was beautiful. He was aware that Central Park had a "dangerous" reputation, particularly – *particularly*! – in outdated Japanese guidebooks. But it was such a sparkling day, and he was a soon-to-be-somewhat-famous jazz musician, and if any miscreants – he'd known that word for a long time, though he had no reason ever to use it – bothered him, he'd pull out his clarinet and pacify them with a song.

Because it wasn't possible, after all the distance that he'd traveled, that there would be any disasters now.

He wandered for a few minutes, looking at the pretty young women and the angry young men, and found himself in a glen, if that was the right word – a sort of meadow. It was incongruous in the middle of a city that was almost as big as Tokyo, but here was a wide expanse of green with no one at all around. He was north of the zoo, and probably pretty close to 72nd Street.

Hiroshi put down his paper bag and opened up his clarinet case. He didn't know of another clarinetist with such an expensive instrument, a rare, silver-plated pre-war Yamaha model that used the outdated Albert fingering system. His father had more or less forced the gift on him, but he had to admit it was a nice piece of work; he'd decided the students would enjoy seeing a piece of history. And what a beautiful and fitting thing it would be to play some klezmer or a few bars of, perhaps, "Green Dolphin Street" right here in the park with no audience at all, where the only ones who could hear him would be the ghosts of all the jazz musicians he'd ever admired. Practically every one of them had played in this city at one time or another, and he himself would be playing with one of the best working bands in the business just two nights from now.

He picked up the clarinet and began to play. And then, just as quickly, stopped. Out of the corner of his eye, he noticed an odd bobbing motion and looked over to see, underneath a magnificent oak-like tree, an enormous crow pecking at something.

He placed the clarinet carefully back in its case, closed it up, and leaned over to pick up the paper bag, stepping on it in the process and causing the bag to rip. The screwdrivers and awls and miniature wrenches, which had somehow come loose from their little hard plastic kit, spilled onto the patchy grass.

Hiroshi, reminded in this manner that he was having some trouble walking today, stuffed the loose tools and the plastic case, along with a few bits of unanchored grass, into the left pocket of his crisp white slacks, the one that normally held his English idiom dictionary, and the candy egg into the right. This took longer than expected; his hands were a bit numb for some reason, perhaps because of the weight of the luggage he'd carried earlier.

He left the torn bag and the packet of marigold seeds on the ground, amusing himself with the fancy that the next heavy rain would soak the packet and germinate the seeds right there.

When he straightened up to leave, he noticed that despite all his fumblings, the crow had remained unruffled. Hiroshi walked closer to see if it would frighten, but it hunched over its hidden meal, flapped its stiff, curtain-like wings, and pecked away.

By the time Hiroshi approached within a foot or so of the crow, it had backed off irritably – could one say peckishly? – but still had not flown away. Whatever the crow was eating was now partially visible and was, most notably, a brilliant violet color. Hiroshi stared at it a moment before he realized that it was an Easter egg – a real one, dyed that color, not a candy one – and the crow was lunching on the hard-boiled egg inside.

Hiroshi looked at his watch. Fifteen minutes had passed. Suddenly filled with a familiar dread and shame – the Japanese, rather than the jazz, part of his personality – he began running out of the park and in the direction of his class. He stopped once at the park exit to get his bearings and to consult the insanely detailed, intricately folded, hand-drawn map of the

Upper East Side that he'd had in his wallet for the past three weeks, and then dashed across Fifth Avenue. On the entire breathless run to 72nd and Lex, he didn't stumble once.

* * *

BY THE TIME the Master Class was concluded, his students, as well as the faculty that had sponsored his appearance and partially subsidized his trip to America, had completely forgotten his tardiness, which in any event was easily excused by his long flight and his evident genius. For these students, and of course the instructors who had sat in, knew enough about jazz to recognize that this slight young Japanese man playing an out-of-fashion model of an out-of-fashion instrument was the real deal.

Hiroshi sat in front of the class soaking in the students' adulation, one hand pushing back his floppy black hair with the powder-blue streak, his only outward concession to hipness – he also had a silver-gray streak, no wider than a pin, that interrupted his right eyebrow, but that was an accident of nature – and his other hand dandling his clarinet on his bent knee. He'd played "April Mist" and "Bossa Antigua" and a couple of his own typically soft and poignant compositions, and talked a little bit about his theory of improvisation. His giddiness had almost disappeared, and his customary modesty was reasserting itself, but still he was enjoying every minute of this. He felt, much like the saying he'd once heard, like the kid in a candy store.

He was no kid. He was twenty-three, and was not only an up-and-coming jazz musician, but an accomplished amateur judo practitioner with an interest in hardware, merengue, and sports cars, and with a beautiful girlfriend back home. Why was he reminding himself of all this right now, he wondered, as the students gathered around him?

Because he wasn't back home? Or because his girlfriend was?

He began to realize that, of all the fifteen or so students, there were only three young women and, of the three, only one that was attractive. He wasn't the type of guy to make a point of classifying crowds in such a manner, but he wasn't the type of guy to play his clarinet in the park, either. Sonny Rollins had practiced on the Brooklyn Bridge, but that was New York, and he was from Tokyo. He wasn't even really from Tokyo; until he went away to college, he'd spent his entire life in a little country town called Ichikawa.

Except that he was in New York right now, and he had two weeks of intensive exploration ahead of him.

Her name was Maureen, the pretty one, and she was a petite, burstingly energetic redhead, with an intelligent, skeptical, narrow-eyed gaze. She knew a couple of words of Japanese – "arigato," pronounced incorrectly, and the like – and she used them playfully on Hiroshi when it became her turn to thank him for the class. She talked a bit about her instrument, the soprano saxophone, and her idol, Jane Ira Bloom. Hiroshi, in turn, complimented her again on her playing – some of the students had been given the opportunity to play a short piece to be critiqued, and Hiroshi had given her a detailed but positive evaluation then and simple praise now. During the class, she had apparently been too nervous to react with great pleasure, but now she gave him a genuine and uncomplicated smile.

A couple of other students crowded her out. They'd both decided that Hiroshi looked like Ichiro Suzuki, the baseball player; he didn't. Then, in the general after-class commotion, she was gone.

Hiroshi managed to catch a glimpse of her as she departed – her compact little form, her ponytail gathered up with a green rubber band, the slap of her sandals. She was a bundle of something or other, Hiroshi could see that. Maybe trouble. Trouble or fun. He hoped he'd find out; all of the students had been invited to his weekend gig.

When Hiroshi hit the street, he was again elated, though in a way that seemed to entail a certain degree of gravity that hadn't been there before in the park or in the hardware store. He meandered for a while, stopped for a papaya drink at a dirty little hot dog stand, and then strolled into a very narrow and astonishingly long and well-stocked magazine store, with the delicious sense that he had nothing at all to do before his first rehearsal tomorrow night. He could see the songs from the set list whole. Indeed, the first or second time he listened to a new song, he could see the entire thing in his mind; better yet, he could see the arc of his improvisations from beginning to end too, just at the moment he launched into them – it wasn't in any way planned, and, if not quite the opposite of, then at a very different angle from the majority of players, who had in mind new chord changes or bits of melody they'd been practicing when they began to solo. Unlike them, Hiroshi didn't have any plans about where he wanted to go in his solos, but there was an absolute and pleasing inevitability once he'd gotten there.

As he flipped through a copy of *Car and Driver*, he saw out of the corner of his eye a pretty young woman, and surreptitiously looked over at her pleasing profile. The young woman turned and smiled directly at Hiroshi, which shocked him unutterably. In much less than a second, he realized it was Maureen, and he felt a different sort of shock.

Maureen was holding in one hand, its pages flopping loosely down, a copy of *Hemming's Auto News*. Hiroshi was only able to read its title by looking down at the level where she was letting it dangle and got, in the process, a quick glimpse of her sleek legs. She didn't look, Hiroshi thought, like the sort of young woman who'd be interested in cars. But then it occurred to him that he was standing in the automotive section and that perhaps she had picked up a title at random in order to be close to him.

It was incumbent upon him to say something. He thought about slotting his magazine back into its correct position on the rack, but decided it would take too long and, if the magazine refused to slide in neatly, bore too much potential for humiliation. So he held onto it and said, "I was very impressed by your playing. You've put a lot of work into your craft."

Hiroshi immediately felt foolish – this was now the third time he had complimented her – but she flushed to the roots of her red hair, smiled, and seemed pleased. Crazily, Hiroshi stuck out his hand to shake hers, and she was forced to quickly jam her magazine back into the rack to shake his back.

He never shook hands in Japan, it just wasn't done, but he'd felt in that instant that he had to do something. And indeed, as she took his light grip, he felt that what he had done was alright. Their hands moved up and down together. Hiroshi, minutely relieved, moved to withdraw the grip, but Maureen held onto it, would not let go, and gave Hiroshi a smile both skeptical and, he thought, flirtatious.

At this moment, at this very moment on an early spring evening in Manhattan, holding this young woman's soft hand, Hiroshi experienced – within the space of perhaps a second-and-a-half after the up-and-down motion stopped and before the separation of hands had commenced – so many different emotions that he felt he might once again sway or stumble in the middle of the blindingly bright store:

More than anything else he felt surprised, for although Japanese people didn't customarily shake hands, he knew enough about how Americans did it to know that they didn't customarily *hold on.*

He also felt puzzlement: What exactly did she mean by doing this?

And he felt a thrilling sense of anticipation, as if, at this moment, he were at the edge of a long, complicated tunnel that, once entered, would hurl him downwards through the interior of a cliff, emerging, about to fall, hundreds of feet above a sparkling sea.

He felt, for precisely the same reason that he felt this anticipation, fear.

He also felt embarrassment that people would see the two of them and assume something odd was going on – an embarrassment exacerbated by his foreignness and more specifically by his Japanese predilection for feeling embarrassed.

Beyond the embarrassment, he also felt shame, shame that she had somehow "caught" him, figured out (though it wasn't exactly true) that he'd praised her only to intrigue her, "get" her.

And beyond the shame and embarrassment, or perhaps as an instantaneous and self-protective corrective to the shame and embarrassment, he felt pique – she had no right to catch him attempting to catch her, and thereby make something unnecessarily complicated out of simple praise.

And yet, more fundamentally than embarrassment and shame and fear and pique, he also felt sexual excitement, very nearly lust, due not only to her physical proximity and to her smooth hand inside of his, but also because she was so clearly willing to be caught.

And, yet again, another layer of shame, but now of a different sort — that his sexual desires were so easily manipulated.

These were some of the emotions he experienced, without being fully aware of them, in the first second or so that their hands lay warmly but motionlessly together. There were still others, occurring perhaps a half second later, as their hands parted, and which were stationed, emotionally, at a slightly more distant remove.

He felt self-righteousness, a sense (though he knew it was insincere) that he was merely a disinterested observer, and that the handshake she had held for an extra second was merely an interesting American phenomenon along the lines of a miniature set of pliers and screwdrivers.

There was, as well, a tinge of self-pity, a sense that once again, as had happened to him so often in the past, he was being misinterpreted. What was the big deal about just shaking someone's hand?

Then there was a sense of calculation. How, he asked himself, do I get this pretty girl out of this overlit magazine store and into my bed at the Gramercy West Hotel?

But along with this calculation came a feeling of paralysis.

Which is to say, how indeed?

And self-doubt dwelt there as well – her expression was half-skeptical for a reason. Did she suspect that her playing wasn't as good as he thought it was? And was she in fact right? Where was his taste? Did he suspend his judgment of her musical ability because she was sexy?

And along with this, a deeper reassessment, a disturbing flicker that came and went in an instant, that maybe he didn't have the ability to teach music at all. Or to play it.

But above it all, transcending it all, wiping out all but the barest margins of the other emotions, there was pride. She likes me. She likes me!

And finally, though he wasn't fully conscious of more than a few of these emotions (the actual count being sixteen) at the moment, and would have confidently asserted in other circumstances that such a large number couldn't possibly be experienced by any human being, even below the level of consciousness, in the space of a second and a half (although, to be precise, some of them lingered in the next second or two after their hands finally drew apart), nonetheless, concerning the relative handful of emotions he did register at the moment their hands were clasped, and the few others he recollected in the few seconds after their hands parted, there arose a seventeenth emotion: a sense of wonderment that he could feel so many overlapping and partially contradictory emotions at once.

He was also aware (at least until he became aware of its non-presence) that none of his emotions or thoughts concerned his beautiful girlfriend back in Japan.

Outside of Hiroshi's mind, in the middle of a magazine store in the middle of Manhattan, his hand and Maureen's hand, which to an outside observer hadn't been joined for a period of time so long as to appear in the least bit odd, slid gently apart. Hiroshi finished thinking about all of the things he was capable of thinking about as he smiled at Maureen and Maureen smiled back at him.

His hands still felt numb.

And then Hiroshi realized that, at the moment he had first held out his hand to Maureen, she had been forced to jam her magazine back into the rack – which made him feel a little guilty, now that he thought about it, though that wasn't at all the point – the point being, she had been forced to jam her magazine back into the rack because her other hand had been gripping a small canvas shopping bag.

And yet (continuing this same thought) he had maintained his hold on his own magazine before, during, and after the handshake.

In short, one of his hands had been holding her hand, while the other hand had been holding the *Car and Driver* magazine.

So which of his hands – he had two, not three – was holding the case containing his one-of-a-kind $4,000 clarinet?

His smile faded, and he experienced an instantaneous eruption of acid in the base of his stomach, which flooded his mouth with the taste of rancid papaya and rotten pastrami and which washed out every one of those seventeen interesting emotions his mind had been playing with.

"Oh my God."

Maureen looked genuinely concerned and puzzled. Somewhere behind his panic, he liked that fact.

"What is it? What's wrong, Mr. Mori?"

"Hiroshi. I think I lost my clarinet."

"Did you go back to your hotel?"

"No, I came straight from the class to this shop."

"Well, then, you must of left it at the class. Don't worry about it. We'll just walk back and get it."

"No, because I remember having it with me at the hot dog store."

"What hot dog store?"

"The one where I had my fruit drink."

"When did you have this fruit drink?"

"Right after I left the class."

"So you didn't come straight here from the class."

"No."

"So, Hiroshi," she said very slowly and carefully, "if you had it at the hot dog store – do you mean a *restaurant*, or a *stand?* – and you don't have it here" – she quickly scanned the narrow store to make sure the clarinet case wasn't lying in the middle of the floor – "then I think the thing to do is to find this place where you think you had your fruit drink and go back there and see if they have it."

"I think that's a good idea," Hiroshi said. "Thank you."

"You're welcome. Now, do you know either the name or the location of this particular establishment?" Hiroshi observed with some irritation that a note of condescension had begun to enter her voice, but he was too worried to care.

"I'm not sure, but I think I could lead you there. I just stopped there for a papaya drink."

"Papaya? *Papaya?* Then I know exactly the place you're talking about." She whirled around and marched out of the store, her eagerness and alacrity instantly wiping out in Hiroshi's mind the bad feelings he'd had about her momentary lapse into condescension.

They ran down the street together, and though he was beside himself with worry and panic and nausea, he couldn't help feeling a certain sense of excitement that he was running down the street with the likes of *her.* And that she was running down the street to help *him.*

* * *

THE LITTLE COUNTERMAN at the little hot dog restaurant looked suitably sympathetic. "You left your clarinet here?"

"I think I probably did," Hiroshi said. "Yes."

"How much was it worth?"

Hiroshi was concerned with the past tense in the question, but Maureen quickly whirled around Hiroshi, interceded herself between him and the counterman and asked, like his attorney, "Why would you want to know how much it's worth? To sell it?"

The little counterman laughed. "Naw, just wondering. I like clarinets."

"Do you play?" Hiroshi asked irrelevantly.

"No, but I listen to a lot of jazz."

Hiroshi was impatient, but interested. "Like who?"

"Oh, Boney James, guys like that."

Hiroshi had never heard of such a name. Maureen said, "Alright, listen, could you please check in the back to see if you have it." It wasn't a question.

The counterman said, addressing Hiroshi, "I do remember

you bringing it in here. You ordered a hot dog and a papaya drink. You put the clarinet case on the counter next to your tray, drank your drink and left the hot dog without touching it."

"I ordered a hot dog? I don't remember that."

"Yeah, I'm sure you did. Because I remember wondering if it was the first hot dog you'd ever tasted."

"They are not so uncommon in Japan."

"Anyway, I brought the tray and the hot dog behind the counter in case you came back. I still have it."

Maureen was close to bursting. "You saved the hot dog? The sixty-nine cent hot dog! What about his $4,000 clarinet? Why don't you check behind the counter for a $4,000 clarinet and forget about a fucking hot dog!"

The counterman shrugged. "I figured he took it with him. Listen, this is a small place. I know the clarinet's not here. Probably someone else picked it up off the counter while I was busy ringing up another customer. You wanna check? Be my guest. Come on back and look around."

Maureen and Hiroshi did just that, scouring every corner of the little restaurant, looking in every clarinet-shaped and – sized cranny in the kitchen and behind the counter.

"Probably," the counterman said as they searched, "you just got a little distracted because you just got here from Japan."

"How did you know that?" Maureen demanded.

"Because he told me," the counterman said. "We talked about all kinds of things. He probably just had bad jet lag. I mean, he was acting like he had bad jet lag. How can you get right off an airplane from Japan without any sleep and not be screwed up?"

Hiroshi had had plenty of sleep on the plane. During the thirteen-hour flight, he had read nine magazines – six in Japanese and three in English. He had flipped through a

Colors of Bennetton book, had read the first twenty pages or so, in English, of John Le Carre's novel *The Honourable Schoolboy*, had listened, on his portable CD player and only when the flight attendant had said he was authorized to do so, to Monteverdi, Moby, Haydn, the Hollies, Lambchop, Lester Young, Count Basie, Tim Buckley and Clifford Brown, and had eaten, in addition to the regular airline meals, a small bag of wasabi peanuts, drunk two small bottles of bourbon on the rocks, and consumed half a bottle of pickled ginger to combat airsickness, which he had never in his life actually experienced. And he had slept.

Now he felt not particularly tired at all. Depressed and elated. Panicked and relaxed. Hungry and overstuffed. But not tired. He looked at the tray containing his uneaten hot dog – which he still had no memory of ordering – and contemplated taking it with him back onto the street, since it was the only object belonging to him he was likely to find in this little place. Then he started to worry about mad cow disease, and the hot dog was again forgotten.

Hiroshi offered to accompany Maureen back to the subway and from there, perhaps, though this part of the offer was unverbalized, to her apartment in Chelsea. It felt very strange. In Japan, it was mostly the women who did the asking. Nonetheless, she assented readily, at least to the spoken, subway part of the offer, though no matter where they ended up parting, Hiroshi told himself, all he wanted was a distraction from his expensive and painful loss.

The early evening was soft and warm. They walked to the subway in silence. Hiroshi, after a moment, said, "Shall we go to the police?"

"Sure, but we might as well wait until tomorrow. You have insurance, right?"

Hiroshi, distracted for a moment by her use of the word "we," didn't answer, causing her, in turn, to look at him with alarm. Then he said, "Yes, of course. I have insurance on everything."

"Good. Because you'll need a police report to file your claim. They're not actually going to look for the clarinet itself, you know. Don't you?"

Hiroshi didn't answer. Maureen said, "Are you upset?"

"I guess I'm upset. Sure. I brought another clarinet with me, a regular Regent for performing, and I've got plenty of reeds, but this clarinet was really special, not just because of the cost, either. But at the same time, I'm happy to be in New York and happy..."

Maureen suddenly grabbed him around the waist and kissed him lightly on the lips. "Hey, Hiroshi. It isn't that complicated. Okay?" She looked at him steadily.

Hiroshi felt himself getting another erection. He hoped it wouldn't collide with one of those loose screwdrivers on the way up. At just that moment, Maureen said, "Oh my God, you really did a number on your pants!"

Hiroshi looked down at his pants in a panic and discovered a little mustard stain on his crotch, right at about the point his erection had just been, but no longer was. But it was such a small and unassuming stain it was hard to see how she could have noticed it. He laughed nervously and a bit wretchedly.

"Listen," Maureen said, "it's been a long day for you."

"Can I accompany you to your apartment?"

"I wouldn't want you falling asleep on me," she said. They walked the last few steps to the subway and she turned, brushing her breast – accidentally? – against the side of his arm. She murmured, "Good night," smiled back at him, and disappeared.

Hiroshi wandered away in a daze. What did she mean, he wondered, by saying she wouldn't want him to fall asleep on her? Did she mean physically on top of her, while they were making love? He would never fall asleep under such circumstances, no matter how tired he was.

Or did "on," in this case, merely mean, "while in the company of, and therefore responsible for?"

Hiroshi pondered this for a while as he walked slowly back in the direction of his hotel, though he wasn't entirely sure he was walking in the right direction. He'd have to hail a taxi eventually. Then, without resolving the question, he turned his attention to her earlier, equally enigmatic statement, "It isn't that complicated, okay?" He was just beginning to sort out its implications when he caught a glimpse of himself in a mirrored display in the darkened window of a lingerie store.

There was a huge, irregular brown blotch staining his right pants pocket, the stain, Hiroshi realized with unendurable horror, that Maureen must have been referring to in her comment about his pants.

Gingerly, Hiroshi flexed the fingers on his right hand and slid them into the blockaded pocket, encountering something unacceptably sticky, along with a sharp corner of cardboard. He watched himself in the mirror as he performed this operation, unable as yet to look directly down at the mess. Amid the shadowy fashions, the advertising-placard image of a beautiful young woman wearing a feathery white bra observed him coolly.

He turned away from the window and looked down. He slowly extricated the lump that the paper was wrapped around and actually had to hold the mess under a street lamp to realize that it was the Cherry Whip, melted beyond recognition.

Hiroshi peeled the wrapper back and stuck one of his few as yet unchocolated fingers into the chocolate-and-cherry mess. A stray Weimaranerish dog trotted past and looked up at Hiroshi with interest; Hiroshi, looking back at the dog, accidentally let the lump of candy slip from his fingers, whereupon it fell with a silent definitive plop onto one of his white sneakers, staining it as well.

The dog moved on. Now, a solitary businessman moved past the streetlight and regarded Hiroshi with brief curiosity before also moving on. Perhaps he was following the dog home.

Hiroshi stood rooted to the spot in the middle of the sidewalk, next to a traffic-signal control box.

It felt like the spot where he had said good-bye to Maureen, though he was now many blocks away. There was very little traffic and no free taxis; he had no idea what the name of the street was. He couldn't move. He really, genuinely, could not move. He considered, but instantly rejected, the possibility that his speculation earlier in the day about a neurological illness had been correct.

He really felt perfectly fine. He was just tired. And his feet, oddly, felt as numb now as his hands had earlier. The traffic signal in the middle of the intersection bathed him in a butterscotchy yellow and then, after some deliberation and a chunka-chunka noise from the signal control box, flooded him with red.

He missed his clarinet, though he felt at the same time a certain amount of guilty curiosity that he didn't miss it more, and that he wasn't terribly upset by its evident theft. He missed the hot dog a little bit, too. And he already missed Maureen.

A group of rowdy, tough-looking teenagers approached. Hiroshi contemplated the effectiveness, if necessary, of stabbing one of them in the thigh with a miniature screwdriver. But they passed without seeming to see him.

A powerful wave of fatigue washed over his body. He raised his right hand to his lips and slowly licked the chocolate from one finger. It was so sweet that, for a moment, he felt as if he couldn't catch his breath. It was rather unpleasant in that regard, but also, with its overwhelming artificial cherry flavor, it represented something interesting and new to taste.

He licked the rest of his fingers clean with his warm tongue, thinking, for the moment, of nothing else.

2

THE NEXT MORNING, at 10:07 New York time, Hiroshi was walking grimly through rain gusts and whipped-up grit on his way back to that damnable hot dog stand. Unexpectedly, Maureen had called him – *called* him! – at eight-thirty a.m., when he was still asleep. It excited him, for just a moment upon awakening, to think that she had tracked him down to his hotel less than twelve hours after they had parted.

But she had only wanted to tell him that she had talked to her cousin, a policewoman in Chicago, who'd urged her to urge him to pursue the problem of the stolen clarinet aggressively rather than wait six months for a possibly unsatisfactory insurance payoff. At the same time, it had occurred to her, Maureen, that maybe the New York police, and certainly the New York tabloids, might be interested in such an unusual crime with such an unusual victim. He was, she therefore instructed him, to find a taxi and meet her at the scene of the crime.

Hiroshi didn't precisely care for either word – "unusual" or "victim." Curled up in his less-than-satisfactory bed in the Gramercy West Hotel, phone jammed between horizontal shoulder and ear, he had listened passively to Maureen's excited voice, unable, ever since the moment it became clear that she was calling about the clarinet rather than something more personal, to match her level of enthusiasm.

Indeed, he was rather extraordinarily tired. After the brief conversation with Maureen, it had taken nearly all of his energy to cradle the phone and re-curl himself. He tried to imagine participating in a demanding rehearsal, but it seemed, suddenly, an impossible thing to do.

After a long while, he twisted with great effort onto his back and stared at his ugly room in the light of day. He had never seen anything exactly like it – there was a thick cable that depended from one wall, bellied umbilically across the center of the room, and attached itself to the television at the other end of the room. There also were ganglia of wormy thinner-gauge wires in one corner of the room near the ceiling, entering his room at the supposedly reputable Gramercy West Hotel from one hole in the ceiling and then exiting, without apparent motive, by means of another hole.

(When he'd gotten into the taxi at the airport and given the Sikh driver the name of the hotel, he'd pronounced "Gramercy" with the emphasis on the second syllable. "No," the driver had instructed him. "*Gram*-ercy. No mercy.")

But what made the wires so disturbing, Hiroshi thought, is that all of them had been painted the same dun-pink as the room itself. Hiroshi had tried not to think then, as he struggled to get out of bed, and now, as he fought his way through the rain to the hot dog stand, that the jumbled pink wires in any way resembled what was going on inside of his body.

Really, he had never before in his life had so much difficulty in rolling out of bed, or so little energy for getting dressed or eating breakfast – he had gulped down a bottle of orange juice and eaten a packet of cheese crackers the same color as the juice – or going anywhere. If this, rather than the way he had felt on his one tour of Europe, was what jet lag was all about, he was more than happy to retreat to the studio, become an obscure jazz version of Glenn Gould, and never tour again.

He had, thankfully, remembered in his lassitude to bring his big green umbrella. But on the other hand, he'd gotten the address wrong and realized only after the taxi driver had let him off that he was still a good five blocks from the hot dog place.

It was terribly difficult to walk. He had to stop once because he saw, in the window of a record store, a poster advertising a new release from Abbey Lincoln, whom he admired, and he'd had to balance his umbrella in one hand to keep himself dry as he fished in the pocket of his other pair of pants for a pen and a scrap of paper to scribble down the title, as well as the titles of a few other recordings he'd seen, on the back of his orange juice-and-cracker receipt. Eventually, he'd had to put the umbrella down on the sidewalk to accomplish this task. Where he dropped it, there was an old newspaper battered to the pavement by the rain, with chunks of side-walk showing through where the pulp had entirely washed away, but there was enough type left for Hiroshi to become momentarily absorbed by an article about a gem theft before the rain and his fatigue forced him to continue on.

Up ahead, a block or so from the restaurant, was a covered walkway protecting the sidewalk from some scaffolded tuck-pointing – which were two extraordinarily cool words, Hiroshi thought – being done on the old brown building above.

As Hiroshi entered the dark walkway, he felt a paper-thin but unavoidable tinge of shame that he was holding an umbrella over his head at a moment when it was not strictly necessary. It felt weak, somehow, feminine. So he closed the umbrella partially and held it in front of him, somewhat phallically, just in time to reach the other end of the walkway and re-enter the rain.

This was miserable. Miserable. The wind, the rain, the low-pressure system inside of his body, his lost clarinet, and his unpreparedness, his absolute unpreparedness, for his first rehearsal tonight. He hated the rain because it obscured everything, made it impossible for him to see anything interesting or new or different. He felt like turning around and going back to the record store he'd passed, but he knew he didn't have the time or the energy to do that.

So in the last block of his walk before the moment when Maureen and the police would surely disappoint him, he made a special effort to look around at the New Yorkers who surrounded him. The young woman approaching him was pretty, but with a prissy mouth. She had a nose ring, he noticed, which he didn't at all mind, but it seemed to clash with that rounded, rather babyish, rather old-fashioned looking mouth.

There was a diminutive old man in front of him, his shock of white hair loaded with bobbing bits of rain, walking so slowly he appeared to be wiping his feet on the pavement rather than moving forward. As Hiroshi's big green umbrella passed over his head, it gave the little man, though he surely was not aware of it, a second's respite from the raindrops.

People. Pretty. Ugly. Wet. All of them more or less miserable but none of them, Hiroshi was fairly sure, as tired as he was.

There, across the street, was the hot dog stand. As he stood on the curb, Hiroshi noticed for the first time the larger building in which it was situated. Up there on the second floor was a chiropractor's office, the word disarticulated symmetrically across four consecutive windows –

CHI ROP RAC TOR

It took a moment for Hiroshi to re-join the separated parts in his mind, but he knew the English word quite well thanks to his judo exertions and was tempted, looking up there, to get a fatigue-defeating adjustment to his spine. Really, he loved chiropractors. He pondered pleasantly on this, and, looking at the ancient brown brick, thought some more about the word "tuck-pointing," which pleased him even more, but then the sight of the building's roof reminded him again of the ugly pinkish wires inside of his hotel room and the something wrong that he felt inside of his body.

At that moment, Maureen spotted his slight figure, overwhelmed by the big green umbrella. "Hey, Hiroshi! C'mon out of the rain!" she yelled across the street. My God, he thought, she has a loud voice.

Hiroshi, again embarrassed by the umbrella, pointedly lowered it as he crossed the street and entered the store. "Good morning. Are the police here?"

"*A* police. Man. Over there." A slender man in nice herringbone wools slacks and a complicated jacket – leather here, wool there, a different kind of leather for the collar – was leaning over the counter, reading the *New York Post*, his back to them.

Hiroshi eyed him for a second and turned to Maureen. "Maureen, thank you for calling me this morning. It was very nice of you. Although I'm afraid that I'm feeling a bit unwell right now."

Maureen eyed him critically. "You seemed a little off center last night. I mean, not that I have any center to compare to. But I wouldn't be surprised you were coming down with one of those damn viruses that circulate on airplanes. You know, with the stale air that everybody breathes."

"You may be right. Shall we talk to the policeman?"

"Sure. Hey, this is kind of exciting, isn't it?"

Hiroshi didn't answer. Maureen tapped the policeman on the shoulder, then leaped back excitedly when he turned around, presenting curly hair and a head of steam from his cup of coffee. "See, this is the guy. This is the guy I was talking about!"

The policeman stuck out his hand. Hiroshi took his hand limply, then pulled his own away rather quickly.

The policeman was rather young and serious-looking, with a long, lean face under the close-cropped curly hair, and soft green eyes that didn't seem to match with the eyes – skeptical, burned out, hard – that he had observed in the actors in American and Japanese police dramas.

"Pleased to meet you, Mr. Mori. I understand you're a musician."

"He's a well-known jazz musician," Maureen interjected needlessly.

"Oh, not so well known. I'm just starting forth."

"Starting out," Maureen said, more helpfully. "But he's brilliant, really brilliant."

"Alright, then I guess you need your instrument, huh?"

"Yes. I think it may have been stolen, although I can't be sure."

"Well, let me put it to you this way. If you left it here, and then it wasn't here when you got back, it was stolen. It wasn't thrown out accidentally in the garbage, okay? A thing that big. So face it, it was stolen."

"Yes," Hiroshi agreed.

"You know, I was in Hong Kong once, about fifteen years ago, before I was a cop," the policeman said. Maureen tilted her head quizzically, waiting for a connection, or to correct him on the matter of Hiroshi's provenance. "I took a ton of pictures with one of those old 110 cameras, with the cartridges you drop in. Afterwards, I spent a couple of days in Tokyo before going home. It's a long story, you know, post-JC, see-the-world kind of thing. Anyway, I rode the Tokyo subway during rush hour and I mean, there was this cute little lady, and it was so crowded her nose was bent sideways against my chest. But she pretended I wasn't even there and I pretended *she* wasn't. Anyway, that has nothing to do with it, the thing is when I got out, I realized I lost the little baggie where I was storing the cartridges. So I go to one of those little police huts you have there..."

"Koban," Hiroshi said.

"Yeah, koban. We've got one in Times Square now. And I asked the policeman – I couldn't speak his language and he couldn't speak mine – if he could look around for it. Can you imagine! In Tokyo, 15 million people or whatever, and he has me fill out a form, I guess for lost or stolen property, and do a little drawing of the cartridge, and he bows to me, like he's actually going to send out one of his lieutenants to look for a film cartridge! I still can't believe I did that."

Maureen looked ready to punch the cop. "Are you trying to tell me this is the equivalent of looking for a film cartridge?"

He blinked and looked a bit hurt. "No, no, I think I was trying to say pretty much the opposite there. They showed me so much respect for such a dumbass thing that I asked. So I figure the least I can do is pay him back in some way by helping your friend out here. I mean, it's my job anyway, but I volunteered for this one."

Hiroshi looked around. Would this place and his ugly hotel room be his only memories of New York? The counterman was different from the guy yesterday, and paid the three of them no attention. There were a few customers, but because the policeman was in plainclothes, they also paid the group no mind.

"Alright," the policeman said, pulling out a fat notebook. "Let me start by asking you some questions."

Hiroshi suddenly felt an onslaught of fatigue so strong that he thought he might vomit. "Wait a minute, I think I need to go to the chiropractor."

Maureen laughed – more of a sputtering bark than a laugh, really – and the policeman narrowed his eyes skeptically. "A *chiropractor? Now?*"

Hiroshi flushed from head to toe with embarrassment. His toes curled. He had to worm out of that idiotic statement, and back out of this restaurant, and yet still maintain his connection with Maureen. He chose pretended stupidity as his method.

He smiled ingenuously at the policeman, who, after all, had just admitted to doing a dumb thing of his own. "Isn't that the kind of doctor you go to if you have the flu?"

"A *chiropractor?* I don't think so," the policeman said, not unkindly. He looked closely at Hiroshi. "You think you got the flu?"

"Perhaps."

"Well, listen, I can take your statement another time."

Hiroshi felt so grateful he could have collapsed right there on the filthy floor. "Another time. Yes. That would be good."

"How about tomorrow?"

"Yes, of course. I would be happy to meet with you tomorrow if you don't mind."

"Not at all. It doesn't make much difference now. I'll ask around the fences tomorrow, just the same as today."

The fences? What was he talking about? But Maureen had slipped her arm around his waist and was smiling at him.

"C'mon," she said. "Let's get you back to the hotel. You take some American miracle drugs and sleep for a while. If you want, I can pick you up before your rehearsal and we can have some dinner."

"That would be good. I think I need to rest. I think I feel a little bit hot, like I'm having a temperature."

"You always *have* one. You mean *running* one. I don't know, I'm always hot myself."

"Really?"

"Yeah," Maureen said. "Hot Spanish blood."

"You're Spanish? I assumed you were..."

"What, Irish? Everyone thinks that. I'm half Spanish and half Sardinian, with a little bit of American Indian. It all makes me very temperamental." She smiled playfully at Hiroshi.

How, Hiroshi wondered, could she be half of one thing and half of another, and still be a little bit of something else? He was thinking about this while Maureen guided him into a taxi, her arm still around his waist, and was thinking about what she meant by "temperamental" when she left him at the door of his hotel room. She told him she would pick him up at that very spot at six p.m. for dinner – rehearsal was scheduled for eight p.m at Xenon, an expensive club near Lincoln Center. He nodded numbly, said good-bye to her, and collapsed onto his unmade bed.

When the maid arrived at 2:00 p.m., rousing him from a deep sleep, he was thinking, or rather dreaming, about something entirely other than Maureen and her ethnic heritage, but he couldn't quite grasp what it was. Something about a train, perhaps.

He sent the maid away and went back to sleep.

The alarm went off at five p.m. He awakened to a room that was already beginning to dim. The hollow sound of horns could be heard in the distance, and the laughter, disturbing to him in his depressed state, of children playing behind the locked gates of Gramercy Park. He slowly removed the sections of his regular clarinet – a Regent, fashioned out of grenadilla wood – from the squarish case with the soft, padded compartments, segmented like a bento box, that had until this moment been jammed into its own compartment in his massive backpack. He selected a good reed and then, wearily, like a soldier assembling his rifle in a black trench, fitted the familiar pieces together in the failing light strictly by feel.

Then he pulled on some clean clothes with great difficulty and sat numbly on the edge of the bed, his furled umbrella across his lap and the clarinet dangling heavily from one hand. Normally, he'd have assembled the clarinet at the club, but he wanted it whole right now; he had the oddest feeling, in fact, that he never wanted to take it apart again. He considered practicing for a bit, but did not raise the clarinet. He considered putting the empty clarinet case back in the backpack or taking some other things out of the duffel bag, or putting the souvenirs he'd bought into the empty duffel bag crammed into the bottom of his stuffed duffel bag, but did not do those things either. He just sat there and waited for Maureen.

He thought, while waiting, of how he used to dream when he was much younger of walking onto a concert stage naked, or in his underwear, but always, in any event, utterly unprepared for the concert that was about to begin. He wouldn't, in some versions of the dream, know how to play his instrument, or he would have forgotten how to read music, or some such humiliation. One time in a dream he'd reached out to pick up his clarinet, and it made a pained yelping sound before he'd even touched it, as if it were outraged at the off notes it knew he was about to play; there were few instruments as sensitive and easily aggrieved. He hadn't had such dreams in many years. He didn't need to. He felt that way in real life – unprepared, like the player, ready to yelp like the clarinet.

When Maureen arrived, Hiroshi had a plan. He knew exactly what he needed to feel better. As they stepped out onto the street, he brought her into the green orbit of his umbrella – it was still raining a bit – and said, "Maureen, do you like Japanese food?"

"Sure, Hero." When had she started to call him 'Hero'? "I like all things Japanese."

"Well, why don't we find a Japanese restaurant? If I had a bowl of katsudon, I know I could feel a hundred percent better."

"Oh, nonsense. You're coming to my place! You need a nice home-cooked meal, is what you need."

"My rehearsal. I'm just feeling a little bit nervous about it. I feel like I need something familiar to eat. Something a little bit warm and nourishing."

"Nourishing? Familiar? *Warm*? Hiroshi, that's comfort food you're talking about! You need, Hero, you *need* my famous mashed potatoes."

Hiroshi was too unhappy to reply. She guided him into a taxi and through the operation of closing his umbrella, and gave the driver her address.

Once they were underway, Maureen said, more softly, "What is this catsup stuff, anyway?"

"Katsudon," he replied, rather bleakly. "Katsudon. It's rice, with strips of breaded fried pork on top of it in a sauce with coddled egg and spring onions and..."

"See, *see*," Maureen exclaimed. "This is what I'm talking about! Comfort food! I know *exactly* what you need. Just leave yourself in my hands – have I steered you wrong yet?"

Hiroshi thought about that for a moment and even opened his mouth to reply, but was forced to acknowledge that as far as the lost clarinet, and the ruined pants, and his overwhelming fatigue, none of it had been her fault. And, envisioning the two of them sharing a quiet dinner at her undoubtedly interesting apartment, he began to brighten a bit.

* * *

HER APARTMENT WASN'T, in fact, terribly interesting. Terribly small, rather, almost as small as a Tokyo apartment. There was one large bookcase containing neatly arranged, official-looking volumes of the same binding and color, like law books. That seemed odd for a musician. And there was another, unmatched, bookcase, with hundreds of jumbled CDs. He wondered if his obscure release was among them.

He could tell, though it was quiet enough, that the walls were rather thin. On them were unframed Damien Hirst posters and concert posters for a sprinkling of slightly-right-of-center jazz musicians, various Marsalises and the like, and, framed, a very old concert poster for Bob Wills and his Texas Playboys and a few hand-colored cowboy-and-Indian photographs from the American West. There wasn't anything particularly feminine about the apartment – nor anything particularly feminine about Maureen, it suddenly occurred to Hiroshi. But everything was clean and well-ordered, and the kitchen table had been beautifully set for their meal, with yellow Fiestaware. Jagabata – buttered potatoes – wasn't exactly something you'd make a meal of in Japan, but perhaps there was something more to her mashed potatoes than that. And perhaps there was something else on the menu entirely.

Hiroshi decided to go to the bathroom, for a sort of precautionary pee – he wouldn't want to get up during dinner. He also wanted to check the condition of his hair and to peer into the mirror to see if he looked anywhere near as bad as he felt.

The tile in the bathroom, black and white hexagons, was very old and cracked in places. The toilet also looked rather rickety. On top of the toilet tank, opened to a page he recognized, was a magazine. It was one of those proliferating New York entertainment guides, with an article about his club appearance, and a picture of him looking rather handsome, he thought, comparing it with his present likeness in the bathroom mirror. There also was what his agent, who had set up the article, had described as a "sidebar," a small colored rectangle inside the main article, in which Hiroshi advanced a brief statement in English about his music — a statement he had written himself.

But oddly, very oddly – Hiroshi struggled to absorb this as he stood there in front of the toilet with his zipper half undone – there was handwriting all over his little essay. The words were rather like scrawls, incised quite firmly with a blue ballpoint pen to make an impression against the sherbet-green background of the sidebar, and what they had to say was not at all pleasant.

This was what Hiroshi had written, after two solid days of effort:

> In my opinion, and perhaps that of others in my profession, we have merely begun to explore the surface of this very recent invention, this music we call jazz. Hundreds of years from now, musicians will look back at our tentitive sound-making, with pity and wonder. Nonetheless, I hope in my little explorings, such as they may be, that I have stumbled over new ideas that may be of interest to some few of my fellow listeners today, if not those of the future.

Truthfully, as Hiroshi re-read his words, he knew they were a little bit insincere – not his own modesty, certainly, which was an integral part of him, but rather his statement that jazz musicians had only begun to explore the surface of the music. In truth, when he listened to the likes of Peter Brotzmann, it was impossible for him to imagine the music going much further.

But the toilet-tank commentary was of a different nature.

Next to Hiroshi's words, "In my opinion," the scrawl said, "As opposed to...?" "And perhaps that of others" was scratched out and would not have been legible at all had Hiroshi not already known what he had written.

The spelling of "tentitive" had been corrected.

Next to "this music we call jazz," the writer had scribbled, "this business we call show." Hiroshi had no idea what this meant.

The words "stumbled over" had been circled with heavy strokes. The comma after "sound-making" had been deleted with a flourish.

Next to "explorings" was the comment "word choice." What was wrong, Hiroshi thought, with "explorings"? And the misspelling of "tentative," he was fairly certain, was the magazine's fault.

That really rankled.

And at the bottom of the sidebar, breaking into the main body of the article so that the blue ballpoint was especially legible, was the single admonition, "rewrite."

Next to the sidebar was his publicity picture – without the blue streak, a relatively recent hair experiment, but with the interrupted eyebrow clearly visible. The caption read, "Clarinetist Hiroshi Mori, who graduated from the prestigious Tokyo National University of Fine Arts and Music only four years ago, has already made a bit of noise in his homeland and in Europe with his ability to swing seamlessly from thoughtfully fractured standards and klezmer recreations as authentic as an egg cream all the way to his own eerie imaginings. His first New York appearance, as a guest of the Grady Granphill Ensemble, begins at Xenon this Saturday at nine p.m."

The word "eerie" had been circled.

Hiroshi wandered back out of the bathroom in a daze. Maureen was busy at the stove, removing from the tiny oven a tray of what looked like glazed pork chops. He stood there at the entrance to the kitchen, waiting for her to turn around.

When she did, her expression was pleasant and expectant.

"Maureen, did you see that in the bathroom?"

"See what, Hero?"

"On top of the toilet. The article I wrote."

"Sure. Of course."

"Well, what I mean to say is, did you see... did you make any comments on it?"

Maureen looked blank. "*Comments* on it?"

"Writing. Editing. Negative comments." She blinked, looked puzzled. He motioned for her to follow him into the bathroom.

"Hiroshi, the food is going to get cold."

"Please. It will only take a moment." She followed him into the bathroom and he immediately pointed, with a mixture of self-pity and triumph, to the offending item atop the toilet.

Maureen looked at it with puzzlement for a second, then laughed her short, explosive laugh.

"Oh, that. You mean the edits? That must be my room-mate. Don't worry, she edits everything." With that, she wheeled around and headed back into the kitchen.

Hiroshi was less than entirely satisfied. "You have a very clean apartment."

"Thanks."

"And you knew I would be coming for dinner. When we met at the hotel, you didn't even listen to my suggestion of a restaurant. And you have the table set nicely."

"You seem angry. What is it you're trying to say?"

"I'm saying, if you knew I was coming for dinner, why would you leave such a thing in the bathroom?"

"Hiroshi, I don't know. I didn't notice, okay? Ask my roommate, alright? You're making a big deal out of nothing."

"But weren't you the one who said yesterday that it isn't so complicated? Well, you're making it complicated."

"How so, Hero, how so?" Her voice was soft and reasonable and, once again, Hiroshi thought, ever so slightly patronizing.

He pressed on. "Well, why would you invite me to dinner? Why would you flirt with me yesterday and invite me to dinner and then allow me to be insulted? Or at least act like it wasn't an insult?"

She smiled gently and shook her head. Her eyes were glittering. "Oh, Hiroshi, you really are making things complicated. *Flirt* with you? I wasn't flirting with you. Do you even know what the word means?"

A double insult, he thought at once.

How much longer would this punishment continue?

First of all, insulting his English – as if he wouldn't know the meaning of such a simple word.

And then, regarding his attractiveness – she was looking at him so condescendingly right now, it was if he weren't even in the category of men that anyone conceivably *could* flirt with. He began, just began, to try to make himself feel better by shuffling in his mind through all of the women who had ever been attracted to him, but very quickly stopped himself as he thought of a third insult implicit in her statement – that he had somehow imagined a thing that was very obvious.

"But you followed me into the magazine store!" he exploded. "You stood right there next to me, and pretended to read a magazine you didn't care about!"

"What, *Hemmings Motor News*? I'm thinking of buying a car! I stopped into a magazine store that's right near the Academy and ran into you. So fucking what? Anyway, maybe you followed *me* in there."

This last sentence she said not in anger, Hiroshi thought, but with a bit of coquettishness. He shook his head. No, he knew for a fact that he had come in first. And he knew how surprised he was to look up and see her. *She* hadn't looked surprised. And here she was, seemingly flirting with him again. What kind of child did she think he was? But he was too confused and dispirited to say anything.

Maureen took up the slack. "Look, maybe this has something to do with cultural differences."

"*Not* cultural differences," Hiroshi barked, startling himself. "That's a stupid excuse."

"Look," Maureen said softly. "Maybe you still haven't had enough rest. Would you still like me to come and see your show this weekend?"

Hiroshi mumbled an assent, and immediately felt weak for doing so. He also recognized that Maureen's last statement might have been her way of disinviting him from tonight's dinner. He felt a little less certain of this when he said good-bye and moved toward the door. Maureen said – shrieked – "Good-bye! What're you talking about? What about this dinner I cooked?"

But Hiroshi said, "I think you're right that I need to get some more rest. Thank you for inviting me. I'm sorry that you went to all this trouble for me, but I have to say good-bye right now." Indeed, he suddenly was terribly anxious to get out of there not only because he was angry, but because he thought for some reason that he might faint at any moment, and that would be too humiliating for him to bear.

This time, she said good-bye back, sounding rather disappointed but making no attempt to stop him. He walked out the door, with the delicious scent of glazed pork chops following him down the stairs.

* * *

41

NOW HE WANTED katsudon more fiercely than ever. There were hundreds of Japanese joints in New York, he thought gratefully, and he intended to stop into the first one he saw. He was grateful, also, that it had stopped raining – he had left his giant green umbrella at Maureen's, and couldn't imagine any circumstances under which he might retrieve it.

He found a place, ordered impatiently, and when the food arrived, tried to gulp it down quickly. He and his friends who observed American tourists and businessmen in Tokyo often laughed at how slowly and delicately they would consume a bowl of noodles or rice. But as hungry as he was, he too found himself eating far more slowly than usual. Was being in America influencing him? Or was the food too hot? A bit, perhaps.

But he also noticed that he seemed to be having a little difficulty swallowing. This was a sensation he had never, ever had before. It was as if the food were in a different language; he couldn't quite get his tongue around it, and with every bite he swallowed awkward lumps. That strange black bird in the park had eaten its egg meat – *egg meat?* – with such unruffled equanimity, but Hiroshi felt as if he had never eaten before.

After managing to finish about half the bowl, he took a taxi back to his hotel and went up to his room, intending to brush his teeth and freshen up before catching a taxi for the club. With a start, he suddenly looked around in panic for his regular clarinet, the Regent, in its little squarish case. Had he left it at Maureen's too, along with the umbrella? But then he looked down to see the clarinet, which, he now remembered, he had earlier in the evening removed from the case and assembled, grasped in his right hand.

His trembling right hand.

Where it had been all evening – in the taxicab on the way to Maureen's apartment. At the apartment, even when he had been reading those humiliating comments in the bathroom.

At the restaurant, even while he had been wielding his chopsticks over the bowl of katsudon. And in the taxi back to the hotel, where he was now safe and intact and dry.

And warm. Sleepy and warm.

He laid the clarinet gently down at the foot of the bed. He went into the bathroom and urinated, realizing as he did so that he must have held it ever since he had left Maureen's apartment. He drank down a small brown bottle of genki drink – a vitamin-and-caffeine concoction he'd brought from Japan. He brushed his teeth. He removed all of his clothes.

Then he unwrapped a CD he'd also brought with him from Japan, though he certainly could have found it here – Lou Reed's *New York*. He intended to listen to it on his Walkman as he fell asleep.

As he tossed aside the cellophane wrapper, static electricity made it stick to the dun-pink wall next to the bed. Hiroshi stared at this phenomenon for a moment, then let the CD slip from his fingers onto the floor.

And collapsed, naked, onto the bed.

He lay there reflecting, not unpleasantly, on the past couple of days. Nothing really so bad had happened to him. Humiliating, perhaps, but also funny in a way. And certainly not, in the great scheme of the universe, terrible.

There was a distant melody audible from the next room. Hiroshi, tired as he was, recognized it immediately as a popular song from the 60s, "Here Comes My Baby."

He was good at that – he could recognize almost any melody, not just jazz standards, but popular music, Broadway show tunes, even some heavy metal. And classical, of course.

When he was a very small child, he'd announced to his mother that the little series of beeps the microwave oven made when it was finished heating up the evening's croquettes or curry was, slowed down a bit, the first three notes of "The Blue Danube Waltz." And, as a teenager, he'd

43

recognized that the chirping tune the traffic signals in Japan emitted to alert blind pedestrians when it was safe to cross consisted of – though this was surely an accident – four of the first six notes, in order, of Michel Legrand's "Summer Me, Winter Me."

It was so comfortable in his bed, his smelly but now-familiar bed. He drifted off to sleep, thinking of pleasant melodies.

And slept through the first phone call from Grady Granphill, the famous jazz guitarist who had arranged for his trip from Japan, checking in at 8:45 p.m. to make sure Hiroshi was on his way to rehearsal.

At eleven p.m., he slept through the second call from Grady, who was now a little angry.

And, just a few minutes later, he slept through the phone call from his girlfriend, Hitomi (Gorgeous Hitomi, Grady had called her when he was in Japan), who was angry, too, because Hiroshi had not called her even once since arriving in America.

He slept through the third call from Grady, now much more concerned than angry, at one thirty a.m.

He would have slept through an apologetic phone call from Maureen, if only one had come.

And he slept through the first time that Carmelita, the Salvadoran maid, knocked at his door at ten a.m. the following morning. He was vaguely aware of the knocking, but was too busy having an odd dream – one that, even as he dreamed it, he was vaguely aware he had dreamed once before, a very short time ago.

In the dream, he was riding in the front carriage of an old-fashioned train in a landscape where he had never been before. It looked like the Swiss Alps, with many soft green valleys, and cows, and wildflowers everywhere.

The train went around a sharp bend. When it did so,

Hiroshi, in his dream, stuck his head out of the window and looked back behind him, seeing, for the first time, the end of the train, which had not been visible when it trailed straight behind Hiroshi's car, but was now fully revealed by the sharp bend.

Hiroshi stared at the last car and realized with a subtle sense of surprise that it was part of the same train he was riding on.

This seemed terribly significant.

So did the fact that there were people in this far car that was a part of the same train he was on, and yet he couldn't talk to them or hear them.

Carmelita knocked again, louder this time, at eleven-thirty a.m. Then she tried to open the door with her passkey, but Hiroshi had bolted the door from the inside the night before.

This time, Hiroshi awakened, fifteen hours after he had fallen asleep. The maid's attempt to unlock the door had startled him. Forgetting where he was, he shouted, "Chotto matte kudasai!"

But it came out more as a whisper than as a shout.

He tried again, adjusting both the volume and the language, but again, his words – "Just a moment please!" – came out as a distressing raspy whisper.

He had entirely missed his first rehearsal.

In a panic, he scrambled out of the bed, but his legs were so weak that he collapsed, face down, on the filthy burgundy-colored rug between the bed and the door.

He tried to get up but realized, to his horror, that the only muscles he could move at all were in his neck and head.

He tried to wiggle his toes, but nothing happened.

He heard the footsteps of the maid departing. Hadn't she even heard him fall?

He shouted after her, as in a dream, but nothing came out.

He lay there, breathing shallowly, and noticed, under the pile of dirty clothes he had worn on the flight over, the package of miniature tools he had purchased. They had been placed neatly back into the little hard-plastic carrying case, and the cellophane had miraculously been re-wrapped around the case.

For a moment, he wondered not about what horrible thing had happened to his body, but about who had reassembled the little package of tools.

3

As HE LAY on the floor, he whispered to himself.

He whispered, in Japanese, "Please, please, what is happening to me?"

In English, he whispered, though he was attempting with all of his strength to shout, the single word: "Help."

A great deal of time passed. How much, Hiroshi could not say. He was naked even of his wristwatch.

His bladder felt very full, which worried him a bit. To distract himself, he looked at everything he could see from his position on the floor.

He stared at the pile of dirty clothes and the package of little tools underneath it. He stared at the Lou Reed CD he'd never listened to. It made him very sad to think he might not ever know if it was a good album or not.

Then he stared at the negligible cellophane wrapper from the CD, which, after the long night, still clung lightly to the wall, stronger for the moment than he was. He stared at the rather dirty baseboards and at the rough fibers of the rug, which made him think of the mat he had stood on in one of his first hours in New York, when his body had sent, and his mind imperfectly received, the very first intimations that something was not right.

At the edge of his vision, he also could see a small bottle of wasabi furikake, which he carried with him everywhere he traveled outside of Japan (before this excursion, one trip each to Europe, South Korea, and Guam, to be precise) and which must have rolled out of his suitcase onto the floor. It was a spice for sprinkling on rice. It contained dried wasabi, seaweed flakes, bonito, sesame seeds, soy sauce, sugar, dried egg yolk and ajinimoto. He would give anything, he thought, to feel its sweet sharpness on his tongue one more time.

He began to sing some tunes to keep himself occupied, or at least to hold back the panic. "Heaven, I'm in heaven, and my heart beats so that I can hardly speak..."

He laughed weakly, not having intended to make a joke about his condition. Why, then, had "Cheek to Cheek," of all the thousands of songs he knew, come to mind? Maybe, he thought, because he was conscious of the way his cheek was pressed against the rug and was happy that he could feel at least that. He felt a tiny sense of triumph at having figured it out.

He tried again, and again failed, to yell "Help."

Then he urinated all over the carpet, though he was unaware that this was happening.

He began to accept that he was going to die, and hoped it would at least happen soon.

The phone rang repeatedly for several minutes. Hiroshi, with grim humor, whispered, "Moshi, moshi! Hello!"

Sometime after he had accepted that he would die, and yet had not died, he began to get extremely bored. He sang a few more songs to himself. Then he began to repeat nonsense syllables over and over again, in Japanese and in English.

"Chi. Rop. Rac. Tor. Chi. Rop. Rac. Tor. Chi. Rop. Rac.

Tor. Chi. Rop. Rac. Tor. Chi. Rop. Rac. Tor. Chi. Rop. Rac. Tor."

He thought of each syllable as a vertebrae, unconnected to any of the others. He tried to reconnect them, but failed.

The phone rang again. And again.

He started whispering more quickly, and was even beginning to enjoy the sensation that at least one part of his body was working, that his tongue and lips, though they could not taste food or water, could at least still form words in Japanese and English. And that, in fact, there seemed to be nothing whatsoever wrong with his brain.

From the room next door, the room where last night he'd heard the strains of "Here Comes My Baby," he heard distinct conversation. There was giggling mixed in, some rustling and bouncing about, and then, after a protracted silent period, the sound of vigorous lovemaking – a woman's high-pitched gasps, a banging bed, something falling on the floor. Hiroshi was thrilled for this diversion, and began to try to picture the identity and appearance of the lovemakers when – it couldn't have been more than a couple of minutes later – there was a loud male groan followed by a softer, somewhat disappointed, female sigh.

In the silence that followed, Hiroshi laughed. He felt a bit superior to the man behind the wall.

Then, without warning, he began to cry, very hard. He felt the prickle of his tears pooling up around his cheeks and brow and dampening the fibers beneath him.

Then he heard his doorknob being rattled. He forced himself to stop crying then, and listened very carefully.

The voices beyond the door were muffled, but he heard a male voice say "he..." and a female voice answer "he..." Hiroshi thought for a moment that it might be the lovemakers from next door, but he could hear them moving about now. It was somebody else, somebody come to see about him.

Suddenly, there was a tremendous buzzing racket, and a jagged blade – a jigsaw, Hiroshi thought it was called – poked through the wooden door, sprinkling sawdust in his hair. In less than a minute, a neat hole had been cut out of the wood, and the resultant disc fell out of the door and landed, propped on its side, against Hiroshi's left ear. A second later, a hairy hand with a shiny watch on the wrist – Hiroshi couldn't lift his head high enough to read the brand or the time – reached in and quickly unfastened the bolt.

Hiroshi whispered desperately, "Wait, wait!" because his head was so close to the door that, when it opened, he would surely be struck.

Nonetheless, the door opened and he was struck. It hurt a bit, but he was glad.

The owner of the hand, feeling the obstruction, stuck his nose into the small crack in the door. It occurred to Hiroshi that this person just as easily could have peered through the jigsaw hole he had cut.

But he must have seen the naked form of Hiroshi lying there, because Hiroshi heard him say, "Oh, my God."

A few minutes passed, during which Hiroshi worried about his nakedness and listened to at least three voices discuss how to get in – the man who had said "Oh, my God," and another male voice, and Carmelita, whom Hiroshi recognized by voice if not by name.

A cool breeze from the hallway came in through the crack in the door and the hole in the door, though Hiroshi could enjoy it only on his head and neck.

After a while, the voices receded down the hallway. More time passed, during which Hiroshi again began to cry. Then he forced himself to stop crying and he began to think about an English textbook chapter on prepositions, in which had been stated, with absolute authority, that something could be "under a door" or "over a door" or "behind a door" but not "in a door." And yet there had been a key in the door, and then a drill in the door, and now a hole in the door, through which a quiet breeze wandered.

Suddenly there came a tremendous shattering noise. Though he could not turn his head to see it, a New York City fireman, followed by two NYC EMTs, a policeman, and the custodian who had drilled the circular hole, clambered in through the smashed window behind Hiroshi, placed his unresisting body onto a stretcher, draped it with a Gramercy West Hotel blanket (Hiroshi worried a bit that taking the hotel's blanket wasn't very nice) and carried him out of the room.

The EMTs transferred Hiroshi from the stretcher to some aluminized rolling unit in the hallway, then rolled him to the elevator. From the creaky elevator – there were no other passengers, thankfully, not that there'd be room – they rolled onto the refreshing street.

During this process, one of the EMTs – the one behind Hiroshi, whom he couldn't see – whistled a tune that Hiroshi recognized as Paul Simon's "Mother and Child Reunion." Suddenly inspired, Hiroshi pursed his lips and blew, hard. Though his lips trembled, he was startled and chagrined – and pleased – to hear a loud, pure tone. If it had only occurred to him at the time, and if a passing maid or guest had somehow managed to interpret that tone as a cry for help, Hiroshi perhaps could have saved hours of agony on the floor.

And yet he knew that was absurd. There were melancholy whistles and happy whistles, but there was no such thing as a frantic whistle.

Nothing to be done. It didn't matter now. Other than being unable to move a single muscle in his body below the neck, Hiroshi didn't feel all that bad. He began, softly, so as not to pre-empt the EMT, to whistle a pitch-perfect rendition of Fauré's *Pavane*.

The EMT, despite Hiroshi's precautions, immediately shut up. Then, all the way to St. Vincent's Hospital in Greenwich Village, while the EMTs took Hiroshi's vital signs, and in between his whispered answers to their questions, he treated them to one of his own improvisations. They might have thought he was demented, but he didn't care. It was the only thing he could still do.

* * *

ON HIS WAY to intensive care, Hiroshi thought principally of three things. The first thing he thought was that he had left everything he had with him in America back in his hotel room.

The maids, the custodians, whoever it was that took care of such things in cases such as this, would find his pile of dirty clothes, including the white pants with the chocolate on the pocket. His dirty underwear. His wallet and his passport. His official picture of Hitomi in his wallet as well as the unofficial (that is, tastefully nude) one he kept tucked in his paperback copy of *The Penguin Guide to Jazz*, on the page with Marian McPartland. His second — and last — clarinet.

The copy of *Nerve: A Magazine of Literate Smut* he'd purchased at the airport. The nineteen CDs, nine of them still unwrapped, he had brought from Japan. The Lou Reed CD, collecting so much dust from the filthy rug that, if he ever recovered it, would probably skip in that yammering, hammering way messed-up CDs had. (Maybe that was his problem – he'd gotten too much of New York's dust in his system.) The piss on the rug, which he'd noticed to his horror when the EMT's were lifting him onto the stretcher. The cellophane clinging to the wall.

All gone.

The second thing he thought of was how, a day or two

before leaving for America, he had changed the windshield wiper fluid in his car (which he almost never drove) and afterwards had eaten a salmon rice ball and a bag of shrimp chips without, he was fairly certain, washing his hands. That stuff was deadly poison, he knew. Could some of it have gotten into him via his lunch and poisoned his central nervous system?

And the third thing he thought was that his prone position in the ambulance had made it impossible for him to see even a bit of Greenwich Village on his way into the hospital. He hadn't even seen the outside of the hospital itself and now might never see it because he might never come out again.

That last thought actually constituted a fourth thing he was thinking about as he entered intensive care.

* * *

LATE THAT EVENING, after Hiroshi had been settled into his room, the resident, one Dr. Subramanian, paid his first official visit. He pulled up a wooden chair and sat next to Hiroshi to hear his soft responses.

"You speak English, I understand." Dr. Subramanian's own English was careful and clipped and even more nearly perfect than Hiroshi's.

"Yes."

"I see by your chart you've been through quite a battery of tests."

"Yes. Thank you. They took my blood, listened to my lungs and heart, looked at my eyes and ears, took my temperature, and they had me squeeze and wiggle many different things, which I couldn't do at all, even though it seemed like some of the doctors didn't even believe me. They kept on tickling my soles of feet, though it was like when you try to tickle yourself – nothing. They did many other things I can't remember. Oh, and they asked me if I was an agricultural worker."

"Exposure to chemicals."

"Yes. I assumed so. Doctor, could windshield wiper fluid have poisoned me?"

"Why, did you drink any?"

"No, of course not. But I didn't wash my hands after I used it and then I ate some shrimp chips."

Dr. Subramanian chuckled. "Shrimp chips, huh? Never tried those. I wouldn't worry about it."

"How about botulin poisoning? I've read that terrorists are planning to use such chemicals to cause paralysis."

The doctor laughed louder. "That's a new one."

"How about jet lag and flu and stress all together?"

"Well, we'd have to check with the psych people, but that doesn't seem likely."

"I'm not mentally ill."

"Of course not."

"They asked me about drugs."

"Do you use drugs?"

"Just, while I was in Europe, some pot. Pot and Irish stout. And when I'm in Japan, I drink a lot of American bourbon. But no real, what do you call them, hard drugs, no." He'd left out speed, which he'd done a fair amount of in high school and a bit after high school, but that was a long time ago.

Hiroshi didn't even smoke. He'd once imagined a Venn diagram, the left circle containing jazz musicians who were non-smokers, the right circle containing Japanese adult males who were non-smokers. Where the two circles barely intersected, there was only one person in the whole world – Hiroshi.

"I'm sure drugs aren't it anyway," Dr. Subramanian said.

"Well, what is it?"

"They haven't told me yet. I'm not a specialist. I see you're scheduled for a lumbar puncture and a brain scan. Why don't we wait and see what shows up on that?"

"They also asked me if I'd had any immunizations lately, which I have."

"That doesn't surprise me. Let's just wait and see."

"Is there anything you can tell me?"

"Well, your insurance seems to be very strong." He chuckled at this. "That's pretty unusual for a jazz musician, I would think."

"So some good news."

"There's a lot of good news, actually. You're breathing on your own..."

This was not news to Hiroshi, but sarcasm wasn't in his vocabulary or in his personality, so he said only, "Yes, I am."

"...You don't need a respirator, your signs are good except neurologically, you're swallowing and digesting food. So we can say there are a lot of things we can eliminate."

"Thank you. And what does that leave?"

"Well, like I said, I can't really say."

"Alright, thank you for what you were able to say."

"You're welcome." Dr. Subramanian patted Hiroshi's insensible arm as if everything were settled. Then he added, as if giving Hiroshi a little something to go on while he tried to get to sleep, "Your spinal column is highly inflamed."

"What does that mean?"

"Well, like I said, I can't really say."

"Alright. Thank you."

Dr. Subramanian smiled and patted Hiroshi's arm again, and again said, "You're welcome. I'll check to make sure the call got through." Hiroshi had given a nurse the number of his agent in Tokyo, who in turn was to be instructed to call a few relatives and friends.

Dr. Subramanian got up to leave. He was the seventh

doctor Hiroshi had seen over the course of the day, and the seventh he had thanked. There also had been four nurses.

One of those four nurses, a Filipino woman named Esther Villareal, possessed of a bit of bristle on her chin and in her manner, stopped by a little later as most of the patients were settling down to sleep, to change the catheter that allowed Hiroshi to urinate. As she worked – the threading of the catheter was a delicate operation, though Hiroshi felt mostly pressure and little pain – she said in her strongly accented English, "They tell you what you got?"

"No. They said maybe tomorrow."

"It's Guillain-Barré."

"Pardon?"

"Guillain-Barré."

"What is that? How do you know?"

"Oh, I know. I've seen a couple of cases over the years."

"Then why don't the doctors know?" Hiroshi felt just a bit of resentment about these uncommunicative American doctors, tempered considerably by his memory of the Japanese ones, like the older physician who had smoked a cigarette while hacking away at a ripped-up calf Hiroshi had suffered in a spill from his bicycle onto a gravel path when he was fifteen. Bits of ash had actually drifted into the open wound. The doctor had been his father's brother.

"Oh, they know," Esther said.

"Why won't they tell me then?" Hiroshi's lip was trembling violently. In Japan, those suffering from fatal diseases were rarely told the truth.

Not to know the truth, in other words, was to know the truth.

Esther looked at him closely. "You think you dying, don't you?"

"Yes."

"You not dying. No one ever die from Guillain-Barré. You

just die trying to pronounce it. Hah, hah, pronouncing the diagnosis. Get it?" She laughed sharply and smacked him on the knee. Hiroshi compared the sensation – the lack of sensation – to that he had felt when Dr. Subramanian had done the exact same thing to his arm. There was no difference. He was equally insensible at every point on his body.

"Hey," she said, looking closely at him. "How many moles live in New York City?"

"I don't know."

"One for each 'borough.'" She laughed raucously. "Borough!"

Esther shuffled off to her next patient, laughing at her jokes. Hiroshi mouthed to himself "ghee-yon bar-ay." The 'r' sound was hard to get exactly right, but it was close enough. It hadn't killed him — pronouncing it or learning of it.

The hospital was very quiet. His roommate, a stroke victim, was asleep. He could hear the faint beeps of his monitors from across the room.

"Pronouncing the diagnosis." That was a pretty good pun, he thought.

It hadn't killed him. He sort of wished it had.

4

AFTER ESTHER, one more nurse came to take his temperature, brush his teeth, and feed him some water. He wasn't sure if "feed" was the right verb when one was passively receiving a liquid rather than a solid, but he couldn't think of any other word and wasn't about to ask this very busy woman.

Without a word, prodding him and pushing him like a large lump of dough, the night nurse wrapped him up very tightly in his sheets and lowered the bed to a full horizontal position. The sheets were as tight as those in a hotel bed, but at least when he stayed in a hotel, he had the option of kicking the covers off and sleeping on top of the top sheet. Here, he was trapped. She snapped off the lights and left, without looking back, as if she'd just closed the oven door.

It didn't take him more than fifteen minutes after she'd departed to become intolerably warm and itchy under the sheets. It occurred to him that it was probably a good sign that he could feel itchiness in some parts of his body, but that didn't make him feel any more comfortable. The doctors had not given him any sleeping pills – probably, Hiroshi guessed, because he had a neurological condition. So he stared at the black ceiling and tried not to think of how much he wanted to scratch, of how much he wanted to sleep, of how much he wanted to die.

It was, of course, impossible not to think of such things. Since he was incapable at this moment of accomplishing either sleep or death, he resolved to focus on the itching problem. It was awful beyond words, because every part of his being wanted to toss and turn, to bathe his clammy skin in fresh air, to rake at his leaden forearms with his fingernails. And yet all this had been denied to him by an officious nurse who had tucked him into his swaddling clothes like a newborn.

There was a call button, of course, but it might as well have been in Tokyo. All he had was his voice, weak as it was, and so he began to shout and shout, fearful that he would awaken his roommate but unable to control himself.

No one came. No one would come. It seemed impossible that he would be able to traverse this endless night – he would die of the heat and boredom first, and yet he could not die.

He began to make scratching motions with his fingertips against the bottom sheet, in the disconnected way that a dog rubs at the air with its rear leg when you scratch its neck. It didn't do anything for the intolerable itch in his forearm, but it made him feel better. He performed this phantom motion for a minute or so before realizing that he was, indeed, moving his fingers. *He was moving his fingers!*

He tested his other extremities. Nothing. He couldn't so much as move his wrist up and down, and his fingers, even had they been at normal strength, were far too ineffectual by themselves to tear the sheet from his body. Still, he felt over-joyed that something had changed. He would spend the rest of the night, he resolved, trying to move another extremity.

Within a few minutes, though, when he discovered that

nothing else would move, he was exhausted and once again dispirited. Even the motion in his fingers didn't excite him anymore, and the response seemed to be getting weaker with each iteration, as if he were using up some precious fuel. There wasn't enough of it for a sparrow.

He thought about his fingers on the keys of a piano – his first instrument before the clarinet – and the idea that he now could play wasn't any less absurd than the idea that he ever had played. It was like the time he had had a terrible case of the flu; it wasn't the illness itself that was difficult, anything could be endured for a finite period of time, it was rather the illusion that began to set in by the second day of aching muscles and spiking fevers that he had somehow always felt this way. And if he had had no memory at the moment of not having the flu, then it was just the same as having the flu forever, except that the eternity stretched backwards instead of forwards.

Still, he reminded himself, as the little muscles under the skin of his forearm jumped and twitched, he'd once deployed his fingers with thoughtless grace on the piano. When he was no more than six years old, he could pick out *"Für Elise"* on his little electronic keyboard with the big-eyed dancing frogs on it. He couldn't do it right this moment, but he had to remember, even if it was painful to acknowledge the contrast, that he could do it eighteen years ago, and he could have done it three days ago.

He hadn't been a genius, not quite, but he'd unquestion- ably been a prodigy. When he'd switched to clarinet in his twelfth year, and to jazz in his fourteenth year, he'd brought with him not only his technical facility and prodigious knowl- edge of music, but added to it a sensitivity to nuance, an adventurous spirit, that he'd never known he'd had when he'd been restricted to a printed score. Now, even at this dark moment, there was absolutely no reason to believe that his sensitivity to nuance or his adventurous spirit had deserted him.

All that was gone was his ability to actually play an instrument. To make a living. To walk to the corner and buy an onigiri and a genki drink.

Oh, and to have sex.

He hadn't even, until this moment, thought about that.

He started to think about Hitomi, how she might be feeling about not having spoken to him yet, or rather how she might be feeling about him not having spoken to her. How would she feel when she found out about his pitiful condition? *Oh, Hitomi, perhaps you should know I'm impotent. And perhaps you should know that's the least of it.*

Until now, he hadn't considered her once since stepping on the airplane, except to think about, and feel guilty about, why it was that he wasn't thinking about her. When would she come to mind directly as a person herself, not as a commentary on or admonition to his person? Not any time soon, he was fairly certain. After all, there was that last evening in Tokyo, the one that he didn't want to think about.

What Maureen had said at her apartment, *that* he wanted to think about. He was still angry at her claim that she hadn't been flirting with him or, more accurately, angry that she had indeed flirted with him and then denied it. It was outrageous; he had more female admirers than he knew what to do with in Japan. Beautiful Japanese girls who were, beneath the surface coyness, direct and un-mysterious about their desires. But this American girl...

He stopped himself, remembering that he had been the one who had ridiculed the idea that cultural differences had been involved.

He'd also told Dr. Subramanian that he wasn't mentally ill. But what else would you call a man who spent the first night of his paralysis brooding over a trivial sexual rejection? Maybe he *was* manic-depressive. He was certainly manic at times, and there was no question that he was depressed right now. Or maybe he was passive-aggressive, a term he'd encountered in one of the American magazines he'd read on the way over. But it was confusing; if manic-depressive meant sometimes manic and sometimes depressive, shouldn't passive-aggressive mean sometimes passive and sometimes aggressive? But from the article's context, it appeared that the term meant the tendency to express unhappiness or disagreement through constant passivity. He must be passive-aggressive, he thought, not to have told Maureen what he thought of her behavior in stronger terms.

He began to examine the notion that he was indeed too passive, forgetting for a moment that he existed now in a physical state far beyond mere passivity, but didn't get too far in his examinations before indistinct rooms of familiar design began to appear before his eyes. He stepped into one of them and finally fell asleep.

* * *

HE WOKE up the next morning, having walked confidently in his sleep through many such chambers, each connected to another as dream is to dream, with painfully cracked lips, a sore throat, and a mouth that seemed coated with mucilage. It was too painful to whistle but, miraculously, a young, thin, rather bouncy Hispanic-looking man showed up within moments, bearing a tray with orange juice, water, a bowl of some sort of hot cereal, and a copy of the *New York Post*.

"Hi, I'm Vincent, and I'll be your orderly this morning." He bounced up and down on his heels to indicate his eagerness to serve. The restaurant reference was lost on Hiroshi, but he eyed the water avidly.

"Don't worry, man, I won't make you pick that up yourself," Vincent said. Vincent had a terrible, pockmarked complexion, devilish looking eyebrows, peaked sharply in the middle with the help of plucking, and what appeared to be a light application of lip liner and a faint dusting of lavender eye shadow. He quickly kneeled by Hiroshi's side and raised the back of the bed so that he was again sitting up. He held the glass to Hiroshi's lips and Hiroshi drank, painfully at first but then in noisy gulps.

"Your swallowing isn't working too well. That's why you make that sound. It's the same sound little kids make when they drink, I guess because their throat is still small."

"Yes."

"Did you know that this hospital was used for the survivors of the *Titanic*?

"No, I didn't."

"That was before my time."

"I assumed that was the case."

"Wasn't in the movie though. Once Leonardo Di Caprio and everyone else drowned, no one wanted to hear about no survivors."

"Can I have some orange juice?"

"Yeah. The thing about us is that we're all survivors in this city. No matter what happens, we always make it, man. Hey, you know, now you're a New Yorker too."

"In what way do you mean?"

"I mean, you're a survivor too. I know about you, man. You're in the paper today."

"I am?"

"Sure. Let me show you. I'm not gonna give you any of that orange juice though."

"Why is that?"

"Your lips are too cracked. It's gonna burn like shit. Then how you gonna play?"

"So you know I'm a musician?"

"Yeah. I'll get you another kind of juice. Maybe cranberry. You guys drink that stuff?"

"I've had it."

"Your chart says you're on an unrestricted diet. You know what that means? It means you're not restricted from eating all of the boring bullshit mashed-up-carrot-shit hospital food you want."

"Could I see that article, please?"

"Sure. Hang on a minute, you're not going anywhere for a while." Vincent unfolded the *New York Post* and took his time finding the article, which was on the bottom of Page 17. "Here it is."

Vincent held the paper in front of Hiroshi's eyes so he could read it himself. The article said:

A rising young jazz musician from the land of the rising sun received a rude welcome to New York earlier this week when he had his rare antique clarinet worth an estimated $4,000 snatched out of his hands as he ate lunch at a Midtown hot dog joint. Hiroshi Mori, 24, of Tokyo, is in town to play alongside famed guitarist Grady Granphill in a one-week stand scheduled to begin this weekend. According to a police spokesperson, Mr. Mori was unable to describe his assailants. There are currently no suspects and no leads.

"That's it?"

"What you see is what you get. Pretty exciting, huh? You're famous."

"I thought it was going to be about this," Hiroshi said, referring to his condition. "Besides, they got everything wrong."

"Wrong?" Vincent looked surprised, as if he didn't know that a newspaper could be wrong.

"Yes. For example, the article makes it appear as if someone grabbed my clarinet from me while I was eating, while in actuality, I left it behind and it wasn't there when I returned."

"I guess they have to make it sound more exciting."

"Besides, I'm skilled at judo. I don't think anyone would have such an easy time grabbing such a thing from my hands."

"Is that how you ended up here?"

"What do you mean?"

"You know, judo, accident, hurt your spine or something?"

"No, no. I don't know how it happened, but it wasn't an accident."

"Wow, that is some scary shit. Let me get you some cranberry juice, then I'll feed you your cream of rice. It's usually oatmeal, but I figured you were used to eating some kind of rice for breakfast, right?"

"Would it be possible for you to read me a few of the headlines while you're feeding me?" Hiroshi suddenly felt very eager to know what was going on in the outside world.

"I'd be happy to turn the pages for you," Vincent offered. He held the folded newspaper in one hand and positioned it in front of Hiroshi's eyes while feeding Hiroshi small spoonfuls of cream of rice with the other hand. It occurred to Hiroshi that perhaps Vincent could not read.

"Thank you. You're very kind." Vincent was showing him the sports, which he had no interest in.

"Knicks did it again, huh? This is usually a nurse thing, but we're a little short this morning."

"I appreciate it."

"If you need to have a bowel movement, just let me know and I'll set up the bedpan for you. Everyone here seems to have a BM right after they finish breakfast."

A bedpan? Hiroshi hadn't even thought about how he was going to have a bowel movement. He hadn't had to go yet, but he couldn't hold it forever. He nodded numbly.

"Anything you need, man. I mean it. I really respect musicians, man. I have a little DJ business myself on the side."

"Yes."

"You know what they call me around here? They call me Saint Vincent."

"Why?"

"*Why? Why?* Because this is Saint Vincent's, man. The hospital!"

"Oh, you're right. I'm sorry. That's funny."

"But I mean it, man. Anything you need. You have to have a BM, just let me know and I'll get you set up. Don't give it a second thought. The nurses and me – that's our job."

"How did you know I was worried about doing that?" Hiroshi said.

"Hey, it can't be easy shitting in bed, right? At least not the first time. This your first time in a hospital? Don't worry, you'll get used to it."

* * *

DOCTOR SUBRAMANIAN APPEARED after breakfast to accompany him to the MRI unit for his brain scan. Hiroshi was terrified, even though the doctor assured him it would be painless. As he was wheeled through the hallways, Hiroshi closed his eyes tightly, preferring to look at his own stock of private images rather than the bright lights overhead. Hiroshi wondered why they didn't put interesting pictures or advertisements for painkillers on the ceiling, since so many people passed by flat on their backs.

He remained flat on his back for the MRI, which indeed was painless except for the boredom, and for another in a seemingly endless series of neurological exams, during which the soles of his feet were scratched and tickled – he still didn't laugh – and other body parts were poked with pins. It was like a torture session, though without the pain. He tried to pass the time by thinking of something at once pleasant and irrevocable about himself, something that wouldn't pass like a thing of the flesh, which no longer could be relied upon.

Print, at least, was permanent. He'd seen, and saved, articles about himself in Japanese papers, of course, and then there was that dreadful *New York Post* item and the article in the New York entertainment guide, now forever defiled in his mind. But there was a better article, the only substantive mention he'd received in any of the cities he and Grady had visited on his one tour of Europe, and he decided it was worth holding in his mind and savoring as his irrelevant flesh was tested.

It was in a paper in Amsterdam. It had said, as Hiroshi remembered it, "H. Mori is very young and, in truth, he plays that way. Still, one imagines that his playing, already impressively fluent and appealing, will be determined by the life experiences he has more than players with a more academic bent. Already, his touchingly sad (though somewhat meandering) original compositions mark him as distinctive. And when he solos, he handles his instrument like a glassblower, breathing soul into the melody, shaping it in unexpected ways, and then presenting it to the audience for inspection, oddly shaped but pleasingly whole and complete."

That was nice, but it wasn't as nice as when he had first read it. Trying to remember the exact words, Hiroshi felt that things were missing or maybe misstated. Wasn't there maybe a whole other sentence in there, something about his interaction with Grady's group? Was it "oddly shaped" or *"sometimes* oddly shaped"? But battered by circumstance like that newspaper on the sidewalk the rain had disintegrated, he felt the gaps between the words growing bigger. He couldn't play any more, and soon he wouldn't be able to remember *how* he'd played.

The neurologist, Dr. Lillet, had a long and horsey though curiously delicate face, and long thin fingers that he wielded with much adeptness, as if demonstrating his own neurological fitness. While he worked, Dr. Subramanian stood watching.

"Is there any more idea on what condition I have?" He tried to address his comment to Dr. Subramanian, but the neurologist answered.

"All we can say is non-specific polyneuritis."

"A nurse told me that I had Guillain-Barré."

Dr. Subramanian laughed. "That's why they call it non-specific. Guillain-Barré is a specific diagnosis of a very particular syndrome." He looked at the neurologist for confirmation.

Dr. Lillet spoke up. "Right. A diagnosis of non-specific polyneuritis is just a place-holder until we figure out what's behind it. It's almost certainly Guillain-Barré. You should consider yourself lucky, all things considered."

"Why?"

"Well, because these days with plasmapheresis and intravenous immunoglobulins and other treatments, virtually everyone who gets this syndrome in a Western country, you know, a modern, technological country, survives. And not only survives, but recovers almost completely."

"You mean I have a good chance of recovery?"

"Yeah, because you're a good candidate for plasmapheresis in light of the fact that you had an acute, serious loss of muscular strength. You're luckier in some ways that someone with a long, gradual onset of weakness. The plasmapheresis isn't a magic bullet, and we're not completely sure what it does, but best guess is it removes certain antibodies that attack the myelin around your nerves and some other substances that contribute to your illness. Anyway, you should gain back almost all your faculties when this is all done with," the neurologist said. "About 95 percent of all GBS patients do."

"What exactly is this disease I have?"

"Guillain-Barré? It's an acute demyelinating neuropathy."

Hiroshi sensed instinctively that further questions about the nature of the disease would not necessarily lead to further illumination. He turned, instead, to his own prognosis.

"And when will this all be done with?"

"Could be as little as two months or so and you'll be playing the sax again."

"Clarinet."

"Or it could be a couple, three years before you're back to more or less normal. But you'll definitely get there."

"Does that mean walking?"

Dr. Subramanian answered. "Of course."

Hiroshi had decided not to be passive-aggressive anymore, just aggressive. "But Doctor Lillet, I've spent every moment in this hospital until right now thinking I would never walk again."

"But you had no reason to think that, since we didn't have a diagnosis yet."

"But doctor, how else could I feel, given that no one told me anything they knew?"

"Because we *didn't* know. We weren't 100 percent sure."

"But why is it that a nurse knew?"

"A nurse made an educated guess. She had no business doing so."

"So why couldn't you make that same guess? It would have saved me many hours of depressed feelings."

"Mr. Mori, we made that guess the minute you came in and told us you'd been immunized before leaving Japan. Guillain-Barré is a rare auto-immune disorder that can be triggered by certain immunizations."

"Once again, Doctor Lillet, if you had an educated guess, why not tell me?"

"Because the human body is a supremely complicated mechanism. Because there are literally thousands of syndromes and diseases walking around out there. Because if we had been wrong, we would have told you that you'd be out playing tennis in six weeks. And then we'd have to come back again to tell you that we were wrong, throw your false hope out the window, you're in a wheelchair for life, or worse. Or maybe just the opposite – we take away all your hope and then come back and say oops, we made a mistake. Would you have liked that, Mr. Mori? Or would you have maybe sued us?"

Hiroshi was silent. He was a little bit angry, but he also felt an unexpected sense of pride that he had stood up to this doctor. It was something he never could have done with a doctor in Japan, because they were so intimidating and distant, and besides, it just wasn't done. Even when every doctor you had ever been to since childhood was one of your relatives. *Especially* when.

When he returned to his room, Vincent was waiting with his lunch – reddish soup and redder Jell-O – and some news.

"You're having a very special visitor tomorrow. Someone who's coming from Japan."

"Who is it? Hitomi?"

"I don't know. Is Hitomi a man's name?"

"No."

"Then it's not Hitomi."

"Then who is it?"

Vincent was rocking up and down on his heels. He reminded Hiroshi of Tigger from Winnie the Pooh. He reminded Hiroshi of himself, at least the way he was a few days ago.

70

Vincent smiled broadly. "I'm not supposed to say. But it's your father."

* * *

HIS FATHER. This was very bad.

Because there was no one who loved Hiroshi like his father.

Other than Hiroshi, his father was practically the only male member of his family, either on his side or on his mother's side, who was not a doctor. He was known in the family, in fact, as Not a Doctor. He was a famous Zen poet, famous at least in the exceptionally narrow circles that Zen poets traveled in. He had a very complicated love-hate relationship with doctors, though there was no such term as "love-hate relationship" in Japanese, and in any event his feelings were much closer to hate. He tormented Hiroshi with his support.

Vincent had pulled from his shirt pocket a folded piece of lined notebook paper he brandished in front of Hiroshi's eyes. "Look at this, man. Not just your father. All the people who called you." Hiroshi had a little trouble getting his eyes to focus on the thin sheet, which kept on flopping over Vincent's hands. He saw his father's name, an uncle, some Japanese friends, all egregiously misspelled, plus Grady Granphill, also misspelled, and a couple of other musicians in New York. No Hitomi, no Maureen – not that the absence of either one mattered, he told himself.

He was coming here tomorrow. His father was coming here tomorrow. Hiroshi was just beginning to absorb this acid fact along with his tomatoish soup when another very special visitor arrived, bearing a very large cardboard carton.

She looked vaguely familiar to Hiroshi. Maybe she was one of the nurses who'd first attended to him when he'd arrived. But she wasn't wearing a nurse's uniform.

"Mr. Mori? My name is Carmelita."

"Yes. Hello."

"Mr. Mori, let me introduce myself. I was the maid who cleaned your room at the Gramercy West."

Sheets, pillows, linens. No wonder he'd thought she was a nurse. Hiroshi had no idea why she was here.

"Mr. Mori, I brought you some of your things from your room. The hotel had to give your room to someone else. I'm very sorry."

"I couldn't be going back there anyway. Thank you for bringing them."

"I am very sorry, Mr. Mori."

"Thank you. I'm feeling a little better each day."

"I am glad. But I am very sorry about something else. When I see the "Do Not Disturb" sign on your door in the morning, I do not disturb. This is what the manager tell me is the rule. But I know something is wrong. I hear funny sounds."

His crying, probably. "Did the hotel tell you to come here to the hospital?"

"No, they put the suitcases in the..."

"Storage?"

"Yes. Storage. I should come in earlier or tell the manager that something wrong. So you have to lay on the floor so long because I know something is wrong but I don't do anything. I'm sorry."

"It wasn't your fault. I got sick."

"I'm sorry, Mr. Mori. So I just bring you the things I think you need now, because you seem so nice and interesting man when I clean up your room and then when I see the polices carry you away..." She started to cry.

He wondered whether she had seen his dirty magazine. He wondered whether she had packed it in the carton. She placed the carton in the tight space between his bed and the powderblue curtain separating him from his roommate. And as she did so, he got a clear view of his Regent clarinet. He, too, began to cry.

"What is the matter? Do you need the nurse?"

"No, it's only that you thought I could use my clarinet. But...thank you. Thank you for bringing it. You didn't have to come here, but you came."

After she left, Hiroshi was left alone again to contemplate his father's imminence. He was very hungry for distraction, for news, and he gazed at the copy of the *New York Post* with the article about him that Vincent had left at the head of the bed. Using his nose, he tried to open the newspaper to read something, anything. He managed to get the paper open to a page where he could see, so close to his eyes that it hurt to focus, an ad featuring a woman in a one-piece bathing suit holding over her head, Atlas-like, a volleyball. It advertised inexpensive air fares to Bermuda.

Holding the page open with his nose, looking at the volleyball, Hiroshi felt a bit like a trained seal. He thought of the way seals looked out of the water, with their palsied flippers and slippery paralytic bodies and, with a loud groan, pulled his head away from the unreadable paper that now bore a faint grease spot where his head had been.

"What's the matter?"

It was his roommate. Hiroshi turned his head. "I'm sorry?"

"What's the matter?"

"I'm sorry I disturbed you. I don't even know your name."

"Harry Blenwen. I know your name. Hiroshi, right?"

"Yes. Nice to meet you."

His roommate appeared on the other side of the powder blue curtain, moving laboriously with a walker. He was wearing the same light grey hospital gown, open at the back, that Hiroshi had worn since he had first entered the hospital naked. Hiroshi had seen him only horizontally until now and was surprised to see that he was a relatively young, though lumpishly constructed, man. Reading his thoughts, Harry said, "I'm thirty-eight. Never expected to have a stroke at this age."

"What happened? I understand that high blood pressure can cause such a thing."

"Nah, cocaine, probably. I own a chain of 6 furniture stores in New York and New Jersey. A fuck of a lot of pressure and a fuck of a lot of money. Mix the two together and you get cocaine. Fun while it lasted. I've been here about a month. Not nearly as much fun."

"I didn't know you could get a stroke from that."

"Yeah. Not just cocaine. Crystal meth, tequila, shit like that. They should print warning labels, huh? I'm moving to a rehab center tomorrow for the next couple of months. After that, probably back to work. So what happened to you?"

"Guillain-Barré. No one knows for certain from what it comes. Perhaps an immunization or a previous bout with food poisoning or the flu. The body has an auto-immune reaction and attacks the spinal cord."

"Is it permanent?"

"No, temporary." Hiroshi felt bad saying this, because one side of Harry's face sagged, and he spoke with a strong slur that made him a bit hard to understand. Nothing about his condition looked temporary.

But Harry looked happy for him. "Well, that's great. Get the hell out of here and fuck some broads, right?"

"Yes."

"I didn't do enough of that. I regret that now. Too much damn work. Actually, that's bullshit. Too much fucking coke."

"I'm sorry."

"So how did you learn such good English?"

Hiroshi smiled, the first time he'd done so since collapsing on the floor of the Gramercy West Hotel. He took a deep breath and concentrated very hard. "Now I think I would have preferred not to have been becoming then what I probably will have become a year from now until I had at least become what I had wanted to be at that time before then."

Harry looked upset. "Am I supposed to understand what you just said?"

"No, I'm sorry. This was just a sentence I invented in English to practice my tenses, which are always very difficult. I thought of it just now for some reason."

"Good. I thought I was having another fucking stroke."

"I'm sorry. It actually makes perfect sense, but you have to think about it for a while."

"Maybe you have to. I don't. You still didn't tell me how you learned."

"Well, like all Japanese people, I had many years of English study in school. But that only teaches us how to read and write to some degree, not to speak. My parents were very ambitious for my education. My mother wanted me to be a doctor, and my father wanted me... he just wanted me to be educated. So I went to English-language conversation schools all through high school. And since then, I have spent a lot of time with musicians who play in Japan, and we always speak English." Hiroshi, sensitive to Harry's regrets, didn't mention that much of his near-idiomatic fluency had derived from a two-year relationship with an Australian girl living in Tokyo named Kerri, his last girlfriend before Hitomi.

"So what were you groaning about?"

"I was trying to read the newspaper, but of course I can't pick it up. I'm very anxious to see the news."

"So? You never heard of TV? We're in this expensive semi-private room with a TV and a DVD player. Geeks like us, what else we gonna do?"

Harry shuffled back through the curtain. In a moment he

re-emerged with the remote control and turned on the TV over Hiroshi's bed. "Whaddya wanna watch?"

Hiroshi repeated Harry's sentence softly to himself. Casual English was so beautiful.

Whaddya wanna, whaddya wanna? I wanna go home, Hiroshi thought.

Harry, waiting, said, "So?"

"I don't know the channels so well in New York. Is there CNN, perhaps?"

"I'll find it for you. Gotta keep it low, though. I'm supposed to be asleep."

Hiroshi settled back to watch CNN – settling back, in his case, meaning that he let his head rest comfortably against the pillow instead of thrusting it ahead like a terrapin, as he had been doing all the time he'd been talking to Harry. He had held his head forward with particular care and rigidity while reciting that complex sentence he was so proud of, and now he had muscle cramps on the side of his neck, running up into his temple, and at the base of his tongue. The only part of his body that worked, and it was sore. He realized that he must have been thrusting his head forward from the moment he'd entered the hospital in an attempt to project his enervated voice.

When he swung his head gently back and forth to relieve the cramp, he felt and heard slippery popping sounds, as if his neck were packed with slimy chow mein noodles and bean sprouts. With a disgusted sigh, Hiroshi focused on the screen.

On CNN that day, Hiroshi learned that North Korea had fired another long-range missile over Japanese airspace. There were recessionary rumblings in Western Europe. Japan's Nikkei stock index had hit its lowest point in more than a decade. Reports from an Iranian defector to Kuwait suggested that Iran had obtained long-range ballistic missile technologies capable of delivering payloads to Western

Europe, and Israel and Iran were engaged in a war of words that some analysts feared could degenerate into an actual war that could embroil the entire Middle East.

Then there was a feature story about a philosopher-scientist from Cambridge University who had written a book positing that the overuse of computers was eroding the imaginative faculties of the human brain.

After this story, there was a commercial, the first of many, featuring a man riding on a commuter train whose cell phone signaled him – though this was not at all the point of the commercial, but rather an incidental detail – with the opening notes of "Ode to Joy."

This bothered Hiroshi obscurely, because the melody wasn't accidental, like the first notes of "Blue Danube Waltz" that he'd heard coming from his family's microwave when he was a child. It also bothered him more directly because he worried that the constant repetition of such mechanical melodies on commuter trains and in other public places would erode the ability of people to appreciate their original elegance. Not to mention that the ease with which they could be summoned would make people think that they were equally easy to compose.

The concept of "eroding" made him think, very briefly, that his muscles must already be eroding from his prolonged inactivity. He made a mental note to ask Dr. Subramanian about that.

And then the report before that annoying commercial, hadn't that been about "eroding," too? Hiroshi tried to recall what he had just seen moments before, even as, on the screen above his aching head, the reports rumbled sententiously on. It was, he remembered, some odd-looking philosopher who said that our ability to think imaginatively was beginning to – think of another English word, a synonym, Hiroshi chided himself – *atrophy*, because of the overuse of computers.

Everything was eroding. Eroding and *atrophying* – how on Earth would such a word be pronounced? – and devolving and decaying and disintegrating.

If people could no longer think imaginatively, how on Earth could they appreciate jazz anymore, a music that, as it was, accounted for only 1.2 percent of CD sales anyway?

Of which his one release, "Obitadashii" – an obscure Japanese word that meant an immense number, as in notes – had accounted for perhaps .000001 percent of that already minimal total. Most of his sales had been in Germany – "Obitadashii" had been released by a small German jazz label Grady had fixed him up with – and, of course, in Japan.

How could he ever hope to record another, more successful, CD if nobody was capable of listening anymore?

How could he have a successful CD release if there was indeed a war in the Middle East? A war in the Middle East would mean many deaths, perhaps chemical and biological warfare this time around, and certainly another disruption in global oil supplies. This would mean a severe blow to the global economy. There probably weren't many jazz fans in Syria or Iran, but a serious recession would make it difficult for jazz fans elsewhere in the world to buy a lot of new CDs. And they would certainly be less likely to risk their money on a new release or search out a new download by an obscure Japanese clarinetist.

There also had been a report on new advances in human cloning, but Hiroshi couldn't think of any reason why a clone would be either less likely or more likely to buy a jazz recording.

But the Nikkei was plunging. In the case of Japan, that meant fewer purchase of CDs, and in particular his CDs, than would otherwise be the case. And if one of those North Korean missiles actually hit Tokyo, it would be horrible. The death, the destruction, the recording studios and record stores and potential buyers of his CDs up in flames...

What on Earth was he thinking of? Esther had appeared in the room with a rolling cart bearing a basin slopping over with soapy water and a sponge. He could barely look at her as she snapped off the TV and prepared him for his first sponge bath since early infancy. If she knew what I'd been thinking, he thought, she wouldn't want to even touch me.

I am nothing less than a monster of selfishness, he thought. The fiery deaths of millions, and all I can think about is the success of my new CD. Awful, awful, he told himself as Esther roughly stripped off his bedclothes and hospital gown. Awful, awful, he thought as he tried to remind himself of all the selfless and altruistic things he had done in his life. But he'd barely begun to go through that list when he was consumed by guilt at the thought of Hitomi consumed by flames. A monster.

Esther began rubbing the sponge over Hiroshi's naked body. Punish me, he thought, flay me with that razor-sharp sponge.

He could feel next to nothing, of course, which only reminded him that, even if the world were not to be consumed in a fiery conflagration, he was not physically capable of recording a new CD. At least, he reflected after a moment, the smell of soap was pleasant, and, even though she wasn't attractive, Esther's physical proximity to him made him feel warm and secure, as if he really were an infant. She probed gently with the washcloth underneath the plastic bracelet he had been given upon his arrival, in case he were to be mistaken for any other paralyzed young Japanese men with interrupted eyebrows and blue streaks in their hair.

How did he know she was probing gently and not harshly? The fact was, he knew. The sponge actually felt good on him as Esther sluiced off the grime of the Gramercy West Hotel.

Perhaps it was just the warmth of the soapy water he was feeling, the way its scent reawakened a skin-memory of relaxing in a hot tub at an *onsen*. But on some spots, his ankles for example, and the small of his back, he was certain he could feel something.

He fell asleep focused on these physical sensations rather than on his complicity in the death of millions, and was awakened once to have dinner and once to have his teeth brushed and his signs checked by the night nurse. Otherwise, he slept straight through the late afternoon and evening of his second day in the hospital and his fourth day in America.

And awakened the next morning freshly bathed and nicely scented for his meeting with his father.

In the time before his father came, Vincent fed Hiroshi his breakfast again – cream of rice again, though Harry had had oatmeal – and he talked basketball, mostly to Harry. Harry's move to the rehab center was happening later that day.

"Hey, Saint Vincent," Harry said as Vincent was feeding Hiroshi his cereal. "How come I get oatmeal and he gets cream of rice?"

"Just trying to make him feel at home, man."

"You could make me feel at home by bringing me a fucking slice of sausage pizza every once in a while, gay-wad."

Vincent guffawed. "I'd have to chew it up for you first, cripple."

Hiroshi was perfectly aware of American-style humor and didn't find exchanges such as these unfunny. But he found himself looking forward all the same to speaking to someone who spoke his own language, even, he reflected, if that someone was his father.

He got his wish that evening, after his first plasmapheresis treatment. The treatment, which was administered right in his room by a technician operating a grandfather-clock-shaped machine that silently filtered his blood, took about ninety minutes. The treatment left him feeling deeply fatigued, though not quite as dispirited as he'd feared when the technician explained how his blood was to be removed from his body and disassembled, his plasma removed and replaced. Indeed, when it was done, Hiroshi imagined himself as cleansed internally as he had been, after his sponge bath, externally.

Then his father walked in bearing a beautifully wrapped parcel. Hiroshi inclined his head slightly – the nearest approach to a bow his father was going to get. Mr. Mori responded by raising his considerable eyebrows, which were pure white and large enough to rival the reach of his nose when seen in profile. His ears had their own, more modest complement of soft hairs. The eyebrows were famous in Japan, appearing in thick Japanese literary magazines and on the occasional talk show. Hiroshi's father was a powerfully built little man, not unhandsome, with calm, rather watery eyes and a deeply lined face – he had been forty-two when he and Hiroshi's late mother had conceived this child who once again to all appearances was no different than an infant.

Forty-two. Hiroshi had read not too long ago a report that sons conceived by fathers over forty were more likely to develop prostate cancer when they themselves were in their forties.

One more thing to worry about, but it would have to wait, he decided, until he was a little bit recovered.

Hiroshi's half brother, Manabu, would have more to worry about when he was old enough to begin brooding about such things. Hiroshi's father and his new wife, Miyoko, had conceived Manabu five years ago, when the old man was sixty.

Mr. Mori handed Hiroshi the parcel – handed it, that is, by placing it carefully on the bed next to Hiroshi's now-too-prominent ribcage. It probably contained fancy cookies or rice crackers, and — through a process that Hiroshi had very little control over — would in the course of the next few days end up on just the other side of his ribs.

Mr. Mori pulled up a wooden chair and seated himself at the foot of the bed, one leg crossed over the other and his hand gripped tightly around the protruding knee. A long and familiar silence ensued.

Hiroshi broke it. "How was your flight over?" It was the first full sentence he'd spoken in Japanese since he'd shouted "Chotto matte, kudasai" to the maid knocking at his door.

"It was fine. Very pleasant." Mr. Mori had been to New York several times before for readings and appearances, meetings with translators, awards from Buddhist literary societies.

"Did it arrive late?" Hiroshi and his father both knew very well that the JAL flight from Narita to JFK arrived every day at about eleven-thirty a.m. It was now nearly seven p.m.

Mr. Mori looked around the room with distaste, but said nothing. Finally, he said, rather cautiously, "Is it very painful?"

"Actually, only my head and neck hurt."

"I understood that the problem was in the rest of your body, and that your head and neck were unaffected."

"That's right. If the rest of my body hurt, that would be a good sign, because it would mean that I'd regained some sensation. Not feeling anything is the primary symptom I'm facing."

"I get it. But then I'm not clear as to why your head and neck are hurting."

"Well, because they're the only parts of my body I can use, I've been overusing them. I build up a lot of tension there. Listen, would you like to talk directly to one of the doctors? I'm sure we could find one who knows some French."

Hiroshi's father knew very little English, but could get along in French. Nonetheless, at this suggestion, he gave a sidewise wave of his hand, as if to say that this wasn't necessary because... because he trusted Hiroshi's account of his own illness? Because he wasn't concerned with the details? There was no question that Mr. Mori was very good at paring away from his life everything that was extraneous. "Pure," "allusive," and "spare" were the adjectives most commonly attached to his tropes.

"You know," his father said, "I had the impression from talking to your agent that I'd find you in a wheelchair, which would be bad enough. This is surprising."

"I'm sorry that you found me this way."

A wave of the hand again. "It must be awkward and embarrassing for you."

"A bit."

"Well, at least you'll have time to think." At this, an old joke in a new context, both father and son laughed a little. So far, the old man was on pretty good behavior, though this lightened Hiroshi's earlier apprehension only imperceptibly. Mr. Mori's effect, as with low levels of radioactive contamination, was cumulative.

Hiroshi asked, "Can I call a nurse to get you anything?"

"I'm fine. Just a little tired from my trip. I have to go to my hotel and get some sleep, so I can spend more time with you tomorrow. How about you? Anything you need?"

"No. I'm fine now."

"Are you well-cared for here?"

"Actually, I am. I had a sponge bath yesterday, and this evening they're clipping my nails." Back in Tokyo, a typical evening would involve, after rehearsal, a disco, or dinner at Hitomi's, or merengue dancing, or an occasional scheduled or fill-in gig at B-Flat or at Sometime, the subterranean club in Kichijoji where he and Hitomi would hang out. It was close to both of their tiny apartments; when he wasn't performing there, he and Hitomi listened to other musicians and talked to them about their lives. In truth, there were so many places to hang out in Kichijoji that Hiroshi used to feel frustrated that he could be in only one place at a time. Now he was looking forward to getting his nails clipped.

He sighted down along the sheets to where his hands lay and wondered, if he were able to bring them to his eyes, whether he would find his nails dirty and ragged. He suddenly felt a bit self-conscious in front of his father, and tried to pull his hands back under the covers, but of course was unable to. Before the family baths he used to share with his parents and sister, his father had scrubbed him from head to toe outside of the water, just as the nurse yesterday had done. He wondered if his father was remembering the same thing.

"Well, then," his father said.

"Well, then." Discounting alcohol-related illnesses, which were not inconsiderable, Hiroshi's father had never been seriously ill once in his life, not even during the war years. He hated hospitals as much as he hated doctors. He had often told Hiroshi that he believed the reason he had never gotten sick was that he didn't allow himself to think about sickness or hospitals or medicine. This didn't explain, however, why Hiroshi's two uncles and the other family members who were doctors, and therefore surrounded by sickness, rarely got sick either.

It did explain, however, why his father had arrived at the hospital more than six hours after his flight had landed.

Hiroshi's father got up to leave. "Remember, Hiroshi, we need you on our team. When it comes to the grownups, it's just you and me, isn't it?"

At this moment, just as Mr. Mori was saying, "You and me," Maureen appeared at the door. She was wearing a light-brown leather skirt with fringes and a blue cowboy shirt with colorful piping in a lasso pattern.

Hiroshi thought she looked ridiculous.

She was holding a lumpy gift-wrapped package that

appeared to contain large balls of some sort, or perhaps small grapefruit. The shape, whatever it was, was appalling.

In her other hand, she carried a small canvas shopping bag that held a couple of magazines. Hiroshi could see the top of one magazine. Above its title, which he couldn't quite make out, was the admonition, in a bold font, "Get Spiritual NOW!"

"Ah, a cowgirl!" Mr. Mori said in English.

Maureen walked over to Mr. Mori, who was rising very slowly from his wooden chair to greet her. Before he had fully straightened, she tossed the lumpy package and the shopping bag filled with magazines onto the room's other chair – a copy of *Elle* sliding onto the floor – and shook his hand vigorously. "You know about cowgirls? Cool! I'm Hiroshi's friend Maureen. You must be the dad."

"Yes, I am Mr. Mori. I am pleased to meet you."

"Hajimemashite," Maureen replied, pronouncing it passably well. It was the standard phrase, literally meaning "for the first time," that Japanese people used upon first meetings.

Hiroshi couldn't believe it. "Where did you learn that?"

"I've been practicing," Maureen said. She walked over to the bed. "How you feeling, Hero?"

"I'm alright, considering. Thank you for coming to visit me."

"Do I detect a note of irony in your thank you?"

"I'm not even a little bit an ironic person."

"You're still mad at me, aren't you?"

"No."

"Of course you are. No reason to be, but you are." She peered over the bed at the box of his possessions that Carmelita had brought. "It took me a while to find out where you were. I called your hotel a couple of times and left messages, but you didn't call me back. Then I tried the club and the Academy, and they had no idea where you were. I wanted to talk to you about that article in the *Post*."

"Did you talk to the reporter?"

"No, it must have been that policeman. Maybe he thought a little publicity would make it harder for the fences to sell it, so it'd be easier for him to track it down. Anyway, your agent eventually called the club, and the word got back to the school, and here I am."

She walked around the bed to the carton and began looking through it. "This all your stuff from the hotel?"

"Yes, but it's personal."

"Don't worry. It's only me." She picked through the box for a minute. "I thought you might like to hear some of this music while you're in bed." She pulled out his portable CD player. The wires were tangled around a small box of condoms Hiroshi had brought to New York just in case. She tossed the gold-colored box onto Hiroshi's bedside table. The box slid open, and a few foil-wrapped condoms, also gold-colored, spilled out. Mr. Mori, who had been watching all this with his usual bemused expression, laughed.

"I think you won't be using those for a while," he said in Japanese.

"What'd he say?" Maureen asked.

"Nothing," Hiroshi said stiffly.

"He probably said you wouldn't have a lot of use for those things," Maureen said. "Oh c'mon, Hero, you gotta laugh. You think I didn't talk to your Doctor Lillet before coming in here? This is temporary, and the better an attitude you have, the quicker you'll recover."

"Thank you for that medical analysis. However, perhaps you should bear in mind while you're cheering me up that even if I meet my doctors' most optimistic goals and I'm one of the ninety-five percent of patients who recover..."

"No, Hiroshi," Maureen cut in. "It's that a hundred

percent recover in the sense that they don't die and gradually get better, and ninety-five percent of them regain most or all of their abilities."

Hiroshi paused. He was certain that Dr. Lillet had said that only ninety-five percent of sufferers recover at all. He closed his eyes to gather his thoughts, and then, with just as much certainty as he had felt just a second before, realized that Maureen was indeed correct. He collected himself, having no intention of permitting Maureen to see that he had been certain in his error.

"What I mean to say was, if I am one of the patients who recover almost all of my faculties..." He paused. The sentence was a bit too long for him. "It depends on what 'almost' means. Is ninety-five percent 'almost'? If there's just a two-percent permanent loss of my faculties, that missing two percent is probably the difference between being a professional musician and a talented amateur. And what if it's five percent? Or ten percent?"

"Duly noted, Hero."

Mr. Mori said to Hiroshi, in Japanese, "What is she saying?"

Hiroshi said, in Japanese, "Mostly, she's interfering."

His skin had started to itch again, rather badly. If Maureen hadn't been Maureen, he'd almost be tempted to ask her to pull back the covers and scratch his forearms and chest.

Maureen watched Hiroshi's exchange with his father and then continued. "But in fact you don't know where the five percent or ten percent or whatever the percentage loss of faculties will show up, do you? Maybe you'll drag your foot from now on. That's not such a good thing, I agree, but I can't see how it'll affect your playing. Maybe your shoulders will be weak and you'll have to take more frequent breaks while playing, and maybe you won't be quite so good at judo.

"Or maybe you just won't be able to wiggle your butt anymore. I don't know. *You* don't know. All I know is your doctor said you have to start rehab exercises pretty soon, and there's no point going into it with the attitude that your career is over."

Hiroshi sighed. "As you just said, 'duly noted.'"

She opened up a CD from the box and loaded it into his Walkman. "Here, lift your head up and I'll put the earphones on."

"My neck is very sore."

"Yeah, yeah, but this won't kill you. This is music. You need some music."

She hadn't even asked what he felt like listening to! He didn't think he could bear to hear Benny Goodman, for example. But it happened to be his rare copy of Tim Buckley's *Star Sailor*, which in fact was exactly what he felt like listening to. He closed his eyes as the melancholy voice surrounded him.

Immediately, Maureen interrupted. She was back at the carton, pulling at his things.

"Hiroshi, where's your wallet and passport?"

"You mean they're not in there?"

"They're not in there."

"Then I have no idea." Probably an EMT had stolen them, or they had just gotten lost in the confusion. He looked over at his father, thinking he should explain the situation in Japanese, but Mr. Mori was staring off into space, smiling faintly – an expression, or rather lack of expression, that Hiroshi had seen many times before.

Hiroshi closed his eyes and tried to picture the contents of his wallet. Four $20 bills, he was fairly sure. Maybe 10,000 yen, a couple of credit cards, pictures of Manabu and Hitomi and his late mother, and the crisply folded and insanely detailed map of the area around the Academy that he'd drawn. But all of those were replaceable. What really had him worried – what wasn't replaceable – were his lists.

There were six in all. One, written in very small script on six very thin sheets of paper, contained a list of 697 CDs he hoped to buy or at least listen to at some point in the next few years. An additional 80 or so titles, already purchased or listened to, were scratched out. There were other lists, a little less ambitious, of 64 places in the world he hoped to someday visit, the 65th, New York City, just recently scratched out; of 31 very specific career goals, none of which, certainly not the gig in New York, had been scratched out; of 16 foods he wanted to try while in New York; of 44 experiences he hoped to have before dying (the handful of sexual ones written, thankfully, in code); and, mostly to please his father, a list of 19 books he wished to read someday.

Losing these lists was almost as bad as losing his ability to move. He could, he supposed, try to reconstruct them from memory, but forgetting even one item on even one list would be painful to him, because whatever it was he forgot was likely to be the most important item of all. Even if it were an unimportant item that he forgot, the list would no longer be complete, and besides, he'd have no way of knowing if the missing item were important or not, and he'd always wonder what it had been. Then it occurred to him that having the lists but not being able to accomplish anything on them was an even worse torment. So if that were the case, maybe he was marginally better off now than he was a few minutes ago before he'd discovered, or rather before Maureen had discovered, that his list of life goals was lost forever.

Still, it was maddening. He wanted to be able to clench his fists so he could dig his fingernails into his palms until they bled all over his hospital gown.

Just then, Maureen said, "Oh, never mind! False alarm!" She had opened the drawer next to Hiroshi's bedside table, and by turning his head painfully, Hiroshi could see his wallet and passport nestled side by side.

He felt joy at this discovery, fury at Maureen for the false alarm, and profound irritation at himself for having forgotten that, when he first was wheeled into the hospital, one of the EMTs had handed his wallet over to the admitting nurse, who had extracted from it his Choki Sogo Hoken card for long-term total medical insurance and then peered at it, and him, from over her half glasses.

Maureen was thumbing through the wallet. "Looks like you got about forty bucks and some Japanese money. Who's the cute kid?" She put Manabu's picture aside and pulled open one of his precious lists. "What's all this tiny Japanese writing?"

Mustering all of the peremptoriness he could manage with his weak voice, Hiroshi said, "It's both highly personal and of very little interest even to someone like you."

She shrugged. "Well, I just thought I'd say hi. I know you're not going anywhere, so don't try to avoid me!"

Hiroshi could only half-hear her. He nodded. She motioned to his father to come with her. Hiroshi had almost forgotten that his father was even in the room. Hiroshi expected Mr. Mori to refuse, even though he had been about to leave at the moment when Maureen had first walked in. But the great man, this subtle intellectual force and tough-minded societal scold, got up with painful slowness from his wooden chair, said, in Japanese, "Well then," and meekly followed her out of the room.

Hiroshi breathed a sigh of relief. He was glad the two of them were gone, and amused himself trying to imagine the awkward silence as the poet and cowgirl rode down the elevator together. He hoped Maureen would at least think to help his father into a taxi back to his hotel.

There was something that Maureen had said that had intrigued him, though. What was it?

His buttocks – maybe, she'd said, the continuing weakness would show up only in his buttocks.

Or maybe, he thought bitterly, those would be the only muscles that still worked normally. He tried to will them to move and discovered, to his surprise, that he could wiggle them rather easily.

He began to move each one, alternately, in time to the song he was listening to, "Monterey," and after a minute or so of this looked up to see Grady Granphill standing in the doorway. A very skinny, light-skinned black man with reddish freckles and thinning reddish hair, he had aged considerably since the last time Hiroshi had seen him in Tokyo.

Hiroshi shook his head slightly and knocked the earphones off his head. He could hear Tim Buckley's toy-like voice faintly from the pillow next to him.

"'Roshi?"

"Grady, hello." He felt deeply irritated for some reason, even more so than he had with Maureen and his father. Was Grady here to lecture him too? Could he tell he'd been keeping time with his buttocks?

"Man, what the hell happened to you?"

Hiroshi tried to listen to the distant sound of Tim Buckley's voice while also appearing to listen to Grady. "It's something called Guillain-Barré. I'll tell you about it, but some other time if you don't mind."

"Hey, not a problem. Not a problem at all. At all. I'm just glad it wasn't something worse when you didn't show up for rehearsal."

"What do you mean, worse?"

"Hell, a lot of things could've been worse. A lot worse. By one a.m., believe me, I'd thought of every one of 'em. Murdered. Stabbed. Suicide. Every one."

91

"I would have called you if I had been able to."

"Of course, of course. I don't care about that."

"Is the gig canceled?"

"Listen, don't worry about that. Don't worry about a thing except getting better. Nothin' but getting better."

"I think that's your way of telling me that you found someone to fill in."

"So we found someone to fill in. Sure we did. Yeah. Your place is waiting for you as soon as you get better. As *soon* as you get better."

"*If* I get better. Enough."

"Your friend Maureen told me it was a sure thing."

"This woman seems to know a lot of people. How did she find you?"

"Hey, 'Roshi, don't get irritated. Okay? Don't get yourself knotted up. I just saw her in the lobby with your father. Course I didn't know who they were at the time. They were talking Japanese. Then I guess she recognized me, and she told me all about your condition."

"I'm certain she did. So I can say it's probably quite unnecessary for me to tell you anything myself."

"I didn't say that. Did *not* say that."

"And what do you mean they were talking Japanese? She and my father?"

"Yeah, I guess. I wouldn't know Japanese from Martian. But they were talking somethin'."

"Grady, I'm a little bit tired right now. Would you mind leaving?"

"By the way, this Maureen chick is fine looking. She asked if she could audition with me. I said sure, c'mon by."

"I would really prefer you leave quite soon."

Grady hesitated for a moment. "Sure, man. If that's what you want."

"That is definitely what I want."

"Alright, then. If that's what you want. Here, I brought you something." Grady left a thin, square package on the bedside table next to the condoms. It couldn't be anything other than a CD, and most likely wasn't anything other than one of Grady's own recordings. "Listen, I'll stop by again in a day or two, okay?"

Grady waited for a moment for Hiroshi to respond. When he didn't, when in fact he turned his throbbing head away from Grady to face the curtain that divided his side of the room from the now-empty half vacated by the cocaine-addict furniture-store owner, whatever his name had been, Grady walked slowly out of the room.

Hiroshi felt very tired, and a bit stunned at his own rudeness. Grady had been extraordinarily kind to him over the years and had stuck his neck out to help him come to America. And he hadn't made a joke about the condoms. Hiroshi moved his buttocks a few more times, but felt like a fool and stopped. He looked down at his left foot, which was sticking out from under the sheets, and tried to wiggle his toe. It didn't move at all. Looking at his distant foot like that, Hiroshi suddenly remembered the dream he'd had last night, and remembered also that he'd had it several nights previously as well – the one about the distant car of the train.

He wasn't sure how many times he'd had the dream, but his memory of it was like a picture reproduced on a clear acetate sheet that had been placed over a nearly identical picture on acetate, which in turn had been placed over yet another nearly identical version, and so on. The edges of each weren't precisely aligned, and there were little differences visible around the margins, but the overall image on the top sheet was quite clear, and it was difficult to tell exactly how many iterations there were underneath, only that there were quite a few.

Could he have been dreaming this dream for a long time,

even before his illness, but become aware of it only lately, because the intensity of the recent dreams had made him remember the more indistinct iterations that had occurred earlier on? Could these dreams have been a premonition, somehow, of what had happened to him?

A nurse he didn't recognize, a hard-bitten little woman of indeterminate ethnicity, came in to clip his nails. She stood there for a moment, looking at him. Hiroshi noticed the present from his father still on the bed and was about to ask her if she could move it to the box in the corner, but before he could do so, she said, "I don't know how you can do it."

"Do what?"

"Sit there in your own stink like that. It's disgusting."

Hiroshi was too stunned to say a single word. She picked up his father's present and, just as if he had asked her to, placed it on top of the carton in the corner. Then she quickly and efficiently clipped his nails, her nose wrinkled the whole time. Hiroshi kept his eyes closed most of the time to avoid having to look at her, an arrangement that seemed to suit her as well.

After she left, he closed his eyes and exhaled wearily. Did he stink? Did Maureen notice this odor? And what difference would it make if she did?

He looked down at his foot again, thinking that perhaps the odor, if there was one at all, was emanating from there. Suddenly, without thinking about it, he understood his dream. It was about his own extremities. They were there, his hands and feet, exactly as they had always been, but now he was aware that they were there only when he made a point of looking down at them.

And his brain couldn't communicate with them at all, so they might as well have belonged to someone else. They were far around the bend and had no business with the rest of his body, nothing to do with his head.

He pulled his head back into his own dark compartment and fell asleep.

5

HIROSHI PASSED the time during his first few plasmapheresis treatments staring at the ceiling, thinking, and using the length of his tongue to investigate the interesting parallel ridges and little hard bumps, like the almond pieces in a Hershey bar, on the roof of his mouth. When he got tired of that, he could touch the tip of his tongue to the tiny gill-like slits in the center of each cheek (which had no discernible anatomical purpose) or pass his tongue across his salivary glands, which, when he made a sucking motion, would inflate like a miniature scrotum.

There was no end to the fun.

With few exceptions, there hadn't been a day in his life since his teens when he hadn't practiced his instrument. And there were very few days where he hadn't also stopped into a record store or a bookstore, or given a performance, or gone out for the evening, or had sex. Preferably all of these things. Now, when he wasn't at play on the roof of his mouth, he might wiggle his buttocks, listen to music, and have desultory and quarrelsome discussions, the real activity in his life happening at the cellular level where misbehaving antibodies were being booted out of his logy bloodstream.

* * *

HIROSHI MUST HAVE CLOSED his eyes for a moment during his second round of therapy, because one moment the technician and his ungainly machine were there fractionating his blood, and the next minute they were gone, replaced by Vincent, who was looking down at him.

"How you doing, man?"

"Well, perhaps I stink."

"What you mean, stink?"

"I was told that I stink."

"Everybody stinks in this stinking place, man. Deal."

"Deal?"

"Cope. Actually, you don't smell that bad. No raw fish or nothing. You want me to open all these presents?"

"I don't care any at all."

"You know that expression in English, 'I don't give a shit'? That's what you're trying to say, right?"

"Right. I don't give a shit at all."

"Well if you don't give a shit, how can you expect me to give a shit? So I'll just open 'em, right? Man, I love presents. Getting. Giving. Snooping." Vincent looked over at the carton.

"First of all we have this beautiful package." Vincent began ripping it apart.

"From my father."

"Yeah, I could tell by the weird writing. You got two packages of food inside. Damn, each one's got its *own* wrapping. One of them's some kind of cookies that look pretty good, and the other is these weird shiny little logs with green paper around the middle."

"Seaweed. Those are rice crackers. Help yourself."

"Hey, you probably think I'm chicken. But I'll eat anything." He ripped open the package of rice crackers and bit into one. "Fuck, these are hard. I don't see how you could eat this shit even when your jaw muscles are normal."

"Have a cookie instead."

"Nah, they look too fancy. I'll feed you a few later. Let's see what this is." He opened the package from Grady. "Looks like a CD."

"Probably one of Grady Granphill's."

Vincent looked at the label, which featured Grady standing in Minetta Lane in Greenwich Village, laughing hysterically at the camera. "What makes you say that?"

The name was right there on the label, so Vincent definitely couldn't read. "Because he is the person who gave it to me."

"Give you his own CD, huh? Not sure if that's a good thing or not. Saved him some money, I guess." Vincent then turned his attention to the lumpy package from Maureen. "Man, I guess it's like Christmas around here."

"I guess."

"Alright, so it's a boring fucking Christmas." Vincent ripped open the package and, sure enough, three bright red rubber balls came tumbling out. He leapt after them, catching two, but missing one that rolled under Hiroshi's bed.

Hiroshi let out a little cry of frustration.

"Hey man, don't worry. I'll get it for you."

"No, I don't care. I don't..." He thought for a moment. "I don't give a shit about a ball. It's just that this girl is mentally ill or something."

"Who, the chick who brought you this? Why do you say that?"

"She brought me as a gift juggling balls. I'm paralyzed and

can't even scratch my nose, and she brought me juggling balls."

Vincent scooted under the bed and brought out the third ball. He placed the balls, and the CD, inside the carton from Hiroshi's hotel room. He placed the cookies and crackers from Mr. Mori onto the bedside table. "Hey, I'll see you later, man. Don't go anywhere without telling me."

* * *

LATER THAT AFTERNOON, Hiroshi found that he was able to wiggle his toes for the first time. The first person he told, after Dr. Lillet and Vincent, was Gorgeous Hitomi.

He hadn't planned it that way. He had given Vincent Hitomi's telephone number to dial for him periodically, which absolved him of his guilt over not having spoken to her. At the same time, he'd assumed that Vincent would be unable to master the myriad digits required to connect him with the unpleasantness that awaited. But right after lunch − creamed chicken croquettes, mashed potatoes, orange Kool-Aid, and some of his father's cookies, all patiently piloted into his mouth by Vincent − Vincent was kneeling by his side, cradling the telephone receiver against his head.

A moist, miniature breathing could be heard, and a few wispy bits of crosstalk that could have been in Finnish, for all he knew.

"Hello."

"Hello, Hiroshi. How are you feeling?"

"Better. I could wiggle my toes a bit today after my treatment. What time is it there?"

"Your voice sounds so distant. It's about eight in the morning. You caught me just as I was running out the door to work." Hitomi was a graphic artist who designed the boxes and did the storyboard illustrations for a small maker of video games. In her early twenties, she had done a little modeling, but detested having her picture taken. She'd also trained in modern dance, and auditioned for a couple of modern dance companies in Tokyo, but learned that even with no cameras present, she loathed being looked at. She liked looking at others. Now, as succor from her unsatisfying job, she created skillful sketches of her friends and of people she'd remembered from the subway and the street. The only way, she said, that she could bear being in a crowd was singling out a distinctive face, particularly that of a foreigner, and focusing on it so she could draw it later. If the owners of any of the faces, mostly American and European in appearance, were perturbed to discover their caricatured likenesses on video games they bought for their children years after their stay in Japan, Hitomi never heard about it.

"How is work? Do you need to get going?"

"Horrible. I can't even begin to describe it. Anyway, what treatment? What exactly happened to you? Your agent was a little vague."

"I can't move anything."

"Then how are you holding the phone?"

"You say that as if you caught me in some sort of lie. My friend Vincent is holding it for me." Vincent smiled at the mention of his name.

"I wasn't accusing you of lying. I'm just a little upset that you're not finishing up your gig and getting ready to go home right now, like you said you'd be. But I understand that you're sick."

"It's more than just sick. It's completely incapacitated. I'm like an unstrung puppet. I know you can hardly hear me, but that's the part that's working the best, believe it or not."

"I'm so sorry."

"It's only temporary. They've started cleaning my blood. "

"I've been sick recently, too."

"What's the matter?"

"Mostly throwing up."

"You say that so casually! This is serious, isn't it? Why are you throwing up?"

"You're immediately afraid I'm pregnant, aren't you?"

"Why would I be afraid of that when we've barely been together recently?"

"It's food poisoning, anyway. I ate something bad a few days ago, chicken croquettes, I think."

Hiroshi had never known Hitomi to be sick with anything, other than menstrual cramps or an occasional cold. He pictured her clearly now, for the first time since they'd begun talking, her bright-eyed, irritable beauty. She had two remarkable qualities he had never in his life encountered in any other woman. First, and best of all, was what happened to her eyes when she smiled or laughed, though she did neither often enough: her eyes, which had a natural sparkle to begin with, would narrow almost to the point of disappearing, but at that point the sparkle became concentrated, brighter, and leapt out like sparks. The effect was all the more remarkable for the rarity of its occurrence, like the flash of green one sees in one sunset out of a thousand. The second quality was the way her vaginal muscles would seize up with such strength at the moment of her orgasm that Hiroshi's penis was forced out. There was nothing better, as far as he was concerned, than sliding back in again after the wave had subsided.

This would happen five or six times every time they made love, at least until recently.

How could a woman with such rare qualities not be happy? But the image of Hitomi that most frequently came to mind was not how her eyes sparkled but how they teared, the way she was always catching bits of grit that seemed to bother no one else in the vicinity. She'd rub at her eyes until one of her long eyelashes came loose and made her even more miserable. The image of her rubbing at her eyes while she sketched, or in the middle of a pleasant lunch, or while they were in the midst of an argument, kept driving away all of the other images he had of her – she was terribly sensitive, or terribly irritable, it was hard to say which. Her skin was always dry and itchy. The bones of her feet ached. Her breasts always ached. Though she was almost never ill, she nearly always felt unwell. He had never known her to be happy, not even once.

Usually, his awareness of her unhappiness made him go easy on her. He wasn't in the mood for that today.

"Are you listening, Hiroshi?"

"Yeah, chicken croquettes. I was just thinking that's pretty funny, that's what I had for lunch here at the hospital. In any event, I'm sorry you're not feeling well. But this whole conversation is going sideways, as far as I'm concerned."

"What do you mean sideways?" For the first time in their conversation, Hitomi sounded alarmed.

"Well, to begin with, you said you're a little bit upset that I'm not on my way home yet. First of all, I won't be home for a long, long while, unless they stow me in the baggage compartment on a stretcher. Second, it's not that I'm not there that you're objecting to, it's that I said I would be there and I'm not that you don't like."

"I don't see the difference."

"I just believe that it isn't the lack of my physical presence that's angering you, it's that I failed to do as I promised."

"You're making a very fine distinction."

"Really? I think it's an enormous distinction. Furthermore, I was expecting you to be far more than a little upset that I haven't even called you once since arriving in New York. I mean, if you're not angry about that, how could you possibly be angry that I'm not there with you? It doesn't make sense to me."

"It makes perfect sense. I'm upset because I miss you. I'm not angry that you didn't call because I understand that you were unable to call."

"I was perfectly able to call before this disease struck. The fact is, I didn't want to call, and you know why I didn't want to call, and because you know why, I think you're being dishonest in pretending that you're upset that I didn't call."

"But I just got through saying I'm not upset that you didn't call."

"No, but the way you've avoided talking about it suggests to me that you are upset."

Hiroshi was beginning to get tired, but Vincent continued to hold the phone steadily, smiling slightly at a conversation he could not understand.

"Wait a minute. You're losing me, Hiroshi. You're making no sense. I'm telling you I'm not upset, and you're saying you don't believe me and you think I *am* upset, but that I'm only *pretending* to be upset? Even the devils aren't that devious. Furthermore, you say you didn't want to call, and I should know perfectly well why you didn't want to call, but in fact I don't know why. And if in fact you didn't want to call, why did you just do so?"

"I'm making perfect sense. You're only pretending not to understand. The truth is, through your silence, you want me to know that you're angry that I didn't call, something I could only prove by taking the initiative and calling you now. And yet the reason you're angry is not that you value me, but that I didn't do as you expected, and I seemed not to be thinking of you, and that hurt your pride. But actually wanting to talk to me was beside the point, given that you didn't call me first."

"If I didn't want to talk to you, why would I be enduring all this convoluted nonsense from you right now?"

Hiroshi couldn't help laughing at that one. He wasn't even

sure what he was saying anymore. "You know, I think you ought to go see a doctor about your illness."

"It's getting better. I just threw up a couple of times, but I'm okay now."

Hiroshi thought carefully. Certainly that was all there was to it. Just about everyone got food poisoning once or twice in their lives. And yet he couldn't help thinking that indeed she was pregnant. They hadn't had sex more than a handful of times in the past few months, and were always careful. But it could have been someone else.

It could have been Ruud, for example. Ruud was a floppy-haired Dutch software engineer, practically fluent in Japanese, who had come to work for Hitomi's company at the beginning of the year. Hiroshi had absolutely no reason to think that he and Hitomi were having an affair.

Except that Hitomi had left her journal lying around her apartment a few months back.

And Hiroshi had been unable to constrain himself from reading it one evening while Hitomi was in the kitchen making dinner for them. Truthfully, he had been looking for references to himself, but his eyes instantly lit upon the katakana characters for "Ruud" – the Japanese transliteration was "Roodo," – and the sentence in which it was contained, which read as follows:

> *"I got to work early this morning, thinking there was a meeting, but I had the day wrong, so I went out to breakfast with Ruud before everyone else came in and while we were having coffee I suddenly thought that I would like to sleep with him, but then I worried about someone from the office coming into the coffee shop and seeing us, so I changed the subject to work."*

The one part of that painful sentence that was the worst was the last part, "...so I changed the subject to work," which suggested to Hiroshi that it wasn't only her private fantasy, and that the subject had been broached.

There also was the matter of the little note Hiroshi had found plastered on the inside of one of her shoes, where it had probably fluttered, forgotten, as she was changing her clothes. On a slip of paper no larger than a temple fortune, it had said, in English, and in Hitomi's writing, *"I will meet at nudul shop."* Hitomi's English wasn't good at all, and there was no need for her to write such a note unless the recipient was an English-speaker. It could have been intended for Ruud, though he was fluent in spoken Japanese and probably read it fairly well, or it could have been meant for some other foreigner she was seeing on the sly. But whoever it was intended for had never gotten it, and perhaps had never met Hitomi at the noodle shop, because Hiroshi had peeled the tiny slip of paper off of the inside of the shoe and secreted it from there into his wallet, where it was tucked away even now in case he ever needed it to make himself or Hitomi feel bad.

He cleared his throat. "Well, anyway, I'm glad you're feeling better." He hadn't been able to say anything about reading the journal entry for all these months, and he didn't have to courage to bring it up now. It was actually much more damning than the "nudul shop" message, which could have been intended for anyone and which he had found accidentally. But with the journal entry, it wasn't just the subject that bothered him, or the fact that she'd mentioned Ruud by name, it was the thought that she had left it lying around deliberately so that he could read it and get the message. If he brought it up, she'd have successfully delivered the message. She'd have won.

Hitomi said, "I'm sorry you've suffered such a terrible illness yourself. I wish I could come to New York and see you, but it's impossible with work."

"You know, the doctors say that one possible cause of this

illness is an auto-immune reaction to a very serious bout with food poisoning."

"Are you trying to tell me that you think I'll get this disease, too?"

"Of course not. It's a one-in-million chance that anyone could get it. I just thought it was funny that you had food poisoning and I didn't, but I got this disease."

"Is it that you wish I had gotten it instead of you? Does it seem unfair to you?"

"Of course not," Hiroshi said heatedly.

"Alright. Forget it. I guess it's my turn to twist things around. Although to tell you the truth, I couldn't possibly do that as expertly as you just did. Listen, I'll say this as directly as I know how. You're wonderful. I owe a lot to you. And what you do with your music is so much more important and valuable than what I do with my stupid sketch pads. If by some power, I could take on your illness and free you of it, I would do it in a second."

"Thank you. I would never ask that, but it's a nice thought."

"Yeah, it's easy for me to say, but I can't even come to visit you."

"Don't worry about that. I'll be recovered soon enough, and back in Tokyo soon enough. Then maybe we can continue this conversation."

"I want you to stay in touch with me in the meantime."

She said it warmly, but there wasn't quite enough conviction in her voice — not to mention the valedictory quality of her offer to trade places with him. "I'll do my best to call, and maybe when my fingers are working better, I'll find a place in this hospital to send you e-mails. And please stay in touch with me, too. I want to know what's happening with you."

"Of course," Hitomi said.

Hiroshi paused. He suddenly felt very afraid of what he

was about to say. "Naturally, if I want to know what I've missed while I've been gone, I can just read your journal when I get back."

There. He'd said it. After all this time, he had said it. Hitomi betrayed no surprise at this odd statement. They took another couple of minutes then to say their goodbyes, and did so with some warmth. But still, the message had been delivered – hers to him, and his back to her. Even if she hadn't been quite clear about what he meant by reading her journal, she soon would be – she'd certainly be late for work, in fact, as she paged through the past few weeks of entries, thinking about what he might have read. Or knowing quite well what he'd read, but wondering how explicitly she'd phrased it. By the time she arrived at work, Ruud would ask what'd kept her, and why she looked so pale and upset. Or why, rather, she looked so flushed and relieved.

He nodded to Vince to let him know that he was finished. Vince cradled the phone and said, "Man, I'd love to know what all that mushy-mush stuff you said was all about."

* * *

HIS FATHER'S second visit went less well than the first. It began pleasantly enough, or at least familiarly enough. Mr. Mori ate an orange he'd taken from a fruit basket that Hiroshi's agent had sent, digging at the tough skin with his trembling fingers, spitting seeds fiercely into an emesis tray, and talking about a colleague, a Japanese novelist of some repute who had been bruited about for the Nobel Prize for many years.

"I don't doubt he has his supporters. I myself admire the man greatly. But please don't try to tell me he deserved such an honor."

"He won the Nobel Prize?"

"No, you hadn't heard? The Tanizaki. You still don't read the newspapers, do you? He was awarded the Tanizaki Prize." This was one of Japan's most prestigious literary honors.

"Father, I've never read the man's works. I can't tell you if he deserves the Nobel Prize or the Tanizaki Prize, which frankly I'd never have heard of if you didn't talk about it all the time."

"If you had read his works, which I don't recommend, I don't doubt you'd agree with me."

"Father, why don't you recommend I read his works if, as you said, you admire him?"

"I admire him, but there are hundreds of authors I admire. Who can find time to read them all? I'm thinking particularly of you, someone who hasn't picked up a book since high school."

"That's not entirely true, and I've certainly read your books, but I don't have a lot of time to read, with my performing career."

"I don't doubt your performing career places demands on your time, but your life is completely one-dimensional. There's little enough intellectual content in jazz. I myself am a great admirer of John Coltrane, who I saw perform in Paris once, as you know. But jazz is all emotion and no intellect."

"I couldn't disagree more completely with that statement."

"Be that as it may, you could use this time in bed to catch up on your reading of something other than jazz magazines and manga."

"Sure. As soon as I can muster the strength to turn a page." He stopped talking, but his mind continued to form a sentence: "Maybe I'll start with one of your books – they're small enough." The fact was, his father had built a fairly substantial reputation on the basis of a very slim output – all told, no more than a couple of hundred pages of poems, one modestly successful novel, and a volume of essays of social commentary. There probably weren't that many more words in his poems that in the lists Hiroshi carried in his wallet.

"Father, I'm sorry I haven't read this novelist so I could tell you I agree that it's unjust he received this literary prize. All I know is that he seems to have a very serious and weighty reputation."

"Then you'll have to take my word for it that it's unjust. It's also unjust he received the Shincho and the Akutagawa."

"Look, if he has an inflated reputation, any prize he receives is unjust. So why does each one wound you more than the last? Every time you talk, I don't hear about a new poem you've written, I hear about some prize you haven't won."

"Writing poems at the level I write them is agony enough. It's becoming even more difficult knowing that I'll never be recognized in my lifetime."

"I'm sorry you feel unrecognized, Father. I've often envied you your life of academic appointments and travel around the world and honors. Even if none of them is the Tanizaki."

"Kid, you look at me and all you see is a sad old ingrate who can't even peel an orange properly without squirting juice everywhere. I should be thankful, right? But I am. I'm thankful and I'm deeply offended at the same time. I don't expect you to understand this at your age, but when one concludes one's life, it isn't a matter of deciding if one fits into the category of Success or No Success, yes or no, and that's the end of it."

"You're certainly a success. You couldn't be more of a success."

"That's where you're wrong, kid. I want more." He popped an angry chunk of orange into his mouth. "I want much more. My brothers, your mother's father, all of them, see us as curiosities. Do you want to be seen as a curiosity?"

"No."

"Do you want to recover from your illness, and lay down your clarinet, which I have told you many times you play beautifully, and pick up instead a pile of textbooks and become, let's say, a neurologist who spends his days examining hopeless cases?"

"My case is far from hopeless."

"I'm quite aware of that. That's precisely why I asked you how you wanted to spend your days when you recover. As a neurologist who understands something about neural pathways, or as an artist who understands our inner dwelling places?"

When Mr. Mori talked about inner dwelling places, Hiroshi couldn't help but think, for some reason, of the hundreds of times he had seen him at parties and social events, cramming sushi or sandwiches into his mouth and gulping beer while he chewed. He liked to swish the beer around the half-masticated food, which wasn't quite as disgusting to look at as one might think, but nonetheless a riveting sight. Then he'd spend hours probing with his tongue at his molars and making a loud sucking sound. Hiroshi had once heard a fellow writer sneeringly describe Mr. Mori as a "glutton for subtlety." He was that, perhaps, but he was also just a glutton.

Hiroshi forced himself to attend to his father's line of argument. "So you're encouraging me to continue to be an artist. But I'm confused. Weren't you just criticizing jazz for being an inferior art because it's supposedly all emotion and no intellect?"

"Yes, but at its highest, as I hope you'll understand someday, it transcends emotion and becomes pure spirit."

"Well, in any event, you know the choice I've made. You helped me make it when I was young and wanted music lessons and Mother didn't want me to. I've thanked you for it many times, so I don't even know what we're arguing about."

"I understand. But I wonder how fully you've made that choice."

"I don't know what you mean. Until this illness struck, I was on a tour of America, I have a CD..."

"I mean, do you want to spend your time fooling around, or do you want to become great like Coltrane?"

"It's not as if Coltrane didn't fool around, in a sense. I mean, he was a heroin addict."

"Once again, you miss my point. It's about seriousness. I know what it means to be serious. I *am* serious. Only a man as serious as I am about his art could understand, in fact, what an injustice it is that I haven't won the Tanizaki. Or for that matter that some bizarre illness has left you flat on your back."

"So what is it you're saying? What is it you want me to do?"

"I'm saying that you have to use all of your physical and mental strength to recover. Your doctor told me about this blood-cleaning machine, and he admitted they don't even fully understand how it works to improve your condition. So don't rely only on that, but rather on your inner strength."

"I'm doing the best I can. You can't understand until you have this how debilitating it is."

"It doesn't matter what I understand. You have to get back to where you were, and then far beyond that point, and do so quickly to make up for lost time. I want to see you succeed in an unequivocal way. I've talked to some of your colleagues, and there is no doubt that I've produced a genius. Don't let me die without proving it to me and to the world."

"Well, that's a pretty substantial order. If it's the 'pure spirit' thing you're talking about, I'm probably a long, long way away."

"Look, you could've been a doctor, and then if you'd been a genius in that field, if there is such a thing, all it would have accomplished is that you'd have saved a few sad souls from their inevitable return whence they came. I can't tell you how sorry I am that the first hands to touch you were a doctor's, and that when you die the last hands will be a doctor's. Worse, it probably will be someone in our family. Instead of me, the only one in this family who understands you or ever will understand you."

"You think you understand me?"

"I understand your life project, and it adds up to a lot more than a tube filled with tubes, which is how a doctor sees our bodies when they're at work on them. This is the difference between a technician, a doctor, and an artist. You think I'm trivial for obsessing over how I've been overlooked? Wait until you reach the end of your life. Believe me, there is nothing worse than knowing you haven't done anything that will last."

"Your work will last."

Mr. Mori waved his hand. "I'm sure it will. But I'm trying to say that for you as for me, it isn't just about performing, and having sex with willing women who think you're brilliant. If you haven't received whatever the equivalent of the Nobel Prize is, or the Akutagawa or the Tanizaki, by the time you're ready to die..."

"I want to point out, if I can interrupt, that I'd be ready to die right about now if not for the doctors you think are so trivial."

"I don't think they're trivial. They're important. Just like firemen are important. But correct me if I'm wrong, all they've done is connect you to a machine. So, good. You'll live. Now what? What are you going to do to win whatever the prize is?"

"A Grammy, I guess. Is that what you want for me, to win

a Grammy? It's a bit of a long shot for me, but I'll try my best."

"Winning a Grammy? If that's what you think I want for you, you haven't been listening this whole time. Get out of bed and figure it out, kid. Your sister was a puzzle from the beginning, and we didn't ever find out the answer to her, did we? So you're my last chance. Figure out what's demanded of you, and then do it."

"*Am* I your last chance? What about Manabu?"

"Manabu is five. And even he's not my last chance, strictly speaking. But I may be dead by the time he does whatever he's going to do. I have no doubt he'll be great at something someday. But you're on the verge of greatness now, and I won't rest until I see you achieve it."

"Well, thank you for your ambition on my behalf, father. But what did you just mean then, about 'even Manabu is not my last chance, strictly speaking'?"

"Well, the fact is, Miyoko is pregnant again."

"Father, refresh my memory. How old are you again, about a hundred and three or so?"

"Sixty-five. There's no age limit on men, as I'm sure you know. And Miyoko is a *very* young thirty-eight," he added leeringly.

"So this new child is insurance, in case Manabu doesn't quite work out according to your plans."

"You think you wound me by saying such things? You should know better than anyone – *anyone* – how vulnerable children can be. Insurance? Why not? Why does anyone have children in this world? As insurance, as a hedge against mortality and meaninglessness. Or is there another reason I'm missing?"

Hiroshi paused for a long while before speaking. "Anyway, I'm a little tired right now. I appreciate your visit."

Mr. Mori stood up abruptly. "I can see that I've said something to upset you. I'll be back tomorrow. Then I have to return home. I have a reading to do."

The phone rang as Mr. Mori was selecting another orange from the fruit basket to take with him, his trembling hands making an irritating racket with the stiff yellow cellophane. Thus engaged, he didn't trouble himself to answer the phone, leaving the job for Vincent, who entered the room on the third ring.

Vincent listened for a moment. Then he held the phone against his side. "It's in Japanese. Doesn't sound like your girl-friend, though. Maybe it's your sister."

"I don't have a sister," Hiroshi snapped. His father, who didn't understand the exchange, left the room. Hiroshi closed his eyes. "I'm sorry. Why don't you just hand me the phone and let me figure out who it is."

Vincent brought the phone over to Hiroshi's ear. It was indeed Hitomi, but her voice had been thickened by crying, which was probably why Vincent had thought it was someone else.

"What's the matter, Hitomi?"

"I'm not sure how to tell you."

It had been only a few hours since they'd last spoken. Hiroshi quickly examined the possibilities as he waited for her to collect her thoughts. She really was pregnant, by Ruud, and ready to acknowledge that fact. Or she was ready to acknowledge their affair. Or she was officially breaking up with Hiroshi. Certainly, it was something like that, and all of it had been precipitated by his comment about the diary. Or more accurately, precipitated by her reading in the diary her own words and her reflecting upon the behavior that had resulted in those words being written there.

It was none of these things. Hitomi said, "I'm afraid I've lost my job."

Hiroshi was both disappointed and relieved that he had been so wrong. "What happened?"

"Well, I've been missing a lot of assignments lately. I guess it was just an indication of how unhappy I've been. Then I missed a couple of days because of my illness, and then I arrived quite late this morning..."

"Because of our conversation?"

"That didn't make any difference. It was only a matter of time. I'm calling you because you're the first person I thought of that I wanted to talk to."

Well, there was a confirmation, if he needed one, that they had broken up. If not, it wouldn't have been necessary for her to explain why she'd called him.

"I'm sorry, but maybe it's for the best, because you were so unhappy."

"It is. It really is. I wouldn't even be crying if my boss hadn't been so cruel about it. It was almost as if he was saying that I'd never accomplished anything."

This unintentional reminder of his father's admonitions was most unpleasant. "You've accomplished a great deal. Maybe when I have a little more strength and you've collected your thoughts a bit, we can have a discussion about what you should do next."

"Thank you."

"In the meantime, I'd be happy to lend you some money."

"I don't need any right now. And you're hardly in a position."

"Actually, I'm okay with my insurance and the help from my father. And I'm the only jazz guy in the world who's saved money from every gig, I think. Maybe I should get hooked on heroin and become dissolute, then I'd fulfill my promise."

"What are you talking about? You have enough problems."

"We are quite a pair, aren't we? One piece of bad luck after another."

"Hiroshi, I do want to stay in touch with you. Take care, alright? I'll call you in a few days. Will you still be at this number?"

"At the hospital? Yeah, there's not much choice about that. I'll look forward to your call."

Vincent waited politely to make sure the call was over. Hiroshi nodded briefly to him, and Vincent cradled the phone.

"Vincent, I'm sorry I became a little irritated with you before. My sister is dead. I mean, she died some time ago."

"I'm sorry. I don't know why I said maybe it's your sister. I thought for some reason you had one."

"Well, like I said, I did. She died. So did my mother. It's my father and me, and his son from his new marriage, and I guess another child soon, and then a bunch of other relatives we two don't like."

"Your father really hates hospitals, doesn't he? I can tell by the way he was sitting uncomfortably, and then he couldn't wait to get out of here."

"My mother died a very painful death from scleroderma, and all of my relatives, who are doctors, couldn't do a thing. Which is one of the reasons he hates them."

Vincent nodded. He picked up one of the juggling balls Maureen had left and gave it a squeeze. He put it back down, picked up another one and then, ruminatively, began to squeeze it as well.

"Hey, you know what's interesting about these balls that chick gave you?"

"Perhaps nothing at all?"

"No, no. It is. The thing is, each one is different. One is soft and easy to squeeze, another is harder and the third one is really hard."

"So?"

"So, I don't think they're juggling balls at all. They're some kind of therapy balls, so you can get your strength back in your hands. You squeeze the soft one first, and then when that gets too easy, you go to the next and the next, until your fingers are strong again."

"I wouldn't have known that, because I couldn't have picked the balls up. I suppose I wish she had told me."

"Sure. Give it a try." He placed the softest ball in Hiroshi's limp hand. Of course, as a musician herself, Maureen would have understood as few others would the importance of the fingers in the playing of the clarinet. To be sure, the instrument didn't require a lot of strength, but certainly a great deal more than Hiroshi had now, as well as sureness and subtlety and speed. Hiroshi felt very ashamed of having called her mentally ill, even if he hadn't done so to her face.

Still, there remained the matter of all of her other rude and inexplicable behavior. Hiroshi flexed his forefinger, which he was beginning to be able to move at will, and pressed it as firmly as he could into the rubber ball. Vincent left him alone.

6

THE THING about Hiroshi's sister was, she didn't belong on either team. One team was Hiroshi and his father – his father had always scared Hiroshi with his opinions, his imperiousness, the sheer heft of his presence – but at least he was on Hiroshi's side as long as Hiroshi was pursuing something of great difficulty and seriousness, be it the piano or the clarinet or even, when he was younger, his judo lessons. The other team, of course, was Hiroshi's mother, who had been a nurse until the day she died when Hiroshi was seventeen, and her father, and her father's two brothers, and Hiroshi's father's older brother, and his two sons, eminent physicians all. On his father's side, the family had operated a clinic for two generations that was located on the family compound where Hiroshi had grown up, and like Hiroshi's father, his father's brother and one of his two sons had married nurses as well, and of the four children the two sons had raised, one of them was already old enough to be a physician himself and one was in training to become a phlebotomist. It might as well have been a circus family where you either learned to ride a unicycle on a tightrope, or you were consigned to cleaning up the elephant's shit.

God knows what Hiroshi's father had been thinking, marrying into another family of doctors. Maybe he hadn't had any prejudices until Hiroshi's mother had become ill. Or maybe his own father, whom Hiroshi had never known, had pushed Mr. Mori as hard as Mr. Mori pushed Hiroshi.

Hiroshi's sister, Shizuka, had acted as if none of it mattered. She had little interest in school to begin with, far less in medicine. As a child, which was practically all she ever was, when she'd closed her eyes, or they'd fluttered in fatigue, there was a violet cast to her eyelids that suggested an inner weakness. The sunlight seemed to shine too easily through her thin skin. But she wasn't the least bit weak. She just wasn't interested.

The only thing she was interested in was secrets. Growing up, because of the six-year age difference, they spent very little time together. Shizuka spent most of her time when she wasn't at school in her room, reading and playing sophisticated make-believe long after most children had moved on to sports and social events. She also took long walks by herself and wouldn't tell the family where she had been. But when she was fourteen and Hiroshi was eight, she introduced him to the Forbidden Pathway.

The Mori compound – consisting of the small Mori clinic, their family home and the much-older Japanese style home, still used for guests, that Hiroshi's father had grown up in – was 110 miles from Tokyo. The family home, where Hiroshi and Shizuka had been raised, was a two-story, four-bedroom Western-style house with a tatami room and a tokonoma, a gleaming kitchen, two Western-style toilets, a solar-powered water heater, and a big, thoroughly fenced-in and lovingly tended vegetable garden in the part of the yard closest to the quiet frontage road, so that all of the neighbors could see

Mrs. Mori working on her hands and knees when she wasn't busy in the clinic.

Next door, connected by a small passageway to the family home, was the Japanese-style house, which included at the far end a tiny tearoom that Hiroshi's mother had used to give tea ceremony lessons when she'd first joined the Mori family. In the part of the yard closest to the Western-style house, after the garden ended, the ground was covered with scrubby grass and small rocks. In front of the Japanese-style house where no one lived anymore was a rather disheveled rock garden that differed to the casual observer from the rocks in the rest of the yard only in degree, not kind. Next to the tearoom, on the far side of the compound away from the family home, were a driveway with a silver MG always parked there, a little tin carport, and an abandoned garden shed where a family of feral cats lived.

The clinic itself was behind the family home. Hiroshi had few memories of the clinic, since he'd hated the sharp medicinal smell and the brusqueness of his uncle, who'd worked there with his wife and Hiroshi's mother as his nurses, appointment secretaries, and custodians. He'd watched patients arrive and depart his entire childhood, but remembered only one specifically, a woman with a huge port-wine stain across her face. All his neighbors had gone to Mori Iin, of course, but he hadn't thought of them as patients, just as his neighbors. He'd gone as a patient himself, all the way through high school, but had no memory of his sister ever being inside its walls, though certainly she must have been there at one time or another.

Everywhere on the compound, even around the sterile little clinic, there were mountain pigeons and the odd ungainly heron visiting from a nearby paddy – the compound was hemmed in on both sides by rice fields, and there was another, larger field just down the other side of the small frontage road.

Across that same road, just next to the large rice field, was the grade school that Hiroshi and Shizuka had both attended in their time, the playground nearly empty except for a pair of bent basketball goals, a shed, and some pigeon cages and rabbit hutches. At night, standing at an upstairs window, Hiroshi could look through the blue-lit windows of the second-floor biology lab, illuminated by a fuzzy blue plant light. Through the back window of the classroom, Hiroshi could see, far off, the Las Vegas-like lights of an enormous, three-story pachinko parlor on the highway that skirted Ichikawa, burning as silently and distantly as a galaxy – an extraordinary celestial sight so close to this country compound.

The Mori compound was only one block away from a busy street, on the other side of the compound from the rice field and school, lined with smaller pachinko parlors, donburi carry-out joints, video rental stores, love hotels, even a small boiler factory. Yet the compound seemed in a mountain town of its own, surrounded by ginkgos and cherries and pines, ringed by gravel and frail lawn. If one walked down the quieter frontage road in front of the Mori compound, where the rice field and school were, one would encounter just past the rice field another, smaller street with tiny grocery stores and clothing shops with sun-faded, limbless mannequins. Every hundred feet or so along this quiet road were vending machines for beer and soft drinks, where gnats gathered at night. When Hiroshi looked out a side window, not the front window where he could see his school and the enormous pachinko parlor in the distance, he could see on this side road a family of four beer machines – a broken family, as each was loyal to a different brand – that hummed and glowed and even, during a brief period when everything automated had to have a gimmick, spoke (though not to each other) in a robot's voice.

In reality, the Forbidden Pathway was just a particular path through their neighborhood; there was, in the strictest sense, nothing forbidden about it at all. It was a children's game. But if the number of permutations possible in the walk one could take cross-town in Manhattan were in the thousands, in this little town of Ichikawa they were in the millions, partly because one was not restricted to walking on sidewalks. Ichikawa was, like most small Japanese towns, highly impure from a topographical perspective. There was no country, there was no city, there were no farms per se – it was like a crumpled map, where every point touched every other point. The idea behind the Forbidden Pathway was simply that by following a precise combination of pathways that no one else could possibly duplicate, one could create a giant key that could open up something buried.

The Forbidden Pathway was nothing more than a formula, a code or a combination, of many of the elements that made up the extraordinarily complicated topography, where so many different things were jumbled together. But the elements had to be strung together – physically, by those who walked the Pathway – in a very particular order for them to lead to anything of value. This, at least, was Shizuka's conception. If you followed the Pathway the way she had invented it, the individual elements – though they all belonged to the people who owned the fields or school or homes – added up to something only she owned, something that took you to a place no one else could go. If you stepped wrong, usually you just ended up on an ordinary walk through the neighborhood, but sometimes it was like punching the wrong numbers into a home security code, where something bad or at least dissonant could happen. Or so she claimed.

It was on a searing summer day, with the locusts shrieking in the trees, that Shizuka introduced Hiroshi to the Forbidden Pathway. It was very simple. She told Hiroshi that she had already memorized all of the steps, and all he had to do was to follow her carefully. He had brought a canteen of water and a half-eaten box of chocolate-filled koala-shaped cookies for the journey.

They began by walking through their house, and then through the passageway to the empty Japanese-style house. The clinic wasn't part of the Forbidden Pathway; as far as Shizuka was concerned, it was just forbidden. They passed through the little tearoom at the far end of the compound and then exited by a small door onto the compound's gravel driveway, where Hiroshi's uncle, who lived thirty minutes away, parked his silver MG. From there, they crossed the gravel frontage road separating the Mori compound from the schoolyard across the way, but instead of entering the baked-white schoolyard where the rabbits cowered, Shizuka steered them past the school to a row of old Japanese-style houses that lived in its shadow. She led them on a narrow wooden walkway between two houses and they emerged in a back-yard, from which the immense pachinko parlor could be seen. The yard was filled with growing gourds and heaps of dead leaves and a tangle of vines and large porcelain jars, broken and unbroken; they threaded their way through this clutter and emerged at the edge of the largest rice field, which was violated at intervals by telephone utility poles.

They skirted the rice field on a sort of dirt road that was interrupted by a number of greenhouses and suddenly emerged in another little neighborhood. Hiroshi turned around and looked back for the Mori compound, but saw only some unfamiliar houses; ahead, he couldn't even see the pachinko parlor. They walked on, Hiroshi following Shizuka carefully as she walked down first this road, then a dirt path, then a wooden walkway between forcing houses, then another road. At one point, they found an unusual-looking butterfly near a small creek, and when Shizuka chased it, she made it seem that the butterfly's appearance had been planned in order to lead them in a particular direction.

Someone's car had gotten stuck in a ditch, and Hiroshi and Shizuka helped the owners push it out while two little girls watched and giggled. The owners were a middle-aged woman and her unsmiling, tangle-haired, and possibly feeble-minded son: they got down in the ditch with Hiroshi and Shizuka and everyone's hands, slick with sweat, slipped back and forth on the bumper and slid on top of each other as they shoved; but when they finally heaved the car onto land, the mother and son barely thanked Hiroshi and Shizuka.

Shizuka continued to lead Hiroshi through her private playland, to a river where they chased a stray cat and where they hunted still more butterflies and dragonflies. All this, every move they made in pursuit of the cat and the butterflies and the dragonflies, was part of the Hidden Pathway, Shizuka insisted. Then they walked along the river some more and encountered a pair of older boys playing samurai with crude swords on a crude bridge.

Shizuka walked up to the bridge and stood so near the older boys that an errant whack from one of their swords could have broken her nose. The boys gradually slowed their game and looked curiously at Shizuka. Then, as if bidden, they backed down off the bridge and let Hiroshi and Shizuka cross.

After they arrived on the other side of the river, the houses began to disappear, replaced by more rice fields stitched together with neglected bramble patches and threatening tangles of spiky weeds. After they had walked another fifteen minutes or so, they came to the largest bramble patch of all, so large that Hiroshi didn't see at first that it had overgrown a small shack, which could be entered only by shoving their thin bodies between the thick weeds.

Once they were inside, it suddenly became cool. Hiroshi took out his canteen and the box of chocolate-filled koala cookies. Shizuka said, "Now, before I let you eat that, you have to promise not to tell anybody this place is here."

Hiroshi tried to peer around in the darkness. There were a few rusty shelves and cobweb-covered advertising placards against the wall. "What is this place?"

"Some kind of old store from before the war," Shizuka said. "I think somebody used to live here after it went out of business. I found a rice ball that was as hard as a rock. He must be dead, whoever he was. Just like you will die."

Hiroshi said, "What do you mean?"

"I mean, if you tell anybody about this place, I'll kill you." She was smiling; she couldn't kill anybody.

"But other people must know about this place."

"No. It's completely hidden. You saw that yourself. Also, you can't just stumble upon it. You can only arrive at it by following the Pathway exactly as I took you here, using the exact combination of steps and turns. Otherwise, if you arrive using a different formula, it won't be here or it'll be here but something bad will happen to you."

A few days later, Hiroshi tried to find the shack by himself. But he got confused about where to go after crossing the river, and never managed to find it. After that, he begged Shizuka on several occasions to show him again, and she actually helped Hiroshi to draw a simple map.

The next time they went to the shack, they spread out a picnic lunch of rice balls, cold green tea, and chocolates, and talked of nothing much at all.

That might have been it, but Shizuka insisted upon going again. She had a secret, she told Hiroshi, that could be divulged only in the safety of their unbreachable hideaway.

On their third visit to the shack, they didn't bother bringing a lunch, only a couple of blankets. They lay down in the cool darkness, watching the spiders float on their filaments.

After a few minutes of silence, Shizuka said, "The thing is, I saw a daddy-longlegs spider the other day in our house. It was huge. It was right on the wall near the T.V. That's what I wanted to tell you."

"Is that so?" Hiroshi felt a little disappointed by the revelation, but kept silent, hoping his sister would say more. He wasn't sure why she had taken him all the way out to this spider-filled shack for a third time to tell him about another spider she had seen back at home. He was beginning to suspect that his sister's Pathway didn't lead to anything very interesting at all. She was a lot older than he was, but he was already beginning to feel bored with this game.

"Yeah. I watched it for a while, and then I figured Mom wouldn't be too happy to have it around the house, so I took one of her magazines and gave it a good whack."

"Did you kill it?"

"Well, the thing is, I hit it at an angle, so at first I only injured it. I knocked off a couple of legs, and left this great big smear on the wall. I guess it was spider blood. The spider hung on for a second and then fell to the table. And then it scrambled around a bit, like it was looking for its lost legs."

"That's really getting me sick."

"Well, I started to feel sick too and kind of ashamed. I could have just picked it up by some of its legs and tossed it into the garden, but I wanted to impress Mom. But then the spider spoke to me."

"It what?"

"It spoke to me. I know that sounds strange. But it said, 'You know, even though I'm a spider, I want to live every bit as much as you do. In fact, when I saw you coming at me with that thing in your hand...' I said, 'Magazine.' I told him the thing was called a magazine. So the spider said, 'Yes, magazine. When I saw you coming at me with that magazine, I tried to run away as fast as I could, but my legs got all confused because I was so terrified. Then I decided there was no point in struggling anymore and I just relaxed my body and allowed myself to get hit, figuring I'd die right away.' 'But you didn't die,' I said to him. 'No, because your aim was poor. I wish I had died. But in a way I'm glad.' I asked him why. And he said, 'Because at least I have a chance to talk to you first. I'll die in just a moment or two, but I just wanted to let you know that I'm not angry with you. And that, when it's your turn, it's really not so bad to die.'"

Hiroshi said, "You mean a spider told you all this?" He was enjoying the make-believe, though he felt a little bit old for it, and he also felt a bit worried about his sister.

Shizuka shrugged. "And then he said he'd see me again when he came back as a different insect, because he expected to be reborn in the same neighborhood. And then he died."

Hiroshi didn't say anything for a moment. Then he said, "And have you seen him again?"

Shizuka didn't answer for a while. "Well, the thing is, what I wanted to talk to you about in private was, just the other day I was in the hallway and I turned on the light and I surprised a cockroach right in the middle of the floor."

"Do you mean that the spider had become a cockroach?"

"Well, no, not exactly."

"Well, what then? Did the cockroach speak to you too?"

"Well, not exactly that either. The thing is, when I turned the light on, the cockroach was really startled. She froze..."

"She?"

"Yeah, I could tell it was a female, somehow. She froze, and then she turned around and looked at me..."

"Shizuka, are you just telling me a make-believe story?"

"That's what my friend Mayumi said. She said, 'I hate to say this, but I don't think cockroaches can swivel their heads on their necks, even if they have necks. And if they could, and if they turned around to look at you, all they'd see would be the bottom of your sneakers.' And I said, 'You may be right from one perspective, but the fact is, that cockroach turned around and looked at me. And it had an expression on its face...'"

Hiroshi had never heard of Mayumi. He didn't even know his sister had any friends, other than one quiet girl who lived near the railroad station, and who would never have spoken back to Shizuka. But he liked this other friend's skepticism. He said, trying to take on the authoritative tone of a four-teen-year-old, "Cockroaches don't have expressions..."

"It had an expression on its face that said it knew, it absolutely knew, it was going to die. The expression was pleading a little bit, like don't step on me, I've got so many things I want to do with my life, and also filled with panic, like this is just too awful to even bear, but it also looked like it had given up and was just waiting for my shoe to hit it. It was very sad."

"So did you stomp it?"

"Of course I didn't. How could I, after what the spider told me?"

"Shizuka, could you be crazy or something?"

"Maybe. But crazy or not, I'm going to have to live my life a different way now."

"What way?"

"I don't know, exactly. Mayumi might have some ideas."

"Shizuka, who is this Mayumi?"

"She's someone I talk to sometimes. You can't really see her, because she isn't exactly real."

* * *

MAYUMI WASN'T REAL. But Shizuka was. So were the cockroach and the spider, but even when he was eight years old, Hiroshi had known she hadn't really talked to them, or rather that they hadn't talked to her. He'd also known there wasn't anything magical beneath the surface of his hometown that you could reach by means of a Forbidden Pathway, unless (he reflected many years later) it was the insight he'd gotten into his sister's illness, the fact that Shizuka had used the distance from the family compound and the bogus mystery that she partly believed in to be able to confess to Hiroshi that something was wrong with her. But Hiroshi had been too young to do anything about it, and besides, Shizuka had managed to get along fairly well without anyone else fully understanding her secret, and had, not too many years later, moved away from home and gotten a job in an office and written some short stories she'd tried, with Mr. Mori's enthusiastic assistance, to get published. A little later, under some pressure from their mother, she'd even gotten married.

* * *

A COCKROACH. A spider. Hiroshi felt a bit lower than even those insects, which at least could wave their legs when they were flipped on their backs. On the other hand, unlike them, he really could talk. He looked up at the hospital ceiling and played a little noiseless rhythm with the tip of his tongue against his teeth. He didn't want to think about his sister anymore. Unfortunately, he was running out of other things to think of, because he also didn't want to think about Hitomi, or his career, or Maureen, or his illness, or jazz, or missiles hitting Tokyo, or his agent, or his father.

It was easy to fall asleep that night, not so much because

he was exhausted by boredom and aversion but rather because it was becoming difficult for him to demarcate the boundary between sleeping and wakefulness: both were equally empty and, when interrupted, equally bizarre.

That was why, when he felt someone crawl into bed with him in the middle of the night – felt it, first, by the bouncing of the bed – and then when that someone placed (his? her?) arms around his thin chest, slightly constricting his thin breathing, he didn't feel particularly startled. It could have been a dream, or it could have been a real person sneaking into his room: really, it hardly mattered. After a moment, he was wide awake in the dark. But the lack of feeling in his body made it hard to tell whose arms they were, only that someone was lightly gripping him.

The room's darkness was punctuated only by the candy-colored lights on the monitors. He felt a rough breath against his neck, and smelled a mixture of alcohol, masticated rice, and stale pipe tobacco.

"Father?"

"Yes."

"What are you doing here? You're supposed to come back tomorrow." Hiroshi thought it was very strange – not just the late visit, but the fact that his father had wedged himself into bed behind Hiroshi and then, apparently, had pushed Hiroshi into a sitting position in order to wrap his arms around him.

"Obviously, as you can see, I've decided to come back tonight instead."

"What time is it?"

"Three thirty-five a.m., Manhattan time," his father replied with some satisfaction.

"So why not tomorrow morning when normal people might come?"

"Because there's no time to waste."

"How did you sneak in here, anyway? And no time for what?"

Instead of replying, Mr. Mori withdrew his hands from around Hiroshi's chest, placed his palms against Hiroshi's back, and shoved. Hiroshi, naturally, rocked forward, and then fell sideways, almost slipping out of bed.

Mr. Mori scrambled out of the bed himself, but rather than help his son back onto the mattress, he grabbed his dangling arms and began to pull him toward the floor.

Hiroshi felt oddly unalarmed. "I know what you're trying to do."

His father grunted and pulled Hiroshi, rather carefully, all the way onto the floor. Then he propped him up into a sitting position again, right next to the bed, and again began shoving him in the back.

Hiroshi said, "This isn't the way to get me to walk, you know." But he wasn't angry about being dragged out of bed in the middle of the night, and he wasn't especially angry about being pushed in the back, either.

Now Mr. Mori was breathing heavily. He wrapped his arms around his son's chest and held him still. His voice came from directly behind Hiroshi's left ear.

"I'm just a little drunk."

"I know."

"I've been in worse conditions by far, I just want you to know."

Hiroshi wasn't sure which of their situations he was referring to. "Is that so?"

Mr. Mori brought his head closer to Hiroshi's ear. It was a creepy feeling. "Yes. When I was eleven or twelve. My friend and I were really drunk..."

"Wait a minute," Hiroshi said. "You were drunk when you were eleven or twelve years old?"

Mr. Mori laughed. "Not unheard of. Anyway, it was right after the war, and we were out looking for mischief, I don't remember what, and I got separated from my friends."

"Where was this?"

"Where? Where do you think? The same miserable streets where you wasted time when you were that age. We didn't go traveling to whatever was left of Tokyo in those days."

Hiroshi always found it hard to picture his father as a child, hanging around the few dusty streets that his hometown must have consisted of back then. But it was nice to imagine, and it was rather nice, actually, to have his father hold him in his arms. Even though he couldn't see his face, or feel that much of his arms around his chest.

"Anyway, I got separated from my friends. Maybe they went home. Who knows? I started feeling really tired, so I sat down right in front of the old tofu shop. And immediately, like it's been waiting for me, this dog, this stray dog, walks up to me. There used to be a lot of stray dogs around in those days, and they were all starving. Everyone was starving in those days."

"Maybe he wanted some tofu, and you were blocking his way."

"You don't think that shop was still in business in those days? No, he wanted me. Most of those dogs were cowards, but this one went right up to me and sniffed my breath. Remember, I'm sitting down, so his muzzle is right at the level of my mouth. He sniffs a few times, then he bares his teeth."

"What'd you do?"

"Those teeth looked huge to me. As young as I was, eight or nine..."

"I thought you said you were eleven or twelve."

"I can't remember exactly. It was during the Occupation, so I must have been really young. But the point is, as young as

I was, I knew instinctively that I was being confronted with a classic, insoluble human dilemma."

"Which was what?"

"The dilemma of the terrorist. Which is to say, if I moved in any way, that dog was going to bite my face off. And I mean that literally. And eat it right in front of me while I bled. He must have sensed that I was weak, because I was young, and tired, and sitting down, and drunk, and on top of all of that I was separated from my friends. So he was challenging me to move, and if I did, he was going to kill me. I mean, whether I tried to escape by bolting suddenly, or tried to casually slip away, or whether I smacked him hard on the muzzle, it didn't matter, anything I did would've been punished by him ripping my cheek open and gulping it down just for starters. All I'd probably had to eat that day was some gruel, so you can imagine what *he* must have had, and how tasty I must've looked, as skinny as I was. But I couldn't just outwait him, either. Because if I didn't move, he would sense that I was that much weaker, and kill me anyway."

"Okay, I guess that was a dilemma," Hiroshi said, trying to picture where, in his hometown, that long-gone tofu shop might've been located, and trying to imagine if there had been streetlights in those days after the war. He wished he could crane his neck all the way around to see his father's face at this moment. "What were you drunk on, anyway, if there wasn't any food?"

"Oh, let's just say it was located somewhere on the vast continuum between cleaning fluid and nihon shu."

"So what happened?"

"What do you mean, what happened?"

"Well, before I interrupted your chain of thought by asking you what kind of alcohol you were drinking... I mean, I'm still a little amazed that you were drinking at all at that age, but before that you were being stared down by a starveling dog in a filthy street and here you are with your cheeks intact, so something must have happened."

His father slowly lifted Hiroshi up by the armpits, laid his upper body across the bed, and then, walking around to the other side of the bed, pulled him all the way back onto his pillow. Then he put the guardrails up and looked at his son.

"Tonight, I drank two glasses of brandy after dinner, a couple of glasses of a middling whisky called Ballantyne's, and then I switched to a much better single-malt scotch called something like MacAllan. I had a lot of that. A *lot*. As far as the answer to your other question..." Here, Mr. Mori stopped and spread his arms out jubilantly. He bowed – not like a Japanese person, but like a performer – and stepped out of the room.

* * *

THE NEXT MORNING, Hiroshi awakened to find that his nose was running, so he turned his head against his pillow to wipe it, but the pillow was too compressed beneath his head for him to reach it with his nose. His father had probably bunched it up that way before making his mysterious exit. There were no nurses about. He pictured his father, back in his hotel room, tucking into his shirred eggs and Bloody Mary.

He was so sick of the indignities he didn't think he could stand it anymore. In frustration, he willed his right arm to move, and, to his shock, it glided easily upwards from the bed to his nose where he touched – and felt! – the bit of cold mucus running down his upper lip.

Hiroshi let out a little cry of delight. His left arm was close to the bedside table, where there was a box of tissues. With only a little more effort, he pulled a single tissue from the box – it seemed to weigh a lot, but wasn't unliftable – and dabbed it gingerly at the base of his nose.

Now, this was something. He tried his legs. Nothing. He could still wiggle his toes and buttocks though, and he could move his arms almost at will. Suddenly remembering that he had a body, Hiroshi began running his hands up and down his trunk.

He went for his heart first, because he wanted to feel it beat, for the first time since his collapse, from the outside of his body. That he could do, though he was shocked to discover how close to the surface of his body his ribs had floated.

Next, he grabbed his penis, weighed it in his hand, and let it drop. Not much more to do there. Then he poked with his fingers as far down the length of his body as he could, attempting to assess how much sensation was there. Once again, he was reminded of those times when, as a child, he had tried to tickle himself – although now he almost laughed in his excitement at being able to feel his finger poking his upper thigh.

Then he explored his stomach and his abdomen. His digestion had been perfect since his illness had begun, but since this morning he had been feeling a bit crampy in the intestinal region, which he perversely interpreted as a sign of returning health. He massaged his gut for a moment and then froze: There was a distinctly palpable lump in the lower right quadrant of his gut that had, he was sure, never been there before.

How much misfortune could one person stand? Torn between panic and self-pity, he squeezed his eyes shut for a second and then, using his newly recovered skill, rang for a nurse. In a moment, Dr. Lillet came in.

"Hi, Hiroshi. A nurse is coming by in a minute, but I was on my way in anyway. Everything all right?"

"No, it's not."

"I see you're moving your hands."

"Yes. I can move them almost at will."

"Well, like I promised, the plasmapheresis works very rapidly. So why isn't everything all right?"

"Because I believe I have cancer."

"Oh, cancer now is it?"

Hiroshi didn't like his tone at all. "What do you mean, cancer *now*? What you imply seems to be that I have just one complaint after another, instead of a legitimate illness."

"Settle down, Hiroshi. Your GBS is absolutely legitimate. But how on earth can you reach the conclusion by yourself that you have cancer?"

"You're a doctor. You see for yourself." Hiroshi motioned to his belly.

"Well, as you know, this isn't my area of expertise. But let's take a look." Dr. Lillet raised the bedclothes and, directed by Hiroshi's feeble hand, discovered the lump.

"See? What else could that be?"

Dr. Lillet laughed softly. "It could be a lot of things." Hiroshi thought of Dr. Lillet's earlier comment about the human body being a supremely complicated mechanism. The doctor rotated the lump with his fingers a few more times. "I'm sure it's nothing. I'll tell you what, I'll bring Dr. Subramanian in, and if he thinks there's cause for concern, he'll bring in a specialist. But it's probably just a subcutaneous fat deposit."

He got up to leave. "Listen, why don't you do yourself a favor and focus on your hands? This is exciting news. I'll stop by in a while, and we'll see what other progress you've been making."

Two hours passed before Dr. Subramanian showed up. Hiroshi spent the time watching television – he had to admit that he felt a certain sense of pride in being able to use the remote control to switch from one inane drama to another. He tried not to think about the lump, which he was certain could not be something called a "subcutaneous fat deposit," but he couldn't pull his mind away from the cruelty of fate – that, just as he had begun his recovery, he had begun his decline as well. Ready to get up and begin living, but stuck fast to the bed, possibly until he died of an intestinal malignancy.

Then he thought for a while about the odd fact that the English word "fast" meant both to move at a high rate of speed and to be completely immobile. Stuck fast. Fast asleep. That meant, he was pretty sure, to be deep asleep and dreaming. Sleep faster, the old saying went, we're running out of pillows. Live faster, he told himself, you're running out of life.

Dr. Subramanian probed and poked Hiroshi's lump with admirable care, Hiroshi had to acknowledge. When he was finished, he said, "It's a subcutaneous fat deposit. It's completely harmless."

Hiroshi wasn't entirely relieved. "Did you talk to Dr. Lillet?"

"About this? Why would I talk to Dr. Lillet? He's a neurologist. Or do you mean, did he talk to me and tell me what to say?" Dr. Subramanian laughed. "Listen, this isn't Japan. If you have cancer, we'll tell you. And if you don't, we'll tell you that, too. Okay? You don't."

"If this is just a fat deposit, why haven't I noticed it before?"

"These things come and go. You might have had it for years, but not noticed it because you probably don't spend a lot of time rubbing your own belly."

"To be honest, I'm still concerned. Because I've lost so much weight, how could I have any fat anywhere?"

Dr. Subramanian looked at Hiroshi and laughed. "Listen,

Hiroshi, you're going to have to start facing up to the fact that your bad luck is about to run out."

"Good."

"Yeah, but, Hiroshi, then what?"

Hiroshi shrugged. "Yeah, then what?" He thanked Dr. Subramanian and then, even before the doctor had left the room, he closed his eyes.

Part Two

Chapter 7

ON JULY 15, about three months after his initial collapse onto the filthy floor of the Gramercy West Hotel, Hiroshi was picking his way abstractedly through the perilous landscape of Central Park. He used for this task a hand-carved Ashanti cane that Grady had sent to him upon receiving word of his discharge from the East Side Rehabilitation Center, where Hiroshi had undergone rehabilitation until just two days ago at the hands of a quiet young woman named Trudi.

He had entered the park at the south end of the Metropolitan Museum of Art and intended to describe a rough semi-circle through the park before exiting again at the north end of the museum and hailing a taxi by means of waving about his impressive cane. He was about half of the way through his journey.

This was his first walk through Central Park since his recovery process had begun. At Trudi's urging (when she urged, she murmured) he had been taking daily walks in Gramercy Park, a gated, child-sized park that allowed him, like a wobbly beginner at a little ice rink, to hold onto the edges during his circumnavigations. Central Park was a much greater challenge, but he was anxious to tell Trudi that he had conquered it. It was Trudi's ingenuity, in fact, that allowed him to conquer it, and that allowed him to wave Grady's cane around when he needed to hail a taxi; she had, among many other things, fashioned a clever little double leather loop that attached at one end to the cane and at the other to his wrist, and this arrangement allowed Hiroshi to hold the cane firmly enough despite the continuing weakness in his fingers. She'd also picked out a pair of high-top basketball shoes for him to help him deal with the weakness in his ankles that made his foot flop down every time he lifted it from the ground.

Trudi and Maureen were about the same age and even looked a bit alike, but Trudi was not Maureen. Trudi wasn't, to begin with, a musician. This was significant, as far as Hiroshi was concerned, because he had become gradually convinced that Maureen's behavior had been influenced by her envy of Hiroshi's relative success as a jazz musician.

Trudi also wasn't neurotic in any way that Hiroshi could discern. She was resolutely practical and phlegmatic, and had guided Hiroshi through the difficult and crushingly dull rehabilitation process with a slightly distant geniality and an unblinking imperviousness to his pain. She was sweet and soft-spoken, but not about to be bent by his cries, nor by his threats to quit. And, unlike Maureen, she did all this without any bogus flirtation and shape-shifting. It helped, as far as Hiroshi was concerned, that Trudi had a childlike mien; though she must have been at least twenty-six, her skinny, late-adolescent body inevitably was clothed in cotton slacks and a loose cotton T-shirt, and her red hair, almost the same shade as Maureen's, was more often than not gathered up in one ponytail or sometimes two – not pigtails, because they were short and unbraided, but the effect was nearly as desexualizing. She operated a weekend dog-walking service to make ends meet. She looked like she could have been Maureen's little sister.

Trudi had, however, been overheard by Hiroshi to ask one of her colleagues on Hiroshi's first day of rehabilitation whether or not Hiroshi was married. This flattered Hiroshi quite a bit, especially considering how self-conscious he had become of his wasted muscles. She probably hadn't known at the time that he was fluent in English, so he enjoyed the compliment without betraying any knowledge that he understood it. She'd been standing only a few feet away from his bed, and he had barely heard her quiet words.

Of course, she might have known at the time that he was fluent, which would have made the compliment even more satisfying because she had made no effort to move away from him when she'd asked the other therapist. But if she had had no idea at the time about his English proficiency, she probably would have remembered later what she had asked her friend once she'd learned he was fluent, and felt embarrassed in retrospect. But if so, she'd never betrayed any feelings of that sort, and indeed, after that initial comment, nothing personal had transpired between them. Though she had grabbed every part of his body, heard him cry, even in the first days wiped his runny nose, all of it was kind and none of it was personal.

Although, Hiroshi reflected, she probably hadn't known he had heard her, even if she did know he was fluent, and had been talking about him in the same way all the doctors had talked about him — though not to him — in his presence. The question, in any event, might have been a matter of idle curiosity, or an attempt to understand his personality for treatment purposes, rather than something personal. Otherwise, at some point, perhaps with her arms (slender, but reined with ropy veins and rather sinewy for such a little person) firmly around his waist as he struggled to walk down

Michael Antman

the two parallel bars, or as she kneeled at his side and stretched his leg backwards over his head, she certainly would have taken the opportunity to say something. She had spent almost a year traveling the world with an elderly Danish industrialist with multiple sclerosis and his wife, paid in food, hotel rooms, and airfare, and responsible not only for his physical care but for travel arrangements and rudimentary translations, so he had little doubt she would not hesitate to say what was on her mind in any situation.

Hiroshi ascended slowly, hardly using his cane, up the side of a small rock outcropping that a six-year-old boy could have bounded up in a matter of seconds. Still, it was exhilarating; his blood felt carbonated. He stepped gingerly up to the top of the rock, which wasn't more than a foot or two off the ground, and inched close to the edge. Immediately, a familiar sharp ache flashed through his groin, the same sensation he had had at times in the past when he had stood at the edge of a path in the Japan Alps, or when he had allowed his toe-tips to slide over the edge of the seventh floor of an unfinished parking garage in Kobe, nothing but asphalt below.

He wondered what caused that ache. What was his body trying to tell him? And why was it sending him that message now, at the top of a small rise in the ground that wasn't enough, even in his weakened state, to cause him injury should he fall?

There was no question that he had become far more sensitive in his period of recovery. There was a game he and his friends used to play as children, where they'd hold the point of a sharp knife over the bridge of their noses without actually touching any skin. But the infinitesimal hairs on their noses and foreheads would stand on end and bristle, and a strange chill would pass over their bodies. Now, he felt that sensation all the time, almost as if, in recovering, his nerves had somehow overshot the mark. Riding on the subway, as he

144

had begun to do recently after his rehabilitation sessions, he'd sit with his cane between his legs and realize that the creeping, lightly burning sensation he felt on his arm was nothing more than the shortsleeved shirt of the guy sitting next to him. The sleeve stuck out just enough to brush against Hiroshi's arm hairs, and that was sufficient to give Hiroshi the chills. Worse yet was when the guy next to him was wearing a T-shirt, and the hair on his arm came into contact with the hair on Hiroshi's arm.

This was something he wouldn't have to worry about in winter. Now, however, it raised a larger worry. If he couldn't bear to be touched, how could he bear to make love?

On the other hand, it was purely an academic concern. Certainly the laconic and low-key Trudi was not a prospect. It was interesting, he reflected, that she had been pulling, bending, and stretching his limbs for three months now, and he had felt none of the skin sensitivity he experienced when, for example, a cashier touched his fingers when giving him his change at the Korean deli. Probably because whatever sensitivity he might have felt was obliterated by the agony of having his muscles worked incessantly.

Surely not Trudi. Though she had invited him over for dinner that night, which was interesting. She had just moved into a minuscule apartment in Chinatown, after a protracted wrangle with her old landlord in Brooklyn that Hiroshi had overheard her discussing with a friend on the phone one day. He couldn't understand why moving out of an apartment was so difficult in New York, but apparently it was. As far as Maureen, she had called Hiroshi several times at the East Side Rehabilitation Institute, and several more times at his hotel. Each time he had answered, or called her back, and had been as polite as he could be.

Hiroshi stumbled down from the rock outcropping and headed for Fifth Avenue to look for a taxi. When he reached the sidewalk, he was able to pick up speed; in fact, he was walking, with the aid of the cane, almost as fast as he had before the illness.

He thought, as he walked, of one of his father's poems – in truth, the only one that he knew. It had been the first poem in the first book his father had published, and his American translator some years later had had the English-language version typeset and framed for Mr. Mori. It hung now in the family home, on a wall next to a slippery tower of old video-cassettes.

Hiroshi knew it by heart – not hard, considering that it was only three lines – though he had never quite understood it.

> *Poetry's a joke!*
> *I walk boldly down the street,*
> *Confident I'll die.*

Hiroshi was confident of only one thing right now, and that was that he wasn't going to die. At least not any time soon. He walked boldly, if slowly, down the street until a taxicab pulled alongside. Then he took so long to fold himself into the backseat that the cabbie started the meter even before they had pulled away.

* * *

HE WAS in a different room at the Gramercy West Hotel – to begin with, a room without exposed, painted-over pipes. His father had arranged for Hiroshi to stay for at least three months, the estimated duration of his recovery, and had paid both for the room and for some amenities, such as fresh, mint-green sheets and pillowcases, heavy new curtains in a darker green, a Southwestern-style throw rug with arrowheads and abstract equine shapes in pinks and greens and turquoise, some Hudson River Valley landscapes on the walls, a small bookcase and a rollaway cabinet, and an aluminum guide bar for the small bathroom. The pictures, the curtains, the rug, the sheets and pillowcases – none of them were particularly sumptuous, yet none seemed the sort of thing his father was capable of, this ethereal glutton who wolfed down his food while staring off into space, and who, in the middle of a walk, was as apt to sit down on a fire hydrant as on a bench.

His father was long gone. He had left after his third visit to the hospital. In theory, Hiroshi could have left not long after him, been met at Narita airport by an ambulance, and completed his recovery in Tokyo. But he hadn't wanted to, his father hadn't wanted him to, and Trudi hadn't wanted him to.

He hadn't wanted to because he couldn't face his friends looking like a stick, jobless, and unable to do the only thing besides speak English that he could do superbly well. He'd always regarded illness as a form of failure and had made a point of hiding from Hitomi whenever he wasn't feeling well. Nonetheless, there was no hiding the fact that his calves were still very weak, as were his triceps. His arms trembled a bit when he lifted the economy-sized bottle of shampoo his father had left him. When he soaped himself in the shower, he buckled at the knees every time the soap passed over one particular point on his groin. His toes, save his big toes, were a little weak, which wasn't a great loss, but his fingers were extremely weak – he couldn't peel an egg – and that was a very great loss indeed. The callus from his clarinet's thumb hook, something he thought he'd never in his life lose, had long since disappeared. This made him very, very sad. His neck still felt at once loose and stiff, and his head continued to ache at intervals. His lips trembled a bit – though a bit was all it took – when he tried to blow into his clarinet. He just wasn't screwed together very well at all.

His father hadn't wanted him to return because, Hiroshi presumed, he wasn't interested in a son that wasn't triumphant. Hiroshi had come here to have a little triumph, and perhaps to make the connections necessary to record his first CD for an influential American label instead of an obscure German one, and his father wasn't about to have him leave until that mission had been accomplished. Or so Hiroshi assumed, surveying the comfortable surroundings Mr. Mori had arranged for him at the hotel; when his father called, he hectored him about his recovery and about how hard he was working his muscles, but his father's intention, it was clear enough, was to get him strong enough to return to his career, not to Japan.

Trudi just didn't think he was ready – physically or mentally. Picturing himself hobbling onto an airplane with a cane, and then having to negotiate the vertiginous stairs in the Japanese subways – there were few escalators anywhere – Hiroshi couldn't disagree.

Although if he got any more phone calls like that strange one the other night, he might have to reconsider. He'd almost been asleep when the phone rang; Hiroshi picked it up, unthinkingly, and heard a rough male voice say, in English, "You die."

Hiroshi had let the receiver clatter from his weak fingers, then picked it up again and called the front desk, but they had no idea who the call might have been from. Hiroshi thought about it, his heart thumping, after a while decided it had been a crank call, probably random, and had gone back to sleep.

All of his belongings had been returned from the hospital, or brought up from the hotel's long-term storage room. He had his regular clarinet (a useless appendage), a couple of boxes of bamboo reeds, and a reed knife that he probably would never use again. He had cork grease and Chapstick for assembling and disassembling the clarinet, something he might never do again. He had all of his CDs, and more he'd bought in the months of his rehabilitation; Chick Corea's *My Spanish Heart* was the official soundtrack to his pain.

He had a microwave, some bowls and plates and forks and knives and spoons, and a portable cabinet that his father had stocked with canned soups, dried apricots, dried seaweed, fish flakes, soy sauce, bricks of shelf-stable tofu, bags of pinto and navy beans, and other such items appropriate for an Arctic exploration. He also had a new bottle of wasabi furikake. He had all the clothes he'd brought with him from Japan, as well as a few new items he had picked up in the days after he'd regained his mobility. He had a crate, still unopened, filled with clothes and "important" papers that his agent had collected from the apartment in Kichijoji, no longer his; his agent had pulled some strings and made some payments to get Hiroshi out of his lease. He wondered if his agent had kept his DVD copies of *Erotic Breast Explosion* and *Sensual Nurse Attack* and *Bare Ladies' Super High-Class Semen Festival Volume III*.

He had a bottle of Blanton's bourbon that his father's brother had sent him. He had an inexpensive blue plastic Remington MicroScreen electric razor his father had given him, since he was now unable to use a blade. He had Maureen's exercise balls, and several other gifts she'd sent him while he was at the Rehabilitation Center – a Michelin guide to New York City, some wrist and ankle weights and a big display box (it looked like it had been swiped from a discount store) filled with individually wrapped bars of peanut toffee – obdurate and indigestible sweets, to exercise his jaw muscles, she claimed. It was difficult enough for him to unwrap one, much less chew it.

In addition to the Michelin Guide, he had a few other books leaning at a sharp angle in his new bookcase, including some fakebooks and the paperback copy of *The Honourable Schoolboy* he'd begun to read on the flight from Tokyo. He had no memory whatsoever of the plot, the premise, or the characters. Sad to think that a writer could spend a year or two of his life constructing a book that was well-written and the product of a great deal of thought, and yet be unable to make any impact whatsoever on a reader. Guiltily, Hiroshi flipped through it, looking for the page where'd he left off, with the intention of perhaps picking it up again. The book obediently flopped open to pages 20 and 21, and presented to Hiroshi two silvery, symmetrical grease spots. Hiroshi scanned the pages, and the page before, to see if he could pick up the thread of the plot, but nothing was familiar to him except his memory of pressing his temple into the open book before he'd dozed off for the last time somewhere over North America. Underneath the oily blotches, the type was slightly smeared – which meant, Hiroshi concluded, that he must have walked off of the airplane, through customs, into the taxicab, and into the Master Class at the Academy, with a blackish smear of John Le Carre's words on his forehead.

Maureen had seen it, and said nothing – one more black mark against her.

He changed slowly into a pair of jeans he had just purchased. The rough fabric was painful enough against his skin, and yet when he had tried on softer fabrics at the clothing store, the cool, floppy presence against his leg had somehow been even more irritating. He really would prefer to go naked – and in fact often did go without clothes, unless one counted the cane, when he was in his room. He put on a crisp long-sleeved cotton shirt, slipped into some loafers, shuddered violently as his skin adjusted to the ensemble, and stepped out of his room.

He cheered up as he approached Trudi's apartment in Chinatown. The seat of the taxi was partially collapsed, causing his skinny butt and hips to sink so alarmingly low that he'd wondered if he'd be able to pull himself up when the taxi arrived. But he used the low angle to look up at the fascinatingly detailed roofs of the richly decrepit buildings they passed. He glimpsed an interesting sign on the top of what probably was an Indian restaurant, which read SWEETS AND UTENSILS. It seemed an odd combination. Anyway, it was a lot more satisfying than the view he'd had from the back of the ambulance when he'd been so frustrated about not being able to see Greenwich Village.

When he got out of the taxicab — it hadn't been as much of a struggle as he'd feared — he saw at his feet a flattened and completely blackened banana peel with, in its center, an as yet unfaded, bright yellow-green oval label that seemed a sort of memorial to the departed fruit. The whole street was dark and dirty, but everywhere were the same patches of unexpected brightness; Trudi's apartment, above an Asian grocery that appeared to be out of business, glowed like an ember in a heap of coals.

Metal grates on the bars and stores. A complex, sour stink. A big dumpster bearing the words, spread across its three green panels, SAM SHAU LING, which Hiroshi pretended to believe was the name of a Chinese restaurant. He had to admit that, aside from all the reasons that Trudi and his father and everyone else had, the real reason he hadn't returned to Tokyo yet was that he truly loved New York's filthy charm.

It was more of an ordeal getting up the stairs than it had been exiting the cab. When Hiroshi arrived at her door, he was out of breath. She answered the door wearing a thick white bathrobe that seemed almost too big, and certainly too luxuriant, for the apartment. Behind her, in the tiny room, ranged buttes, mesas, and sheer cliffs of cartons and upended furniture.

"Hey, sorry, Hiroshi. I'm really running late."

"How could you be late? This is your apartment."

"I'm late. You're literal. I mean that I'm terribly behind schedule. I had to cover half of the next shift, and I haven't even taken a shower. And then I have nothing to cook with yet."

"Shall we reschedule?"

"Reschedule? Of course not. Just make yourself at home. I have a couch at least, so you won't need to sit on a packing crate. I'll finish my shower, and you read a magazine. There's a bunch in the open carton in front of the sofa. Then, if you don't mind, we can order Chinese. This is sort of the neighborhood for it, don't you think?"

"I don't mind." Hiroshi watched Trudi dash into the bathroom. Then he went into the living room and walked very carefully around the clutter, bracing his cane against a tower of cartons, and sank into the couch with some relief, holding onto the pole of a floor lamp for balance as he laid his cane down. The television was on, a tennis match, and even though the sound was rather low, Hiroshi was surprised to discover that he could feel through the pole the vibrations from the crowd noise and the bouncing ball, or at least the vibrations from the television's speaker that reproduced these sounds.

As instructed, he pulled out a slippery handful of magazines, bracing their weight against the heels of his hands, because his fingers could not do the job. He selected an issue of *Entertainment Weekly* with Catherine Zeta-Jones on the cover, an issue of *Smithsonian* with an article about Etruscan pottery, an issue of *Modern Rehabilitation*, and two copies of *Elle*, even though they reminded him a bit of Maureen. He hoped he'd have time before Trudi got out of the shower to at least glance at the many articles that interested him.

He balanced the five magazines on his knee in order of reading preference – *Modern Rehabilitation, Entertainment*

Weekly, Smithsonian and *Elle* – and opened up his first selection, using the side of his hand instead of his useless fingers, to an advertisement for dumbbells featuring a beautiful young woman with little apparent need of rehabilitation. He laboriously pushed his way back with his hands to the table of contents to see if there was an article about Guillain-Barré – there was not – and then became aware that Trudi was calling to him from behind the closed bathroom door, over the sound of the shower. He rose suddenly, spilling the five magazines onto the floor, and just as suddenly sank part of the way back onto her couch, overcome by a sudden wave of weakness in his thighs. With an effort, he rose to his full height, picked up his cane and slid his hand into the leather loop, and walked over to the bathroom to see what was the matter.

"Hey, Hiroshi, c'mon in. You have to see this!" Even her exclamations sounded low-key.

"Are you sure it's all right?"

"Of course. I want you to see this!"

Hiroshi eyed the doorknob cautiously. He doubted he'd be able to turn it. But when he pushed at it, the door swung open on its own. Trudi was standing there with the towel wrapped loosely around her waist, bare breasted. Her towel had slipped so far that he could see a bit of her pubic hair. Her breasts were very round and much larger than he'd expected, and there were freckles on the tops and sides of them. Her areolas were bright red and rather raw-looking, though in a quite appealing way.

"Look at this cool ceiling!"

Hiroshi tore his eyes away from Trudi's body and looked up at the ceiling, noting, on the way, that her hair lay loose and wet against her skin instead of gathered in a ponytail; though the loose hair didn't quite fit her little cat's chin, it made her look much sexier.

There was a tessellated Escheresque bird pattern on the

wallpaper – placed on the ceiling, Hiroshi guessed, to cover water damage – and it was interesting enough, but hardly worth interrupting a shower for. He turned his attention downwards again, trying to look Trudi in the eyes, but again found himself staring at her breasts.

"Yes, that's very nice." Hiroshi backed slowly out of the bathroom because he was afraid that she might get angry at him for staring at her in this way. She had let the towel drop completely now, but rather than following Hiroshi out of the bathroom, or smiling at him, or waiting expectantly for him to follow her, she simply stepped back into the shower and pulled the curtain shut behind her.

Perhaps she's just comfortable with nudity, Hiroshi considered. And the ceiling certainly wasn't uninteresting. But not so interesting that she couldn't have waited until she was done showering, Hiroshi reflected. Probably she was trying to seduce him, though in this country, any explanation was possible. He waited for the image of her nude body to clear his brain, then hobbled over again to the couch and picked up the copy of *Modern Rehabilitation* he'd just begun to read. But he couldn't concentrate on the magazine's annual wage survey. He kept on thinking about those tessellated birds and those freckles.

After a while, Trudi emerged, dressed in khakis and a pretty, appliqued shirt that she must have had hanging on the back of the bathroom door. Her hair was once again in a ponytail. She didn't act any differently than she had before the shower, or indeed any differently than she did at the Rehabilitation Center. She picked up a Chinese menu from on top of a pile of mail and catalogs perched on a carton.

"Hey, have you ever had mabo-dofu?"

"Sure. I like it."

"Well, how about some mabo-dofu and – oh, they've got a

pressed duck dish, which I absolutely love. And some hot-and-sour soup – does that sound good?"

"Everything sounds good. There is not a type of food I don't like."

"In that case, let's also get some Yu Shan Scallops. You okay with spicy?"

"Sure."

"Everything is sure with you. You're an agreeable guy, Hiroshi." She sounded like she was in a very good mood – almost giddy. She picked up the phone and, after a moment, put it down again. "What am I thinking? I won't be hooked up for months. Do you see my cell phone anywhere?"

Hiroshi began to look around the chaos in the living room. It struck him for the first time how unusual it was for a woman to invite someone over to her place for the first time when the apartment was in such disorder. He found an odd thing, a scrawled note taped to one of the packing crates that read: "If you begin to feel unsafe." Nothing else on the note but that, and when he peeked under the lid of the crate, he saw that it contained only sweaters. Then he heard her in the bedroom say, "I found it!" and, after a minute or two, heard her ordering the food, with a couple of additional items – orange beef and crab crackers – tacked on.

When she came out of her bedroom, she was completely naked. Her breasts swayed when she walked. She put the cell phone on the kitchen counter and said, "It'll be here in about forty-five minutes. In the meantime, let's work on your legs for a while."

"Is this therapy?"

"What else would it be?"

"Is it sexual?"

"Sexual?" She seemed genuinely surprised, though not at all offended. "You mean because I'm naked? No, I expect you to get naked, too. We're not in the Rehabilitation Center anymore."

Hiroshi nodded solemnly, though her explanation wasn't entirely comprehensible. He began to pull off his shoes. "Is this a usual kind of therapy?"

"Usual for me. Just get into the flow, will ya?"

"All right. I'll flow." He began, slowly and carefully, to remove his clothes.

Trudi laughed. "Here, this is going to take forever." She leaned over to unbuckle his belt and, in the process, the tip of her nipple gently brushed against the soft skin of his inner wrist. He jumped at the exquisite and unfamiliar sensation — it was almost as if his inner wrist had been an erogenous zone all along and had been patiently waiting all these years for him to discover it — and, almost in the same motion, grabbed Trudi around her naked waist and began to kiss her.

Trudi pulled back after a moment. "Man, it took you long enough."

"I wasn't sure."

She pulled her right shoulder back slightly to indicate that she wanted Hiroshi to caress her breast.

He did, but instead of kissing her again, said, "Isn't this a bit..."

"What? Unprofessional?"

"I guess."

"I'm not at work, Hiroshi. I'm in my apartment. My apartment. I can do anything the fuck I want to do here, and right now I choose to fuck you before our mabo-dofu arrives in forty-five minutes. Any objections? Any questions?"

"No, it's just that..."

"It's just that what, Hiroshi? I've been trying to get you to notice me for the past three months." She stood, arms on her hips, facing him. "What do you think, I'm some kind of robot? I get so fucking pissed at all these idiot patients who think I'm some kind of cliché rubber-doll nurse sex-object bullshit who I wouldn't touch with a twelve-foot pole if my life depended on it, you can't be a cute nurse or physical therapist in this city with normal sexual desires without being pigeonholed as a sex toy playing nursie dress-up for their pathetic wet-dream fantasies. And then you come along and I'm actually attracted to someone for once and you treat me like I'm just there to serve you, like some rubber doll except *without* the sex."

It was the most he'd ever heard her say at once. He was surprised by all the "fucks" and "fuckings" in her speech, he'd never heard her swear at all before, but it was kind of cute, coming from her. He said, "I'm sorry if I offended you."

"You didn't offend me, you idiot. You just made me very frustrated."

"I'm sorry. You have to understand, I'm just afraid."

"You don't have to be afraid."

"You don't know what I'm afraid of."

"Oh, bullshit. I know what you're afraid of. You're afraid of your illness. You're afraid you won't be able to 'perform,' right?"

"Something like that."

"You didn't seem to be having any problems when you were staring at my boobs in the bathroom."

"I know. But I just wasn't sure what you were doing in the bathroom, so I just walked away because I didn't want you to get mad. And then you said it was therapy, but just nude therapy, and not sex."

"Oh, Hiroshi, you are such an idiot. You know English, you're obviously smart, you're a musical genius supposedly, but you're a fucking idiot, pardon my French. You walk around in a daze half the time like your mind is on God knows what, and you wait for things to happen to you and when they do you don't even accept it when it's right there in

157

front of your face. Therapy? What'd you *think*? This is a little fantasy I like to play, Hiroshi. A fantasy. Have you ever heard of a sexual fantasy? I do the 'rehab' thing in the buff and it turns into hot sex. I mean, that's the idea. Just thinking about doing it – not that I've hardly ever actually done it, but I think about it a lot. It gets me through the day, okay? When I'm working with some eighty-six-year-old stroke victim. Oh, are you thinking I'm 'unprofessional' again? Well, fuck you. I do my job better than anybody, but tell me anybody in the world working at their jobs who doesn't get bored once in a while and think about sex on top of their desks, or whatever. Like your mind doesn't wander when the bass player is plucking away at some lame-ass solo that goes on for fifteen minutes." She paused. "That's why I stopped going to see jazz."

"Because the other players were fantasizing?"

"Because of those fucking boring bass solos. God, Hiroshi, what'm I going to do with you?"

"Do you want me to leave?"

"No, I don't want you to leave. This is exactly what I'm talking about. The genius I got here! I just want you to get with the program, okay? And stop being so passive about it. Jump into my fantasy, will you?"

"Okay."

She tilted her head to one side and smiled. "You do find me attractive, don't you?"

"Of course."

She grabbed his half-hard cock and pulled him toward her. "I'm going to go put on my uniform. Then just let Nurse take care of everything. Okay, baby?"

* * *

HE SHOULD HAVE STAYED the night. Instead, he chose to take a taxi back to the hotel. He was so tired he anticipated no problem getting to sleep. But he stared at the ceiling instead.

He had had more than enough of staring at the ceiling in the hospital – a lifetime's supply of staring at the ceiling – but here he was doing it again, this new skill he had picked up. Although he'd enjoyed it, he felt strangely little about having had sex with Trudi; instead, his mind dwelt upon his dwindling funds. The hotel room was paid for only for the next two weeks, and that was it. His insurance would last until the end of the month, which was the official end of his rehabilitation period. His savings – most of which had consisted of gifts from his father – were now gone. He'd already gotten an emergency extension on his tourist visa, and would need a job to get a working visa. Or, more accurately, he needed a working visa because he had to get a job.

But he had never done anything for a living except play music, something that was now impossible. With his money almost gone, going back to Japan at this point would mean moving in with his father. He needed to find something here in New York, at least for the time being, something that he could do in his weakened state. He resolved to go out tomorrow and look.

Having made the decision, he did not move on. He rethought his situation, and remade the decision, and then repeated the process a half-dozen more times. He finally decided to take one of the .50 mg Xanax pills that Trudi had slipped him on the sly for just this kind of problem. By the time he fell asleep, it was after two in the morning, and he awakened to an ambulance siren shortly thereafter. Then he fell asleep again, and awakened at six a.m. to yet another siren. It interrupted an odd dream in which he was racing around the hallways of a hotel, not the one he was in, with his big green umbrella unfurled against a strong wind blasting from behind heavy varnished doors. Every once in a while, he stopped running and let the wind carry him down the hallway.

After a huge breakfast of smoked sturgeon, scrambled eggs and onions, orange juice, Greek olives (the least Japanese food on the planet), and coffee, Hiroshi called his agent, Muni, in Tokyo.

Muni was a little distant on the phone.

"It's good of you to call me," he said stiffly.

"I apologize for not having been in more regular contact."

"I suppose there's no reason for you to be. The gig in New York went on without you. I did as you instructed and canceled the Nagoya shows. After that, you don't have anything scheduled until October. So there's really no reason for you to be in touch with me, is there?"

"Nevertheless, I should have called more while I was recovering. Just to let you know of my progress and to thank you for your hard work on my behalf."

"When are you coming back?"

"To Japan?"

"Yes, Hiroshi, to Japan. Where else?"

"I don't have any immediate plans to come back."

"Are you still suffering from the aftereffects of your illness?"

"Well, yes, of course. But I'm physically capable of flying back to Japan. I'm just not ready."

"Well, I'm sure when you are ready to come back you will. In the meantime, are you practicing?"

"Practicing? What gave you that idea? Of *course* I'm not practicing. I'm not physically capable of holding a clarinet and moving my fingers over the stops. I'm not capable of screwing the mouthpiece into the barrel or the ligature onto the mouthpiece. I'd have trouble holding my clarinet up for more than a few minutes. I'm not even capable of scraping my reeds."

"Of course. I suppose my asking was just wishful thinking. The thing is, I shouldn't worry. I know about Pat Martino, for example, and he came back from a brain aneurysm or a stroke or something, and he completely relearned his guitar technique to the point that he's playing more impressively than ever."

"I'm familiar with Pat Martino's CDs. But I'm not him, I'm me, and I've got my own set of problems. The thing is, you might as well cancel my October bookings now."

"You honestly don't feel you'll be ready by then?"

"I will not be ready. No. Absolutely not."

"How can you know?"

"Because, having lived with it, having contemplated every cell of it in silence and in boredom for three months now, I feel as if I know my body now as well as anybody ever knows their body. I know what I can do, and what I can't do and what I'll never be able to do again."

"Meaning what?"

"Isn't my intention clear at all? I'm quitting the music business."

"Don't joke around with me."

"It's hardly a joke. What it is, now that I think about it, is the stating of the utterly obvious. Of course I'm quitting the music business. No, that isn't even it. What I mean is that my body, this illness that invaded my body, has made this decision *for* me to quit the music business. It really has nothing to do with what I think, or what I've 'decided.' I can decide I want to pick up the clarinet and play today, but all that'll come out will be a tuneless wheeze, if even that much. And that'll be true next month or next year."

"You have to understand, Hiroshi, I'm standing here holding the phone listening to your voice come out, and it sounds like some demented impostor doing a miserable job of pretending he's you. It's like, I don't know, what's a strong man?"

"Huh?"

"Give me an example of a strong man, Hiroshi. I can't think right now."

"I don't know. Arnold Schwarzenegger. Shaquille O'Neal."

"Arnold Schwarzenegger. You quitting your music is like Arnold Schwarzenegger quitting his body. You can't quit the music business any more than you can quit your life. It isn't just what you're all about, it *is* you, in your totality."

"What I'm saying is a simple reality, however difficult it is for either one of us to hear."

"What you're saying, Hiroshi, is a simple absurdity. Quitting music for you would be like killing yourself, plain and simple. Is that what you want to do? Is that what you're trying to tell me, that you want to kill yourself?"

"I have no intention of killing myself. I'm going out later today for an interview with the manager of a Nature Company."

"A Nature Company? You mean a *store*? The best young jazz musician in Tokyo, and you're going to work at a *store*? You might as well *well* just kill yourself."

"I'm not going to kill myself. I'm just going to be a retail clerk."

Chapter 8

SHIZUKA HAD GOTTEN A JOB ONCE. This was a surprise to everyone; Hiroshi had witnessed one neighborhood boy, in fact, say to Shizuka, "But I thought you lived in your own little world of made-up stories." But Hiroshi's sister went off anyway and became an office lady in a small business, right there in Ichikawa, which imported and distributed inexpensive kitchen gadgets and sold cookbooks. The job consisted mostly of making and serving tea to the executives, running small errands, and sending faxes and packages. Hiroshi was too self-absorbed in his intensive daily practice sessions and in his studies – the entrance examination to the Tokyo National University of Fine Arts and Music required several years of preparation – to notice how his parents felt about their daughter leaving the house every day to go to a real job. But she seemed to do quite well; no one ever questioned her intelligence. After a few months, though, she started missing work. When Hiroshi was fifteen and she was twenty-one, she had confided in him that she sometimes spent the day in a local tea shop writing short stories rather than coming into the office.

She'd come to him and said, "I know you're preoccupied with your music and your studies, but I want to tell you about my work experience."

Hiroshi had shrugged. He'd always liked talking to his sister. "Okay."

"The reason I want to tell you is about you, not me. I'm just so glad you're going to go to college in a few years and get away. You're very lucky that you have this talent for music, but you're even luckier that you're going to do something bigger with it." Hiroshi had already, while still in high school, played a few local gigs, but everyone had agreed that he needed to go to University, take some composition and theory courses and learn from some accomplished musicians, to get to the next level.

"Yeah, I guess I feel pretty lucky," he'd said.

"Because if you don't, you'll get stuck having to be an adult," she'd said. "I know I have to go to work, I can't live off of Uncle's clinic forever, but it's truly awful. The other day at the office, I was looking out the window and I thought I saw a bird drop dead right off of a telephone pole and hit the ground. So I ran to the window to look for the little thing, and it wasn't there. Now the thing is, the whole business was just a fraud on my part, because I knew perfectly well that the bird hadn't actually fallen off the pole, it had just swooped downwards before flying away. I mean, if there was a bird to begin with."

"So if you knew that, why did you run to the window?"

"Because it would have been something interesting if a bird really had died. The *only* thing interesting. You have to understand, Hiroshi, what it's like in an office. It's like a big coffin with windows. It's rare that you even see any birds at all outside the windows. They've all been poisoned by the chemicals in the rice fields and the golf course. And then for something to really happen, well, you're just desperate for that."

"Well, at least the bird didn't fly up to the window and talk to you."

Shizuka wasn't easily insulted. She smiled calmly. "You mean how I used to tell you about the cockroach and stuff? Hiroshi, that was real. They *did* talk to me."

Because she was pretty in her delicate way, and had begun to learn how to affect a façade of normalcy when she needed to, Shizuka started making friends at the office, and even went on some dates. But that ended after about a year when a fellow worker she liked agreed to meet her for dinner at an Italian restaurant in Tokyo after some business meetings he had planned there. She took the train there, but her date never showed up for a perfectly good reason – he'd had some sort of emergency. Besides, everybody gets stood up at one time or another, that wasn't so unusual, but Shizuka – this is what Hiroshi had heard from his mother who had called him at college to tell him the whole story – had remained seated in a plush chair just outside the entrance to the restaurant, waiting for her date, until the restaurant closed, and then, even after it closed, refused to move or even to speak, so that the owner of a bar across the lobby had eventually called the police, who had pleaded with the mute girl for close to an hour before physically forcing her out of the chair and taking her to a hospital for observation.

Shortly after that, Hiroshi's parents had arranged a marriage. He was, of course, a doctor, a nephrologist. Hiroshi was too busy with his studies to pay much attention after the very lavish wedding, but he heard through the grapevine that the husband began to encounter Shizuka sitting on her futon in the middle of the day, talking to herself. Shortly after that, she left him and returned to the family home over the vehement objections of Hiroshi's mother, though apparently Hiroshi's father and his new brother-in-law were less displeased by this occurrence.

* * *

HIROSHI WASN'T a big fan of nature, except as an abstract ideal, but the Nature Company was heaven. The manager was thrilled to have a Japanese-speaking clerk to serve all of the Japanese tourists who came through, and Hiroshi was thrilled, comparatively speaking, to have a job that required virtually no heavy physical work but that was busy enough to allow him to forget about everything that had happened. And because there was always a shelf or a cabinet to lean against, he often didn't need his cane.

This was no coffin with windows. There were interesting things everywhere to look at and listen to and pick up and touch. When he wasn't serving customers, Hiroshi amused himself by playing with the inexpensive toys that were stocked in square bins in the middle of the store – plastic lizards and snakes encased in super-hardened rubber balls that Hiroshi liked to squeeze, round noisemakers that mooed when turned upside down, miniature compasses, frogs on springs. He excelled at demonstrating these toys to the children who pulled away from their parents immediately upon entering the store. When older kids made smart cracks about all the plastic toys in a store that was supposedly devoted to nature, Hiroshi informed them that plastic came from petroleum, and petroleum came from dinosaurs. He wore a blue-green smock that made him feel oddly authoritative.

He liked to eavesdrop on the customers, especially the English-speaking ones: "In high school, they used to call me the legend." "Last I heard, he was running the national practice." "It isn't so much to structure as to implement." "It's something in his duodenum." "I can't keep the belt on this coat from falling off."

When things were very quiet, he listened to samples of off-brand New Age music blended with synthetic-sounding nature sounds, or paged through lavish picture books of the California and Oregon coastline, or others devoted to wildly colorful underwater scenes that he now would never get to see. The parrot fish was his favorite, appearing again and again in books about the sea like an A-list celebrity.

Best of all were the neat maplewood cabinets, locked against shoplifters, that were filled with expensive polished stones. Here were marvelous objects every bit as colorful and precious as those fish, but he could hold them in his hand, look at the gold of the tiger's eye and the cool Venusian aqua of the crystals, and best of all, stroke their smooth surfaces, which had a calming effect on his still-jumpy skin. After a morning of this, he'd go to lunch and spend a healthy portion of his day's wages on bi bim bop, gyros, pastrami sandwiches and egg salad sandwiches, nut-covered halvah, egg creams, street-vendor hot dogs and souvlaki, frothy whipped orange drinks, deep-fried mushroom and zucchini chunks, floppy slices of sausage pizza sprinkled with red pepper flakes that made his lips burn twenty minutes after the meal, cold bottles of Heineken and Asahi, cheap sushi, questionable curries, mealy McDonald's burgers, huge bowls of chili, and oily chicken soup. The only place he'd never dared to enter was a tiny take-out restaurant called Fried World.

On his way to lunch, he'd pick up a *New York Observer*, or the *Post*, or the *News*, and read the entertainment news and the world news as avidly as he consumed his food. Except that when he had to eat an overstuffed sandwich, he'd put his newspaper aside to manage the sandwich to his mouth, tilting it gently from side to side, sizing up the location of his next bite with cross-eyed admiration while he chewed the previous bite. He wondered if anyone at the sandwich shop or in the park was watching him make love to his sandwich, but he didn't much care.

He could not stop eating. He was spending all of the

money he earned at the Nature Company on food, along with bus and taxi fare, and would have to call his father soon to ask him to pay for another month at the hotel, or find someone to move in with. Either prospect was humiliating, but he could not stop himself.

It was true that he must have some sort of problem with food. On his one European tour, he and his band mates, the ad hoc de Chirico Quintet — *basse, chant, batterie, guitare,* which is to say Grady, and of course *clarinette* — had played for three days in Paris at a club on Rue des Lombards. The meals he and his bandmates had shared before and after shows at nearby bistros and tea shops had been for him reve- latory, as simple as they were – even the crusty brie sand- wiches, as long as his *clarinette,* had been memorable, and yet when the bus was idling outside the malodorous Hotel des Arennes to take them to the airport, Hiroshi had been struck with a sense of thunderous injustice and impersonal envy, that he had not eaten enough nor experienced enough, and might not be back in Paris for many years to come. So he had lied that he had left his passport in his room in order to dash into the patisserie next door to the hotel, purchased half a dozen miniature pistachio and chocolate *macarons,* and then wolfed four of them down in his vacated room with its view of a tiny Roman arena out back, the others secreted in his jacket pocket to be accidentally smashed, and eaten, later. The windows of the minibus were darkened, so his bandmates had seen nothing of this shameful scurry. He burrowed into his seat and listened to the music the Indian bus driver was playing – some ethereal, ultra-feminine Bollywood theme from Lata Mangeshkar -- and regretted having missed the first part of the song in order to debase himself and give himself the ache he felt coming on in the lower left quadrant of his gut. Chet Baker had destroyed himself with drugs. Coltrane had been addicted to heroin and Life Savers. Art

Pepper, Miles Davis, pretty much all of them had something going on.

Surely he was allowed a bite to eat?

Three or four nights a week, he'd go over to Trudi's apartment. Slowly, her life began to materialize out of the cartons and onto her walls and floors. She put up a poster for the musical *Rent* and a hand-colored photograph of her as a three-year-old, and another poster, very faded and tattered at the edges, that looked as if it had come from a schoolroom wall:

JACK'S WONDERFUL PUMP

- AND THE LIFE STREAM THAT FLOWS THROUGH HIS HOUSE
- THE REINS OF THE HEART WHICH ARE WORKING FOREVER NIGHT AND DAY
- THE FOUR CHAMBERS WITH THE LIVING WALLS
- HOW THE PUMP DRIVES THE LIFE-STREAM ROUND AND ROUND
- WHAT IS IT THAT HAPPENS WHEN WE BLUSH
- THE PRECIOUS THINGS THE RIVER CARRIES
- THE FOOD FOR JACK'S MILLIONS OF SERVANTS
- THE RED AND WHITE SERVANTS WHO GET OLD IN SIX WEEKS AND DIE
- THE WANDERING CHEMISTS WHO HELP JACK IN TIME OF DANGER
- HOW YOU MAY FEEL THE GREAT PUMP BEATING

She also filled her closet with clothes. She had only one tiny closet, but two sets of clothes. One set, the first to appear in her closet, was her usual sweatshirts and baggy T-shirts and jeans. But as she slowly turned her cartons inside out, he came across, one by one, parts of the second set: a stewardess costume – Pan Am, circa 1965, she said – another nurse's uniform, not the one she'd worn the first night, a French schoolgirl's outfit and, her prize, a prison guard's uniform. These she wore to bed.

She was full of tricks, this one. No handcuffs, thankfully, and no costumes of the sort that a young woman might not ordinarily wear; Hiroshi remembered hearing Grady, in the course of an alcohol-fueled riff on his omnisexual experiences, make reference to a possibly emblematic "rubber German shepherd costume." There was none of that scary stuff here. In fact, they had sex in pretty much the same way every time – just that it was sex, she made it clear, with a stewardess, a nurse, or a prison guard. Whatever role he was playing didn't interest her all that much, although she was very clear about hers. One time, feeling better about his strength, he'd tried to enter her from behind while she was standing in front of her bathroom mirror, his palms braced against the sink, but she'd whirled around, in the very spot where she'd first shown him the interesting ceiling, and snapped, "I'm not your little Japanese girlfriend," and he'd never tried that again.

She was on an anti-depressant, she told him; he'd see her taking the pill every once in a while with a glass of orange juice and she would toast herself by saying, "Here's to my health."

She unquestionably had a depressive frame of mind, something she'd never revealed at the Rehabilitation Center, but which became very clear when they were together in the evenings. One time she showed Hiroshi her favorite quote; as she unfolded the square of paper on which it was typed, Hiroshi anticipated exactly the sort of soul lift, most likely Eastern in origin, that a depressed person might crave and that he himself needed, a bit of breezy exhalation from a wisely gentle soul. Instead, what she showed him were twenty-seven word-processed words:

"That miserable patch of events, that mélange of nothing, while you were looking ahead for something to happen, that was it! That was life! You lived it!"

Hiroshi had neatly folded the paper and handed it back to her so he could think about what he'd just read. "Not very hopeful, is it?"

"Oh, I don't agree at all. I think it's very hopeful."

"Who wrote it?"

"Some American writer you've never heard of. *I've* never heard of. Clifford Odets."

"Why is it hopeful? Why do you think this?"

"Well, I just think if you recognize that it's all fleeting, you can grab onto things as they pass, instead of looking back all bitter like this guy."

"Are you grabbing onto things?"

She laughed. "Hey, I grabbed onto you, didn't I?"

Hiroshi thought. She didn't laugh very often. She had been all business at the rehab center, despite her one speculation about his marital status, but she didn't laugh much at her apartment, either. Sex was serious business to her, which required her to close her eyes and concentrate very assiduously on whatever fantasy she was inhabiting as he gently pulled apart her uniform or gingerly maneuvered past the tattered lace panties she sometimes liked to keep on. She crooned to herself sometimes, during sex; she never cried out, and rarely talked directly to him. Drinking was serious, too; she wasn't a mean drunk, but she was an awfully quiet and introspective one. She was a lot like Hitomi, Hiroshi considered, which might have given him pause as regards his tastes in women except that she had picked him; he had not picked her.

He couldn't remember, actually, any relationship where he had done the picking. He tucked that away as a topic for future worry. Instead, he had said, after she'd returned the folded piece of paper to her purse, "Why do you live in this tiny place?"

"It's all I can afford, Hiroshi. It's a miracle I live in Manhattan at all."

"It's just so dark. Doesn't it just make your mood worse?"

"Hey, my mood couldn't be worse. I should tell you what's going on in my life sometime."

But she didn't. She told him, from time to time, that he made her happy, and so he continued to see her after his shifts at the Nature Company and hers at the rehab center, and when he wasn't working or with her, he ate, and read magazines – his list of books remained untouched – and took walks around Manhattan.

They made plans to go together to the Mohonk Mountain House, a popular weekend destination in the Shawangunk Mountains. She decided to rent a car for the weekend, and promised to do all of the driving, since Hiroshi had never driven in America, and in any event could barely grip a steering wheel. She promised to pick him up in front of the hotel at six-thirty a.m. on a Saturday morning, having cancelled all of her dates with the Pomeranians and the wheaten terriers, the borzois and the cockapoos, that constituted her weekend clientele. He waited in the lobby with his jacket, his cane, a carton of orange juice and a paper cup of coffee on his side by the couch, and a small overnight bag riding on one shoulder. He'd had to ask the desk clerk to open the orange juice carton for him.

When seven o'clock came and went, Hiroshi began to worry that she had stood him up, or had had an accident, or that he had his weekends mixed up; it wouldn't be the first time he had done that. But at 7:45, she pulled up in front of Gramercy Park, across the street from the hotel, in a red

BMW convertible, and double-parked the car to help Hiroshi across the street.

As they worked their way out of the city, Trudi was unusually quiet, even by her standards. He looked at her profile; she was driving with both hands on the wheel, very intently, as if she were unused to driving. She was wearing a pretty, sea-green silk scarf and a delicate-looking blouse, the most feminine-looking outfit he'd ever seen her in. He wondered if she'd brought any of her costumes with her.

She was very subdued. After a few minutes, she put the top up, even though it was a beautiful day. He said, "Is everything all right with you?"

"Everything is fine, Hiroshi." She offered nothing more.

"Are you excited to be taking this trip?"

"Very excited. I went here when I was a child."

"Not on your bicycle, I assume."

"No, not on my bicycle. What do you mean by that?"

"Well, I assume you went with your parents."

"Never heard you talk sarcastically before. 'Your bicycle.' You're getting to be like an American."

"So, with your parents?"

"Yeah, of course with my parents."

"It's just that you've never mentioned your parents. I feel a little strange about you, I guess, because you were my therapist, and suddenly we became lovers and there was nothing in between, and there isn't anything I know about you except from what I can figure out from the posters on your walls. So who were they?"

Trudi sighed. "My father was a famous custodian."

"A famous custodian? That's like a janitor, right?"

"Something like that. A little more involved, maybe."

"Are you being sarcastic now? How could he be famous?"

"He began as an actor, here in New York. But he never made any money at it, just little roles off-Broadway and a few commercials when he could get them, just enough so that he could eat. He met my mom when he was doing summer stock – she was trying to be an actress, too. Then they moved to Waltham, Massachusetts where she was from because her father, my grandpa, offered my dad a job in his insurance agency. But it didn't work out."

"Why?"

"They had a huge falling-out about something. Maybe he was having affairs or something, and her dad didn't exactly appreciate it. A 'falling-out' is a fight." She knew, without looking over at him, that he hadn't understood that expression. She was good at that sort of thing.

She'd hardly looked at him the whole time they were driving, intent on following the road.

"So what happened?"

"He kept on falling further and further after that. Working at a hardware store, that kind of stuff."

"I know. Like working at the Nature Company."

"No, this was the real deal, all he could get. Besides, he drank a lot. They had me very late, when he was in his late forties and my mom was almost forty. They got divorced when I was in high school. He got a job as a custodian at my school, and it was unbelievably embarrassing."

Wasn't his job at the Nature Company "the real deal," all he could get? But he still wanted an answer to the earlier question. "But he was famous?"

"Yeah, sort of. In his early sixties, he started fooling around again with community theatre, and by sheer happenstance he ran into an agency producer he'd known from the early days. This guy tells him how hard it is to find older actors who are any good, so sure enough he starts getting some roles. Then he appeared in this series of pizza commercials that ran nationally for a couple of years, something about how the kid delivering the pizza and the old doc delivering the baby get mixed up with each other, some crap like that, and he made a fortune. Then he blew it all on whisky just in time to die of heart failure. So that's my dad, the famous custodian."

"So your parents were both actors. Is that why..."

"Why what? Why I like to dress up, is that what you mean?"

"I suppose."

She laughed. This was the second time. "Hiroshi, if I could tell you why I liked to fuck the way I like to fuck, if anyone could tell you why they like what they like, they know themselves a hell of a lot better than I do. I don't know, maybe I just don't like myself or something. I really have no idea. It just turns me on. Let's not talk about this, okay?"

"Sure. Did I upset you?"

"You didn't upset me. Why do you always ask if you've upset me? You've never upset me. That's why I like you."

"Okay."

"You just don't get me yet, is all."

"I'm sorry I asked about the costumes."

"The costumes? I told you already, fuck the costumes. I'm not upset about that. If I make you a part of my fantasy every time we fuck, I mean if we're fucking to begin with, why would I care if you ask me about it? Listen, Hiroshi. We've got two conversations going on here at the same time and you're hung up on the wrong one. I'm upset because I started talking about my father, okay? He was a drunk. And drunks are assholes. What more is there to say?"

The Mohonk Mountain House was not, as Hiroshi had imagined, a simple lodge. It was a very old, very brown, and very masculine-looking building that was hard to take in all at once, the way it rambled at the foot of the hills. There was a large dining hall and an old library to which Trudi dragged Hiroshi as soon as they checked in; she wanted to see if a book her father had left there all those years ago was still on the shelves. It was an Oxford University Press volume of Byron's *Don Juan*, Trudi said; she'd never read it and had no intention of doing so, but it might remind her of her father in the old days before his decline began.

She took a long time to scan the shelves. The books were in no particular order – guests would leave a book they'd finished reading, and pick up one left by another guest – but it was clear to Hiroshi that, among all the Stephen Kings and John Grishams, there were no old Oxford University Press volumes of Lord Byron. Still, she lingered, and then took Hiroshi on a tour of the hotel, pointing out a hummingbird feeding at a little sugar dispenser right by a ground-floor window, another one waiting patiently behind – a scene almost identical to one that she remembered from her childhood visit – before they finally registered and went up to their room.

After their bags had been dropped off, she said, "I'm going to take a bath," and disappeared into the bathroom. Hiroshi looked out the window for a while at the ancient, rounded mountains and then walked into the bathroom to join her. The weakness in his legs felt particularly bad after the long car trip and he thought that, if the bathtub were big enough to accommodate both of them, the warm water would do him good.

He used his cane to swing the bathroom door open. Trudi said, in a rather alarmed voice, "Hiroshi, I'm taking a bath!"

This seemed a rather odd reversal, Hiroshi thought, of the time just a few weeks ago when she had invited him in to view her naked body by claiming to find her new ceiling interesting.

He walked in anyway, and began to undress. Trudi didn't complain, but made no effort to help him as he struggled out of his clothes. Getting undressed was difficult with his weak hands – none of his clothes these days had buttons -- and was particularly difficult in a small bathroom where there was no place to sit but the toilet seat.

The bathtub was big enough for two, just barely, and as he slipped in to the other end of the bathtub, his neck uncomfortably caught between the faucet and Trudi's feet, he noticed that she had a large purple bruise on the side of her neck. So that, he thought, was why she'd been wearing a scarf.

"How did you get that bruise?"

Trudi closed her eyes and turned her head away from Hiroshi, perhaps unaware that, by doing so, she had exposed the other side of her neck, on which was visible an even larger bruise, but this one with finger-shapes, fish-belly white, clearly visible against the purple.

"Trudi, what happened to you?"

"My husband tried to choke me."

"What husband? When?"

"Last night, when I told him about our trip."

"But what husband are you talking about?"

"What husband? The only one I have." She made a little mouth-shrug. "We've been separated for a few months now, so I didn't see much point in telling you." She sounded relaxed enough, considering what had happened to her and what she was telling Hiroshi right now.

"Is this why you've moved into your own apartment?"

"Yeah, of course. Why else?"

"So you were married the whole time you were taking care of me."

"Yeah, I was. But like I said, I'm separated. I'm already talking to a lawyer."

She pulled herself slowly to her feet and stepped awkwardly over the edge of the bathtub, holding on to Hiroshi's shoulder for a moment to brace herself. It was the first time she'd used him for such a purpose. As Hiroshi looked up at her, he was stunned to see similar bruises, also with long, dead-white finger marks marring them, around her waist just under her ribcage.

Hiroshi pulled himself out of the tub with great effort, yanked a heavy towel from the rack next to the tub and began drying her off, using his palms to push the towel across her skin.

She stumbled over to the bed and, with her head turned to one side, let Hiroshi continue to dry her. She had a faint smile on her face, and said nothing. Hiroshi said nothing, either.

In the twelve seconds or so since he had seen the bruises on her waist while she had clambered out of the bathtub until now, when he was drying the skin at that very spot on her waist, he had felt, once again, too many emotions to absorb. So he took the time afforded him by his task of drying her, and by her peaceful silence, to think.

He was stunned and a bit horrified to have seen the bruises – first the one on the right side of her neck without any finger marks, then the one on the left side of her neck with the very white and ugly finger marks, and then the bruises on her waist that were the most shocking of all.

He thought about why the bruises on her waist were more shocking than those on her neck, considering that her husband could easily have choked her to death. Perhaps it was because it seemed relatively easy to leave such marks on a delicate part of the body like the neck, but it was quite some-thing else to do so on the waist, which was far less delicate. The feral anger and strength that must have been required was really the thing that shocked him.

He could never do such a thing to a woman. Not even before his illness. *Certainly* not before his illness, he reminded himself – it wasn't about how strong you were, it was about how much you respected another human being. Even if that other person had betrayed you, her husband, by seeing another man, it took greater strength not to lash out than it did to do so.

Of course he was shocked, as well, that she had a husband to begin with. And a bit angry that she hadn't told him. But, at the same time, flattered that she had chosen to go to this place with him instead of her estranged husband, flattered that he had made another man so brutally jealous, flattered more than anything else that she had chosen to go ahead with the trip even after her husband had attacked her.

She'd gone ahead with it because she wanted to be with him.

Then he thought that she must be a very strong person to have withstood such an attack and still go on this trip the very next day. She hadn't wanted to disappoint him, that was clear, but she also hadn't wanted to let her husband know how much he had hurt her.

He thought of the fingers. He'd never met her husband, and certainly never would, but he knew the shape of his fingers. He'd never forget how they'd marked her. Yes, he'd tried to hurt her, but whether or not he'd intended it, he'd also marked her. If he'd thought the marks would scare Hiroshi away, he was very wrong; they just made him care that much more about her.

And then he thought of the beautiful scarf she'd been wearing. Wearing just to hide the bruises on her neck from Hiroshi. A wave of love for her strength, for her consideration of his feelings, for her pitiable condition, swept over Hiroshi and he tossed the towel aside and kissed her. Her lips were very warm and soft. Between kisses, they trembled almost imperceptibly, like Hiroshi's own.

Hiroshi was very turned on. Not, he hastened to remind himself, by the bruises themselves, but by the dignity with which she had borne them, and the quiet, slightly shaky placidity with which she'd let him dry off her naked body.

They began to make love and it was so oddly exciting to Hiroshi that he considered that perhaps Trudi was caught up in some new fantasy of her own. No, no, it wasn't that she'd brought this beating on deliberately, it wasn't that, it was just that she was perhaps imagining that she was someone else and that fantasy was not only allowing her to forget her pain and humiliation, but was actually making her excited, just as the costumes did.

Thinking all of these things all at once, Hiroshi entered her roughly, but Trudi indicated by tapping her fingers against his collarbones that she wanted him to slow down. She still hadn't said anything.

Neither had Hiroshi.

Among the things that Hiroshi hadn't said as yet were, "How do you feel?" and "Did you go to the emergency room?" and "Did you call the police?" and "Why did you still come on this trip with me after all this happened?"

He didn't even think of saying these things, in fact, until just after he'd rolled off of her, and they occurred to him as the sort of things he probably should have said a bit earlier. Trudi wasn't crying, which would have been better. Instead, she said, very calmly and politely, without a trace of either coldness or warmth, "Why don't we get dressed and get some dinner?"

She had never said such a thing before, after they had made love. She would say, "That was good." She would say, "That was fun." She would say, "You'd better get back to your cell before the other guards find us."

But she'd never said, "Why don't we get dressed and get some dinner?"

Indeed, they did both get dressed and have dinner, and they spent the rest of the weekend having a pleasant time hiking at the base of the Shawangunks, taking only the baby trails that Hiroshi could negotiate with his cane, and reading side by side in the library, and getting drunk over lunch and dinner in the Granary restaurant. She talked freely about her husband, but didn't say anything more about the attack the night before they'd left.

On the way back from the Mohonk Mountain House, they continued to talk. Trudi had married her husband when she was twenty-three. He owned a statuary business in Queens, inherited from his father, which brought in a solid income, and had paid her way through Nazareth College in Rochester while she got her masters degree in physical therapy. But like her father, he'd been an alcoholic, and had beaten her on a couple of previous occasions. Hiroshi wondered if this time was the worst, but didn't want to ask her, because she didn't seem to want to talk about this time.

Besides, he was hardly listening: He kept on thinking, as they drove back into the city Sunday evening, about how his lust had obliterated every other sense he possessed, and how stupid he had been to have sex with her while she lay there quietly uncomplaining. Maybe the lovemaking had comforted her in some way. He wasn't sure, since she'd said nothing about it at the time, and nothing since then. Nor had he said anything, fearful perhaps that she'd get angry at him for being so inconsiderate. So he never brought it up, and she never brought it up, and they never had sex again.

Chapter 9

THE NIGHT of their return from the Mohonk Mountain House, Hiroshi lay awake listening to a Sun Ra CD. He wasn't thinking about anything in particular, though he was unquestionably afraid that he would have difficulty again going to sleep. He thought about taking another one of the Xanax pills that Trudi had given him, but he didn't feel like struggling out of bed to retrieve the bottle from the bathroom. He kept on thinking about that poster he'd seen in Trudi's apartment, the one about "Jack's Wonderful Pump." There was one line in particular that had stuck with him: "The reins of the heart which are working for ever night and day." When he'd recovered the use of his arms in the hospital, the first thing he'd done was feel the beating of his heart from the outside. It was a wonderful and chastening thing to know that the heart beat continuously, day and night, every day of your life without pause. But what if you weren't paying attention? When you were asleep you couldn't pay attention. What if it stopped beating then? There would be nothing you could do about it except die, and you wouldn't even know you'd died.

Hiroshi thought that dying in his sleep was the most awful

way to die of all, because you couldn't think back on your life and what you'd accomplished, and what you still hoped to accomplish. You just lay down, thinking it was the ordinary end to another ordinary day, and then nothing ever happened to you ever again from that moment forward. And it could happen, this night just like any other night, because the reins of the heart really didn't work forever.

"How the pump drives the life-stream round and round." That was another line from that poster. Hiroshi could feel his pump pounding against the inside of his chest. But he could barely feel his life-stream. His blood felt as if it were barely moving at all. He checked his pulse to make sure it was still strong. Then he checked it again.

He was terrified of going to sleep. More to the point, he was terrified *of* sleep.

After a while, he rolled out of bed and, using a thick felt-tip pen that he gripped roughly between thumb and palm, scrawled a few new entries into the English journal he kept on his bedside table. He wrote down the word "scaffolding" to remind himself to find out why the word contained "folding" when this stretched-out structure of temporary girders and struts was utterly unfoldable. He needed to look up the difference between a "white elephant" and a "pink elephant." Both seemed to imply a type of vulgar taste, though one was thrust upon you and the other you created yourself. He was confused about "cassock" and "hassock." Why was it "tuckpointing" instead of, say, "pointucking," which seemed to do a better job of describing how the little bits and crumbs of loose brick were tucked in and cleaned up? Did one pass muster and cut the mustard, or was it the other way around? A "stitch," he was fairly sure, was better than a "card," the former implying that someone was genuinely amusing and the latter suggesting an irritating, almost always male, sort of "practical joker." Joker Arroyo was a Filipino politician, which made him think of that funny Filipino nurse. He wrote down "burrow" and "borough." But what was "arroyo"? Wasn't it some kind of landscape feature in the desert, like a chaparral? Was "chaparral" in some way connected to chaps, not English fellows, but something that cowboys wore, like leather pants or spurs? Maybe, in any event, he was quite wrong, and scaffolding could indeed be folded up and carted to a new job site for a new round of tuckpointing.

He sighed heavily, beginning to grow weary of words. He started a mental list of new movies he'd like to see, and another list of the slightly older ones he'd missed while in the hospital and in rehabilitation. But he couldn't hold all the titles in his head, so he wrote them down as well.

He felt like he was running a fever; he had to get some sleep. But his mind drifted back to words. There was another word he'd meant to look up, one that he couldn't quite remember. The cheap plastic wind-up alarm clock on his bedside table said 2:06 a.m., which was more or less true. He had to be at the Nature Company by eleven a.m., so he had plenty of time – far too much, as he contemplated the hours he had yet to traverse.

The other word, the one that he couldn't quite remember, was something that Trudi had said. This was important because he wanted his English to be perfect and he wanted his memory to be perfect. And he wanted to stay awake because he was terrified to go to sleep. What had she said? Was it from one of her quotes, perhaps? This was really starting to bother him, that he couldn't remember. Sometimes he thought he spent half of his life trying to remember fleeting thoughts, bits of melody, useless words. He closed his eyes and fell back onto the bed, compacting his pillow into a bar shape and pressing it over his eyes to try to bring the word back. Instead, all that came back was the image of

Trudi's bruised slender waist and livid throat, which glowed behind Hiroshi's eyelids like something radioactive.

There was something terribly significant about the word he was trying to remember, he was sure. But what could possibly have any significance to him now, given that there was nothing of significance to anything that he was doing?

After a while, he pulled the pillow off his eyes and rolled out of bed again. He turned the TV on and jabbed at the remote, using his relatively strong forefinger, trying to find CNN. He turned the sound off so it wouldn't compete with the Sun Ra. There was a commercial for a brand of frozen pizza, which made him think, though he didn't particularly want to, of Trudi's father. The role Trudi's father had played was an old doctor delivering a baby, but someone had somehow mixed up the doctor with the young kid delivering the pizza. They probably both had said something like, "I'm here for the delivery." But what possible point could such a circumstance have? Hiroshi imagined a scene at the end of the commercial with a group of youngish women gathered around a crib, shot from the perspective of the baby, in which the women said such things as "Isn't that the most beautiful thing you ever saw?" and "I've always wanted one all for my own." Then the camera would switch angles to look in over the women's shoulders at the object of their affection, a large sausage pizza.

"You could make me feel at home by bringing me a fucking slice of sausage pizza every once in a while," his roommate Harry Blenwen had said to Vincent, way back when Hiroshi wasn't even able to move.

Out loud, in English, Hiroshi said, "You could make me feel at home by bringing me a fucking bowl of katsudon every once in a while."

The Sun Ra CD came to an end. He suddenly felt like screaming.

But he was silent. The whole room, the whole hotel, was silent. Hiroshi padded over to his box of possessions, which he hadn't unpacked since Carmelita had brought them to the hospital, to look for his Lou Reed CD. He pulled out the same junk he'd been pawing through ever since he moved back into the Gramercy West Hotel, but this time, when he grabbed the tool kit for the dozenth time, he stopped and really looked at it. For the first time, he noticed, with some disappointment, that it bore a small red label on the bottom that said "Made in China."

But that wasn't what interested him. Why, after all, *was* it back in its wrapper? This truly did demand an explanation. And there had to be one; things didn't just happen. It wasn't as if it were a loose wrapper, either, that he or someone else could have rewrapped; it was a tight one, with a thin strip of cellophane around one edge that you had to peel away in order to pull the cellophane apart. Inside, the miniature tools rattled, implacable and untouched. And yet he remembered quite clearly that he had spilled the tools all over the ground in Central Park before stuffing them back into his pocket, loose, and racing all those blocks to the Academy.

Maybe, he thought, Maureen had secretly replaced the broken tool set with a new one.

But even for a meddler like Maureen, that seemed point-less and extreme. She would have had to sneak into his hotel room not long after he'd left her apartment in anger that day, because he'd first noticed the kit was rewrapped when he was stretched out on the floor of the hotel the next morning, after the illness had first struck. Even the juggling balls turned out to have had a purpose. What possible purpose would such a switch have had?

Then he started to imagine that Maureen was there in the room talking to him. "Hey, Hero, instead of racing your brain at a thousand RPM, why don't you slow down for a minute and think? Don't come up with nonsensical explanations just for the sake of saying something. If you're going to stay up all night anyway, why not focus on what's possible and throw away the rest?"

Fair enough. The only thing that Hiroshi could think was possible was that the little awls and wrenches and screwdrivers had spilled loose from the plastic kit because the kit had been cracked or loose at the hinges. And that, irritated at the poor quality of this souvenir, he had at some point gone back to the hardware store and exchanged it.

Exchanged it for the new kit he held in his hand right now!

A sudden chill passed over his body, and his limbs stiffened up. After a moment of panic, he realized that the chill came from a wonderful realization. He must have indeed gone back to the hardware store at some point, and if that point had been after he had visited the hot dog stand, then it was possible that he had left the clarinet not at the hot dog stand, but at the hardware store.

It was hard to tell if it was just his hopeful suggestibility, but a vague memory began to surface, of him walking back into hardware store, brandishing a cracked plastic case. He tried to search within the memory to see if he had been thirsty at this point, or if he was still tasting the papaya drink he'd just had.

But that was beyond the reach of his memory. He couldn't convince himself that he had already drunk the papaya drink, but he could surmise that the reason he had left his hot dog untouched was because he must have been brooding about the broken souvenir, and that he had gone directly from the hot dog stand to the hardware store after bolting down his drink.

All of this was significant because, he next convinced himself, the hardware store might have been keeping his clarinet in its lost-and-found department all this time, waiting for its owner's return.

And yet Maureen, who was supposed to be so smart, hadn't figured any of this out.

Hiroshi, feeling suddenly very good and rather smug, rolled back into bed yet again. He pictured telling Maureen that he'd used his deductive reasoning and his memory and his intuition to find his clarinet. Then he pictured her saying, "That's great, Hiroshi, but if you'd wanted my help, maybe you should have told me to begin with that you went back to the hardware store. Then I wouldn't have wasted my time and that policeman's time."

Hiroshi wondered if she were sleeping with that policeman right now.

Alright, enough. That was ridiculous. He was feeling a little crazed, and had been spending far too much time alone, but he knew there was absolutely no reason to believe she was involved with that policeman who'd shown up at the hot dog stand. The fact that he had been assigned to Hiroshi's case was nothing more than...

Hiroshi tried to think of the English word. It was something like coincidence, but not quite, because coincidence implied something significant about the coming together of two things, like two friends from a small town running into each other at a resort on the other side of the world.

This was more like a stranger meeting a stranger, with the significance developing later, as a result of the meeting.

Suddenly, it was as if the stranger was standing there right in front of him. *Happenstance!* That was the word! That was the word he'd been trying to remember all along! He felt as happy as he'd felt when he'd found his passport and wallet, intact, in the drawer next to his hospital bed.

Happen. Stance. Happen. Stance. It meant something that just happened, for no particular reason. Like one detective instead of another being assigned to his case. Like Trudi's father, who had run into the agency producer by... happenstance, resulting in a new career for him and plenty of money with which to drink himself to death.

Happenstance. If I went back to the hardware store after the hot dog stand, Hiroshi reflected, and then circled back to the magazine store which was right around the corner from the Academy, that would have been an awfully long distance for Maureen to have followed me, especially considering that I was walking at normal speed back then.

Maybe, since the magazine store was so near the Academy, Maureen really had wandered in without intending to bump into Hiroshi.

Maybe it really was, as she had claimed all along, not a form of flirtation, but merely happenstance.

At this, the sixth iteration of a word he would now never again forget, Hiroshi fell asleep.

* * *

HE WOKE UP VERY EARLY, excited, and took a taxi back to the hardware store without even checking to see if it was open yet. It was only eight-thirty a.m. by the time he arrived. The store opened at ten, and his shift at the Nature Company began at eleven, so he'd have at least a half an hour to look for the clarinet in the store. He walked to a nearby Starbucks, had a skimmed tall latte, a caramel-walnut scone, and an apple turnover, perused three newspapers, and waited.

At exactly 10:00, Hiroshi walked back to the store, and double-checked the sign with the store hours, not wanting to face the humiliation of pulling at a locked door. It was indeed scheduled to open at 10:00. Hiroshi walked with his cane across the jute mat, which again made him sway, pulled open the door, and walked into the cool interior.

189

The minute he saw the teenage girl behind the counter, he felt ridiculous. What made him think there was any chance that, even if he had left the clarinet at this store, it would still be here? It was, actually, the height of arrogance to think that someone who didn't know him would care that much about one of his possessions to hold on to it for him.

The girl looked at him curiously as he walked slowly up to her. "Do you have a lost-and-found here?"

She continued to look at him. She was chewing gum. She looked like she was a Hispanic of some sort; maybe she didn't even speak any English. But then she said, "Hey, you're the guy who left your oboe here, aren't you?"

"Clarinet. You remember me?"

"No, but my uncle said to look out for this Chinese dude."

"Japanese."

"He said you were walking around in a daze, and complaining about something. Then you just left your oboe on the counter here and wandered out."

"I guess that's right. I was exchanging a miniature tool kit."

"Pretty weird, if you ask me. And you're just now coming back to get it?"

"Yeah. It's kind of hard to explain."

"My uncle didn't say you walked with no cane."

"I didn't."

"You do."

"I had an illness after that day. Is the clarinet still here?"

"Yeah, where else would it be? I'll go get it for you."

Hiroshi was the happiest he'd been since that moment at the Academy when all the students had looked at him, transfixed, as he played "Bossa Antigua." He called after her, "I must not be the only Japanese customer. How did you know it was me?"

She called back. "My uncle described you. He said you were so weird, he'd never forget."

Well, that deflated him a bit. But within seconds, the clarinet he thought he'd never see again was back in his hands. The case was missing, but that was a very small loss, considering. It looked to be in good shape. He held the instrument against his chest with his right forearm as his left gripped his cane, and said, "Thank you for keeping it all this time and thank you for your honesty."

"No problem. My uncle said it'd be too easy to trace if we tried to sell it."

"Well, anyway, thank you. I'd like to give you a reward."

She shrugged. "Okay."

Hiroshi thought for a moment. "Actually, I don't have very much money right now. But maybe in a few months, if you don't mind waiting."

She shrugged again. "Yeah, sure."

Hiroshi walked out of the store and headed toward the Nature Company. He walked even more slowly than the cane demanded, savoring the counterbalancing weight of the clarinet in his other hand. But after a moment or so, it slipped out of his loose grip and fell with an unmelodic clatter to the sidewalk. He stood there for a moment, trying to figure out how he could hold it as he walked. Then he headed back into the hardware store.

"Would you mind giving me a plastic bag?"

The girl behind the counter shrugged, and pulled out a white plastic bag. She handed it to Hiroshi. He looked at it for a second and said, "Are you sure you don't have the case that goes with my instrument? I can guess I left both of them here, so I'm surprised you only have the instrument."

But she only looked at him with mouth set and eyebrows raised, an expression that Hiroshi interpreted as "You have to be kidding," though he wasn't sure if she meant by that that he should feel lucky to at least have recovered the clarinet, or that she'd decided to keep the case as her reward, or perhaps that she'd never seen the case and was unhappy that he'd given her no reward and now on top of it was implying she'd stolen something of little value. It probably wasn't worth sorting out. He leaned against the counter to gain use of both hands, slipped the clarinet into the bag – it stuck out at the top like a loaf of French bread – and slipped the handle of the bag over his cane, where it caught neatly against the point where the leather strap was attached to the cane. He then slipped his hand through both the handle of the bag and the loop in the leather strap. Bag flapping and clarinet swaying, he hobbled out of the store and headed in the direction of the Nature Company.

He'd decided to walk for a few blocks before getting a taxi, because it was a beautiful day and because he felt good about his triumph of deduction. He walked even more slowly than usual with the cane, to keep the clarinet from banging against the cane. He accidentally kicked a small rock; it cantered and skipped away from him into the gutter.

He was on another track now. He was in the slowest lane of all. A few passersby brushed against the bag hanging from the cane. He passed one of the few walkers slower than he, a hunched-over old man with a cane of his own, puffing on a thick cigar, and found himself, where he once would have brushed through the cloud, dwelling for a moment in the redolent scent. He breathed deeply.

It was odd, having some of his energy back but being forced to walk slower than ever. When he had been walking normally, and someone had cut in front of him, he would raise himself up on his toes to translate his forward motion into an upward one. Or sometimes, when he was feeling particularly happy, he'd make a little corkscrewing motion in the air with one of his legs. Now, when someone was walking slowly in front of him, Hiroshi just fell further behind. When he walked close to a wall, he let a finger on his free hand trail across the rough surface, or traced the spaces between the bricks, the tactile equivalent of doodling.

In front of a Korean deli, he passed over a broken-up section of sidewalk into which thick, octagonal chunks of lavender glass had been set seemingly a century ago, at least half of them chipped or missing, though where they were missing a hexagonal hole remained, and many of the others were obscured by thick drips of tar and concrete. A cost-free way to light a basement stockroom, Hiroshi guessed; it was the sort of thing he'd never have noticed without a cane, and without the need to look down periodically as he walked. He probed at one of the holes with his cane's rubber tip, which unfortunately was too thick to fit – he liked the idea of one of the subterranean workers, bathed in dim lavender light from the street, seeing something like a rubber tip entering the roof of his world.

There was a row of street vendors, selling hardcover books, old magazines, cheap-looking African figurines (which made Hiroshi look with admiration at the superior carving on the handle of his cane), and various other odds and ends. Incredibly, one vendor had among his piled up junk and bric-a-brac an old full-length clarinet case, similar to the one Hiroshi had lost, so he bought it for $5, gave the vendor the white plastic bag, and put the clarinet in the case, feeling incredibly lucky that he'd found such an odd and appropriate item right in the middle of a New York street. He paused for a second, struck by an awful thought, and examined the case carefully – but no, it wasn't the same case he'd lost, just a very similar one, so feeling even more fortunate in that he hadn't foolishly bought back his own property, he continued his slow stroll.

He was very happy now. He passed over a few dead leaves

on the sidewalk, then returned to them and crunched them with his foot. It was an intensely pleasurable sensation.

He ambled on. A little girl in pink dress, pink sandals, and a straw hat was pretending to play a trumpet or some such with her thumb and forefinger held to her pursed mouth: *foo foo foo foo*. She reminded him of another little girl he had seen being piloted around the Ohara Art Museum in Kurashiki in her stroller, gravely licking the reproduction of a Monet on her copy of the exhibition pamphlet. He smiled to himself and then noted an impressively large man with a bulging forehead, who suddenly appeared alongside him and smiled, too – but, oddly, at Hiroshi and not at the little girl pretending to play the trumpet. He'd seemed to be hovering just behind Hiroshi, and then, as Hiroshi noted the discordant smile – discordant because of the otherwise serious face he glimpsed – he walked quickly past Hiroshi.

It was hardly worthy of note, though when Hiroshi arrived at the Nature Company, the same man – or at least one who looked very like him – bulging forehead, thick straight black hair, an angry red shaving rash on the neck, intelligent brown eyes, and an amused smile – asked him where the bathroom was, and then departed without using it.

On his first break, Hiroshi called Maureen. She seemed surprised, pleasantly so.

"Hiroshi, I'd about written you off."

"Do you mean because I haven't been calling you back?"

Her only response was a long laugh. "How you feeling?"

"Very much better."

"Good. I'm glad for you."

"But it's a disaster."

"Why a disaster?"

"Because I can't play any more. My hands are too weak and I can't stand up on my own without a cane. And various little parts of me have a tremble, like when I purse my lips."

"I know. I know. I've been tracking your progress."

"How?"

"Oh, I called the rehab center a few times."

Hiroshi wondered if she'd ever spoken to Trudi. Probably. He tried to think about whether that made any difference to him.

"I guess I should thank you for taking an interest in me to such a degree. I've been using those squeeze balls you gave me to strengthen my hands, though I'm still on the first one."

"Squeeze balls? What're you talking about? I sent you some juggling balls to mock your infirmity." She laughed lightly.

"Who told you about that one?"

"Like I said, I've been tracking you. I talk to a lot of people."

"Like my father?"

"Not really. The language thing. Grady. The hospital. You name it."

"Have you sent some big man around to follow me?"

"Boy, you sure do like to accuse me of things. No, I haven't sent a big man around, or a little man for that matter. I'm perfectly capable on my own."

"Interfering and spying on your own?"

"Well, here we go again. I was hoping when I first heard your voice that we could get through a conversation without an argument."

"Maureen, I wasn't planning to argue with you either. There is something about you that always gets me angry. I wish I could understand why. But I called to say actually that I had some good news."

"What?"

"Well, I know you're just going to get angry back, but I found my clarinet."

"That's fantastic, Hero. Why would I get angry?"

195

"Because you helped me look for it, and even called the police for me, and all along it was in another place I had forgotten about."

"I don't care. So you forgot. You didn't do it on purpose. I'm just glad you have it back and can play it again. Does it still sound okay?"

"I don't know. I don't think you listen to me. I can't play it at all."

"Alright, so you can't play it yet. At least you have it."

"Yes. To sell."

There was a pause at the other end of the line. Then Maureen said, "Hiroshi, you are worse than a moron." Then she hung up. Hiroshi was due back on the floor after his break, but he stood there at the phone trying to remember the nineteenth-century classification system for the mentally retarded. Moron was better than cretin, but worse than idiot and imbecile. So, if he was worse than a moron, that would make him a cretin.

Fair enough. He went back to work with nothing whatsoever on his mind.

Chapter 10

AFTER WORK, he took a taxi back to his hotel and dropped off his recovered clarinet in its substitute case while the driver waited outside. Then he had the driver take him to Central Park near the zoo, close to where he had gone his first day in the city. He wasn't sure exactly why he was there, but it was a beautiful day, and maybe now that he had his clarinet back, at least for the moment, everything might return to where it was when he first arrived. He'd go and look at the marigolds he'd planted, and discover them to be gloriously flourishing, and leave the park, and maybe he'd be restored magically to the condition he was in when he first entered it.

A tall, black-haired man in a satin New York Yankees jacket, both hands jammed into the jacket pockets, smiled pleasantly and familiarly at Hiroshi as he entered the park. Just as he passed, Hiroshi turned his head, trying to determine who he might be, and was instantly smashed across the nose and jaw by the man's open hand.

Hiroshi wavered, leaning heavily on his cane, as he watched spots of blood spatter his white tennis shoes. His eyes immediately filled with tears from the blow to his nose, which in turn caused his whole being to flood with shame and embarrassment. That man must have pulled his hands out of his coat pocket and slapped me the moment I turned around, he thought, maybe because he didn't like me looking back at him.

But that makes no sense, Hiroshi thought fleetingly as the man leaped at him. Hiroshi dropped his cane in a panic, thrust his right leg and hip into the man's midsection, grabbed the man's left arm awkwardly using his practically fingerless hands as grappling hooks, twisted the arm, then flipped him over his own body onto the sidewalk. Hiroshi staggered backwards, his calves quivering, but managed to remain standing. He stooped very cautiously, his eyes on his attacker, and picked up his cane. His thighs were quivering so much that he could barely stay upright even with the cane.

A small crowd had now gathered to witness this confrontation between a bleeding Japanese man leaning heavily on a cane and staggering as if drunk, and the tall young man in the New York Yankees jacket who lay sprawled on the sidewalk. The stranger began to pull himself up onto his elbows. Hiroshi, taking no chances, swung sharply with the midpoint of his cane at one of the man's ears, then the other, causing the man to collapse again. The force of his second swing caused Hiroshi himself to fall to the ground, his whole body now shaking violently and his face so hot and tight he thought the skin might split. He lay there on his back, unable to see anything of his attacker but the black rubber soles of his work boots.

There were calls for ambulances, the police. Several young women in separate sections of the crowd whipped out their cell phones and jabbed at them. The crowd – there must have been thirty or more people by now – had split nearly into two, half hovering over and restraining the stranger, half attending to Hiroshi. There seemed to be a general consensus that

Hiroshi was the victim, the good guy, which pleased him immensely. Someone hoisted Hiroshi up by the armpits and gave him his cane, allowing him to get a glimpse of his attacker, being pulled to his feet almost simultaneously. The man was bleeding from his right earlobe, which looked to be torn. He attempted to point at Hiroshi – both his arms were restrained by passerby – and said, "Let him go. I fucked up. I thought it was someone else."

Whoever it was that had pulled Hiroshi up by his armpits immediately let go, causing him to collapse to the pavement again. Several people in the crowd gasped. But Hiroshi once again was pulled to his feet. A young woman in very tight black pants and a tiny black top produced a handkerchief from somewhere or other and tenderly wiped the blood from his nose and upper lip. She looked into Hiroshi's eyes and said, "Cool flip."

Hiroshi said, "Thank you," though he wasn't quite sure what she meant by that. Someone else in the crowd said, "You wanna press charges?" but Hiroshi shook his head, and stumbled out from the crowd and walked as fast as he could down the sidewalk away from everyone. He looked over his shoulder once to see if the man with the torn earlobe was following him, but he was still standing there, surrounded by the crowd. It was only then that Hiroshi recognized the man as the same one who had asked him about a bathroom earlier in the day at the Nature Company.

He walked for about two blocks, though his legs were shaking so badly that his knees actually knocked together and he almost fell again several times. He waited until he was certain that neither his attacker nor anyone from the crowd of onlookers was following him to rest against the stone wall that separated Central Park from the sidewalk on Fifth Avenue. He touched his nose gently with his weak forefinger. It wasn't terribly painful, suggesting that the slap hadn't broken it, just given him a schoolyard-style bloody nose. His calves trembled even more violently when he stood still, and his right forearm ached terribly as if it had absorbed the full force of his blows to the man's head. The fear and shock of the experience also had left him feeling a bit nauseated, so he swallowed heavily a couple of times, tasting blood, and took a deep breath to calm himself.

A block or so later, he stopped at a souvlaki vendor and bought a can of ginger ale. The flavor was — in order — sharp, tinny, salty, phlegmy, and sweet. It was cold too, then suddenly warm and spittle-like. Tipping his head back to swallow made him realize that his jaw was sore too, and the change in his head's angle made his nose throb. But as he swallowed the drink, he pictured to himself the way the man had smiled at him before slapping him in the face.

It doesn't make any sense that someone would smile like that and then attack, Hiroshi thought. Except that Hiroshi now knew that the smile was a smile of recognition and confidence in his strength. So why would the man claim the attack was a mistake and apologize? Clearly, he had wanted to minimize the incident and make it less likely that Hiroshi would press charges.

And he hadn't claimed that Hiroshi had started the fight because he hadn't wanted to press charges himself. He probably wanted to just forget about the whole thing.

Or perhaps he didn't want the police involved so that he'd have another clear shot at Hiroshi some other time. This time, maybe, with something more dangerous than a slap, something that a judo throw couldn't defend against.

But who was he? If it were Trudi's husband, which certainly seemed likely, why did he seem to know Hiroshi when Hiroshi didn't know him? And could he have been the man who had called Hiroshi at the Gramercy West Hotel to say, "You die"? Again, it seemed likely, but that call had taken place before he'd gotten involved with Trudi. But perhaps Trudi had been talking about him to her husband for a long time before their affair, which suggested to Hiroshi that perhaps the affair had been nothing on her part but an attempt to get her husband jealous. She'd succeeded.

The souvlaki vendor was looking curiously at Hiroshi, and tapping his own nose, then gesturing to Hiroshi. Recognizing immediately the significance of the gesture, Hiroshi staggered over to the rearview mirror of a car parked alongside the stand, craned his head painfully to capture his image in the tightly angled mirror and caught a glimpse of a bloody little chunk of dried mucus sticking out of his right nostril, the only one visible.

"Fight, huh?" the vendor said, smiling conspiratorially.

"Yes," Hiroshi said. "I won."

He dropped the can of soda into a garbage can and walked on, brushing gently at his nose while he looked for a taxi. There was something else he'd seen in the rearview mirror that he wasn't sure of, so he let one empty taxi go by and ducked down to look into the mirror of another car.

Sure enough, there on his jaw was the faint red mark of a finger.

It was reddish, not dead-white, and it was the kind of mark left not by choking, but by slapping. But there was no question in his mind that the earlobe he had just ripped belonged to Trudi's husband.

Ripped and flipped. When that girl had said "cool flip," she'd probably been complimenting him on his judo skills. Hiroshi smiled to himself. His illness hadn't slowed him down one bit. He imagined what he could have done to Trudi's husband, if that was indeed who it was, if he were truly healthy. He also realized that, once Trudi's husband was ready to attack again, it wouldn't be a matter of mere imagining.

After work that evening, he called Trudi's apartment

repeatedly, but there was no answer. He called Grady, but he knew before the phone began ringing that he wouldn't be at his apartment; he'd be at a club somewhere, working. He thought about calling Hitomi, but decided against it. Finally, he called Maureen and told her what had happened. He also asked for his umbrella back.

She came to the hotel about an hour later, carrying his big green umbrella. She was wearing cute blue overalls and a white T-shirt.

She handed him a small, gift-wrapped CD. "How're you feeling, Hiroshi?"

"Thanks. What is this?"

"Some Brazilian music. So? How?"

"I'm doing okay. I'm mostly just flipped out."

She sat down on the edge of his bed. "And who was he? Police have any ideas?"

"I didn't call the police."

"Why not, because you got your clarinet back without them?"

"No. I don't know why, really. He told the crowd that was around us that he was sorry and thought I was someone else, so I guess I didn't see much point at first. But later I thought I recognized him."

"As who?"

"Well, I'm not sure, I mean I recognized him as someone who was following me around before, not someone I know, but I'm guessing he's the husband of a girl I was seeing."

"Wow. Husband. And *was* seeing. You pack a lot of interesting stuff into your sentences, Hero."

"They were going through a divorce. He attacked her for taking a weekend trip with me, so it's only logical he might attack me too."

She looked up at the ceiling and sighed. "I suppose it's futile to ask if she called the police too."

"Not to my knowledge."

"Serious?"

"I think so. He strangled her."

"Yeah, I'd say that's serious. She's dead."

"So strangled is like drowned?"

"Or asphyxiated or suffocated. They're absolutes. No half measures."

"Well, I guess I meant 'choked' then. Is that okay to say?"

"Yeah. Sorry. So how's she doing?"

"I'm not sure. I haven't talked to her since yesterday afternoon."

"Why? Scared you'll give him one more reason to be angry?"

"Maybe. I didn't think so much of that at the time. Mostly, I was just ashamed."

"Of what, Hiroshi?"

"I'm not sure I want to tell you."

"Okay."

"'Okay'? Just 'okay'?"

"Well, either you want to tell me or you don't. Don't get all outraged when I don't try to dig out of you something you claim you don't want to talk about to begin with."

"That's a good point, I suppose. But you've been digging out about me since you met me. You yourself said so. Grady saw you in the hallway talking Japanese to my father. You said that with the language barrier, you couldn't talk to him."

"Grady said that, huh? He's not high on my list these days. He asked me down to the club to hit on me."

"Anyway, were you talking Japanese to my father or not?"

"Hiroshi, I know about six phrases. Did it ever occur to you that since Grady knows nothing, *nothing*, about other languages that he'd interpret any kind of rudimentary gibberish I'm trying out on your father as 'speaking Japanese'?"

"But I don't understand what you're finding to talk about with my father to begin with."

"About you, you idiot."

"I've noticed you call me names like 'idiot' a lot."

"Well, stop acting like one and I'll stop calling you one. Your father loves you very much and is very worried about you. So he asked me to help out a little bit behind the scenes."

"Help out how? And why behind the scenes?"

"How? Who do you think picked out all the furniture and stuff for your room and bought it all? Your father? I mean, he wrote the check, but can you imagine this mystical poet who probably doesn't even use a chair because he floats two inches off the ground whipping out his credit card at IKEA? He and I actually managed to communicate between French, which I know a little, and English, because he knows a few phrases. As far as doing it behind the scenes, I guess it's because you act like you can't stand me. Why, I'm not entirely sure. But I appear to be about your only friend in this city besides Grady, because who do you invite over when you get mugged, or whatever it was, but me?"

"It wasn't 'mugged.' And I beat him up."

"Good for you, Hiroshi. So you invite me over, then you obviously have a deep, dark secret about your girlfriend but you don't want to tell me, but you clearly want me to sympathize."

"I don't want you to sympathize at all. In fact, I'm ashamed."

"That doesn't mean you don't want sympathy."

"And I'm supposed to get it from you? You think every thing I do is moronic and idiotic, so how will this be any different?"

"Hiroshi, I get impatient with you because of what you

do. Yeah, I think you do some dumb things." Softly, she added, "But I think you're brilliant."

"What did you say?"

"I said, I think you're brilliant. I mean, everybody's a genius or brilliant or 'remarkable' these days, right? But your music is the real thing, I think, and I think I know enough to know. That's why I take this interest in you. Maybe I just want to say I knew you when."

"You think I'm brilliant and you take an interest in me. Both of these statements are contradicted by the way you edited my essay."

"Y'know, I've explained to you before, that was my roommate."

"Yes, you did. And that explanation never made any sense."

She paused for a moment. "No, it didn't."

"Because why would your roommate, even if she is someone who is..." He searched for the right word. "*Compulsive* about editing, why would she care about me and what I had to write?"

"Because my roommate is my lover."

"Yes?"

"Yes. And I guess they were jealous."

"Who are 'they'?"

"Like I said, my roommate."

"And why jealous?"

"I don't know, because I was talking about you after your performance. Saying how cool you were and stuff."

"Can I ask you a question?"

"Sure."

"Why would you help my father decorate my room, and send me those exercise balls, and keep on calling me, if you have a boyfriend?"

"You seem to have been under the impression from day

one that I was somehow interested in you. I mean, I am, but not sexually. Not at all."

"Thank you for clarifying that."

"Hiroshi, listen. Let's go out to dinner or something, okay? We can talk about it then."

Maureen hailed a taxi for them and they went to the Grand Central Oyster Bar. It was just the kind of place that Hiroshi would like; it was clattering and crowded, and the menu was immense.

They had to wait a few minutes for a table. They said little as they stood there and then, after they were seated, they absorbed the menu in silence for a moment. Then Hiroshi said, in a tone approaching awe, "I've never seen so many oysters in one place in my life."

"Are you getting some?"

"Maybe some Cape Ann, from Nova Scotia. I've heard they're good from there. Or maybe a half dozen of the cutty-hunk, just because I like the name. And maybe the pompano filet, and a Bass Ale. Who's paying, by the way?"

"You are, Hero."

He shrugged. "Yeah, I guess I am. I forget that you're still a student. Maureen, the reason I was feeling ashamed is when I saw the bruises on her neck and waist, she was naked. I don't know why I'm telling you of all people, but the fact is I got excited and had sex with her."

"That's a Japanese thing, though, isn't it, getting turned on by women tied up and beaten up?"

"I suppose, but it's not my thing. I wasn't excited by the bruises themselves. I just wanted to have sex with her then, and she never said no." He shrugged.

"Yeah, so maybe it comforted her."

"But I didn't even ask her afterwards if she'd been to see a doctor or anything."

"She's old enough to figure out for herself when to go to

the doctor. If she spent the weekend with you, she must've been feeling okay."

The waitress arrived. Hiroshi lowered his voice to a whisper, which made him realize that his voice had for some time been back to normal volume. "I shouldn't have ignored it, though. I hardly said anything about it, even after we had sex."

"Well, you said she was married. Maybe you just felt funny about helping her cheat on her husband."

"No, I didn't know! I didn't even know she was married until I saw she was beaten up!"

Maureen laughed. "Okay, so then maybe you were a little too much in shock from finding out your girlfriend was married at the same time she showed you her bruises. Hiroshi, you can dwell on this all night or your whole life if you want, but the fact is, she didn't bother telling you she was married, and she was cheating on her husband, so she had two things to be ashamed of herself. Not to mention that, worst of all, she didn't even warn you about the bruises before she got undressed, so you wouldn't know how the hell to respond. I mean, she could have cancelled the weekend, or said here's what happened, please don't touch me, or here's what happened but I want to make love anyway. Instead, she left it up to you, so of course you'd be beating yourself up about it no matter what you did. Like if you *hadn't* tried to touch her she wouldn't have gotten all sulky anyway. I mean, women, they're unbelievable. Oh, and I forgot to mention, try not to forget you weren't the one who beat her up in the first place. It was him. He's the one who ought to be feeling guilty, not you."

"I suppose. And then he tries to beat me up, I guess. Although I don't know for sure if it was him."

"So call her up and ask her if he's been stalking you. Ask her what he looks like."

"What does *your* roommate look like?"

"About five foot one, Korean, with long black hair and really nice tits. So I guess you can cross her off your list. Besides, she knows tae kwon do, so she would've whipped your ass if you'd tried that judo shit on her."

Hiroshi's oysters – two platters of a dozen each – and Maureen's smoked trout arrived.

Again, he lowered his voice. "She's a woman?"

"Yes, Hiroshi, she's a woman. Don't you know what 'my lover' means?"

Hiroshi doused an oyster with lemon juice and swallowed it. "Maureen, one-third of my friends in Tokyo are gay or they like to fool around in different ways. So don't talk to me like a child. I just didn't know the phrase 'lover' meant 'same-sex.' Like I didn't know the exact meaning of 'strangled," that it meant 'killed.' Do you know what 'baka' means, Miss Japanese Speaker?"

"Yeah, I can guess. Stupid or something, right? I'm sorry. Anyway, she's a law student and she really does love to edit stuff. She saw your thing and went bat shit because I was talking so much about you. But I gotta say, once she got started, I kind of encouraged her."

"Why?"

"Love-hate, baby, love-hate."

"Because you were jealous of me too?"

"Not jealous. Envious. The way you play."

"Well, you have nothing to be envious of now."

"Why don't I have anything to be envious of now?"

"Because I've destroyed my life."

Maureen laughed. "Yeah, you've made quite a mess of things, haven't you? "

"Do you think it's amusing?"

"Yeah, a little bit. Honestly, I do. I mean, Jesus, it's not like you have cancer. You're strong enough to beat people up and healthy enough to eat oysters. So lighten up."

* * *

AS THEY WERE WALKING upstairs into the terminal, Maureen said, "Did you know I'm an identical twin?"

Hiroshi looked at her profile. "Are you going to tell me now that she was the one who followed me into the magazine store and came to the hospital in a ridiculous cowgirl outfit and talked to my father in Japanese?"

She laughed. "No, no, she lives in Boston. She's married and has two little kids, and she still works full-time as an investment counselor or something. Actually, I'm not sure exactly what she does, but it isn't music. I mean, she can't even read music. So why am I telling you this? I don't know. It's just that she and I are genetically identical, down to the fact that our middle toes are crossed over our whatever that toe is called that's next to the big toe. And see this?" She pointed to a perfectly round and minuscule depression on the underside of her brow, just above her tear duct. Hiroshi had never noticed it before; it looked like a B-B could fit inside it. It was rather cute. "I've never seen another human being, ever, with that little pit, whatever you call it, except for my sister and me. So I'm saying genetically we're exactly the same. But she's ten pounds lighter, and she's married and got two kids, and I'm gay, and she knows how to trade futures on government debt, if there is such a thing. So how hard-wired can we be? You know what hard-wired means? I mean, I left out another part. When I was seven years old, I had cancer. Childhood leukemia. I had it and my sister didn't. That's why I said, hey, at least you don't have cancer, okay? I wasn't being flippant, because I was there."

"So what does this all have to do with me?"

"What, everything has to do with you? I had several courses of chemotherapy and lost all my hair, thanks for asking." She laughed. "Anyway, I'm not sure what this has to do with you. I just get the sense you're feeling like you're fated to something, like you're in this downward spiral and you're absolutely helpless. But my life is different from my sister's because we chose to make it different."

"You chose? You chose to have cancer?"

She paused. "No. I don't know what the hell I'm trying to say. I didn't choose a lot of things. I knew I was gay from the time I was five years old, maybe younger, though I couldn't have put it into words. And I always knew I'd be a musician from I guess the same age."

"So now you're saying just the opposite, that we're fated to be what we're born to be."

"Exactly. I'm trying to say you were born to be a musician just like I was, and that's what you were fated for, so don't try to fight it or fight anything in your essential nature, but you can make choices and change things that aren't in your essential nature, like..."

"Like what?"

"I don't know. I just feel you giving up on life, and I think you shouldn't let that happen."

"Well, Maureen, the thing is, maybe that's my essential nature, too. Giving up. Being a loser."

* * *

WHEN THEY GOT BACK to Maureen's apartment, she invited him in. Her roommate, she told him, was back home in Pennsylvania. She made them both some tea, and settled in next to him on the couch. Despite the long shelf of law books looming over his head, it was very comfortable; Hiroshi was beginning to believe that Maureen could in fact be a great friend. They flipped through television channels for a few minutes, looking for something to watch. Then she shut off the TV and turned to Hiroshi.

"Look, I know I was confusing you with all that stuff about my sister. It confuses me too, why we're so different when we're exactly the same. I just think there are small choices you can make, like whether or not you want to waste your time with a married woman with an angry husband, or selling rocks at the Nature Company."

He didn't want to get angry, he liked her too much at this moment, but he couldn't help himself. "I'm not surprised you want to tell me now how I should live my life. That's been your specialty since we've met."

"Yeah, actually, it is. Because I look at you, Hiroshi, and I have a problem with you. I'm actually offended by you."

"And what's that problem? Why are you offended?"

She closed her eyes for a moment and exhaled heavily. "I enjoyed dinner with you tonight. I really don't want to say anything negative."

"But you will anyway."

"Yeah, I will anyway."

"Because you make that choice."

"Yeah. I make the choice. Honestly, I make it because I like you so much. And because I like you so much, I feel I've gotta do something, say something. Okay?"

"Listen, Maureen, why don't I just leave."

"Please don't leave. I want you to listen, and while you listen I want you to brace yourself, okay? This is what my conversation was circling around all evening, but I couldn't figure out how to say it because it was just too painful. What I'm trying to tell you, Hiroshi, is that you can make choices about how well you can support your essential nature."

"Yeah. So?"

"So, Hiroshi, what I'm saying is, you've failed to make those choices."

"I've *had* no choice."

"Yes, you have. You've had the choice, and every time you've made a choice, you've made a choice that's trivial. And now that's what you're starting to be."

"What?"

She said, very softly, "The expense of spirit in a waste of shame is lust in action."

"What was that?"

"Nothing. A quote. Never mind. You're a clerk in a store who gets into low-life scrapes. At this stage in your life, because of what you've chosen to do with it, I'm sorry to say that you've become trivial."

"Trivial."

"I'm sorry, Hiroshi. Thank you so much for dinner, it was wonderful and generous of you, and then I have to go and say something like that. But I had to, I really did."

After Hiroshi said good-night and got in a taxi, he thought about Maureen's verdict. It didn't sound all that bad. But she had delivered it with the air of a final and irrevocable judgment. And he had to agree she was right. He was a genius. A trivial genius. But the "trivial" part was a lot stronger than the "genius" part. He knew that the word, and the judgment behind it, was likely only to grow through the long night ahead, and would very soon be throbbing like a wound. And yet he didn't care what she thought any more, or what anybody thought. *How can you lie there in your own stink like that,* that nurse had asked him. But he was perfectly capable, apparently, of lying in his own stink.

Chapter 11

HE HAD A LONG, long night of complicated dreams. He went to a Japanese statuary shop to confront someone, but this person, terrified, had flung stone Buddhas and cherubs and bird baths to the pebbly ground as he approached, as if shattering these objects at his own feet would somehow preclude Hiroshi's devastating attack; he was making love to Kerri, his Australian girlfriend, and had her pinned against the door of his hotel room here in New York, her legs around his waist, the pounding and moaning so loud that the police and some doctors had broken in to investigate; and he was having a concert, playing a saxophone while simultaneously juggling four red balls in front of a rapturous audience, and the juggling, more than the music, somehow made him realize – a dream realization, not a real one – that his whole reason for creating and playing music from the beginning was that incredibly pleasurable sensation of being able to do something really, really well.

All of them, all three, and probably others that he'd forgotten, were the same: They were dreams of mastery. But dreams of mastery were only dreams.

After a morose breakfast, Hiroshi brought the recovered clarinet in its new case and his wristwatch to a pawn shop in Queens that one of his co-workers at the Nature Company had recommended, then took a taxi directly from there to the hardware store. After looking for only a moment at the two items, the pawn shop owner had forced Hiroshi to name a price first, and the speed with which the owner had accepted Hiroshi's wild guess led him to believe that he had been ripped off. Actually, he'd been quite aware at the moment he ventured it that it wasn't merely a wild guess, but rather a deliberately understated wild guess, given that the one outcome more potentially humiliating than being taken for a fool and ripped off was the possibility of being mocked for his greed. So he'd ripped himself off. Still, he pushed the 30 $20 dollar bills in his pocket without protest; it would have been far too difficult to unfold his wallet and place the bills inside, even if they'd have fit. Now he was without his wristwatch and his antique clarinet, but the pawnshop owner hadn't been interested in the case that Hiroshi had bought from the street vendor, so now at least he had a long case for his regular clarinet, which he still had not bothered to disassemble.

He'd stood outside the pawn shop for a long time, looking for a taxi back to midtown. He was worried about all the cash in his pocket. The street was noisy and fascinating, but he turned his back on it and pretended to read the sign in a dusty office next to the pawn shop so that he would be inconspicuous. The sign was constructed of little plastic letters that were slotted into grooves in a board covered with dusty black cloth. The sign read, "LETUSS AVEU$ $$ O MPAREOV RR AT NA UTO & L IFE INS." Hiroshi was trying to decipher it, and in fact had gotten out a pen to record the jumble of letters, the case held between his knees, when a taxi cruised by.

A moment later, after he was seated inside the taxi, he'd

gripped as best he could with his fingers and used an upward shrug of his shoulder muscle to pull a couple of the new bills out of his pocket as if it were a recalcitrant ATM. He held the bills loosely but anxiously in his hand waiting to pay the fare even though there was still a long ride back into the city. After arriving in midtown, he pulled another one out to pay for a cup of latte, a pecan roll, and a chocolate éclair at a Starbucks near the hardware store, noting with pleasure – as if he were accomplishing something – the way his pocket was slowly returning to normal dimensions. After bolting down the coffee and the pecan roll, he pulled out still another sheaf of crumpled bills and walked into the store.

The same young woman was behind the counter. Hiroshi said pleasantly, "Hello, I'm back. Do you remember me?" She said only, "Uh huh." Hiroshi, feeling suddenly self-conscious, blurted out, "I brought you some reward money to thank you for finding my clarinet for me." This time, the woman said nothing. Hiroshi handed the bills to her, having no idea how much was in his hand.

She used her thumb and forefinger to take the clump of twenties from Hiroshi's limp grip and then slowly pulled the bills apart, smoothed them out and stacked them, making sure that the high-collared, high-haired portraits of the white-haired gentleman all faced the same way. There were eight portraits in all.

The young woman put six of the bills into the cash register and stuffed two of them into the pocket of her uniform apron, then bent down under the counter and came up with the original clarinet case. She handed it to Hiroshi and said, "Here you go. Sorry about the case, but my uncle said I had to hold onto something. I hope you're having a good time in New York." She looked with some curiosity at the similar-looking case that Hiroshi was gripping along with the squishy éclair in his free hand, and laughed somewhat unkindly.

Hiroshi accepted the original case and, once out on the street, placed the chocolate éclair into it so it would be easier to hold both cases in one hand, and gripped his cane in the other.

When Hiroshi came home from work that evening, the phone in his room was ringing. It was his father. Hiroshi, feeling profoundly irritated, said, "Hello, father. I'm a little bit tired from work. Would you mind much if I called you back tomorrow?"

There was a silence, slightly longer than the satellite delay might account for. Then his father said, "I'm afraid that wouldn't be convenient for me. I'm traveling tomorrow."

"Where are you going?"

"A reading. Which reminds me, I've been meaning to ask, does your new job require much out-of-town travel?"

"I really don't understand. I thought I explained to you that I'm basically a sort of clerk, or salesman."

"Yes, but I was just wondering if you had to lend your expertise to other stores of a similar sort in cities across America. Or whether they need you to come to their headquarters building from time to time to talk to younger employees about what it takes to succeed."

"Father, I really don't have the energy or the strength to respond. Do you want me to become a salaryman, is that what you're saying?"

"A salaryman? I don't even recognize the word. No, I'd actually rather you continue to sell rubber snakes to six-year-olds than to be an office drone. In fact, as far as I'm concerned, I'd be happy for you to continue to work at the Nature Company for the rest of your life, if you were also practicing your instrument and performing, which you are not."

"And who told you I haven't been? Maureen?"

"Yes, Maureen. She and I barely understand each other,

but at the same time, with a little bit of French and English, we communicate perfectly well."

"And did she tell you that I have the strength of a four-year-old in my fingers?"

"I think I understood her to say something like that. I do understand the English expression 'give up.' Are you aware, by the way, that when you really *were* four years old – or maybe five, or six, it hardly matters – I placed a little trumpet in your hands and you began to play? You worked the stops, or whatever those things are called, and after a few days you pushed out a little melody."

Hiroshi remembered vividly the War of the Toys, the way his father had piled on the miniature musical instruments and sumi-e sets and CDs to counteract the chemistry sets and stethoscopes he got from everyone else. The two toys he remembered with the greatest fondness from his early childhood were a miniature gold-colored plastic trombone with a slide that really moved, though it couldn't actually be played, and a tiny plastic glass of beer with real bubbles that Hiroshi liked to pretend to drink. Between the toy trombone and the real trumpet, his father had won that war. But now the battleground had changed.

He said, "I'm afraid that at this point in my life I wouldn't be satisfied with pushing out a little melody."

"You wouldn't have to. It's only your fingers that you have to retrain, not your brain. You didn't suffer brain damage, did you?"

"Father, I'm not saying I'm going to give up entirely. I'm just taking a break from my career."

"This life is not discontinuous. You understand? It is not to be interrupted. Do you stop breathing when you get tired of it? Is your heart beating too much of a routine? Do you need a vacation from chewing your food and swallowing it? If

I had ever taken a break do you think I could live with myself?"

"I suppose it depends on how you define 'break.' Your time on the road didn't always correspond exactly to readings or lectures or whatever it was you claimed you were doing. And whether or not you define vomiting red wine and sake into the garden as a 'break,' I don't know, but you sure weren't writing at that moment, were you?"

"If you're going to regress, as I suspect you are, to a smart-mouthed adolescent, why don't you just return to Japan? I mean that quite seriously. You seem to be slipping, both physically and mentally, and given that you're my last adult child and as long as you seem to be losing control of yourself and your life, I would feel it my responsibility to care for you until you get better."

"And what would I do in Japan?"

"Like I just said. Get better. What are you doing in New York?"

"There's nothing for me in Japan. Just you. As you so artfully pointed out, I'm your last adult child, but you've got some real children whose lives you can mold. I can't be that any more."

His father shouted loud enough to make Hiroshi pull the phone away from his ear. "You *can't* be that? You have no choice but to be that. You *owe* me that!"

Hiroshi could not bring himself to say any more. "Well, anyway, I will consider your proposal to return. Now I'm going to get my dinner. I'm really very hungry." With that, he hung up.

Was he getting better in New York? That was one of several things to consider from that conversation. He made himself a Cheddar cheese sandwich with sliced tomato and mayonnaise, opened a can of Miller Genuine Draft and, while eating, squeezed the second of the three exercise balls. When he finished his sandwich, he placed his Regent clarinet into the newly purchased case and clicked the little latch firmly shut. The thought of picking up his clarinet filled him with nausea, but squeezing the balls wasn't so bad. When he finished the can of beer, he tried to crumple it, but managed only to squeeze the middle, leaving the top third of the can bent downward like someone doubled over in pain.

* * *

HIS FATHER often reminded Hiroshi that he was his last child, the only one who'd made it to adulthood. Hiroshi couldn't really dispute that that was largely his fault. One summer night when he was sixteen, he and a school buddy, Toshi, had purchased some beers at a vending machine – it thanked them in its robot voice – and lay out in the garden, looking up at the stars.

Once, twice, three times, his mother had called him in to go to bed – his father had been out of town – but Hiroshi and his buddy had ignored her. It was hot and stuffy in the house, and it was breezy outside. So the two of them had fallen asleep right there in the garden, with no pillows or blankets, just lying on their backs. At least Hiroshi assumed his friend had fallen asleep; when he awakened a little later, the friend had gone.

At that point, having enjoyed the cool air, it probably would have been smart to go back inside, but he was too tired and sluggish from the four beers he'd had. Also, he could hear his mother and his sister arguing intermittently, and he hadn't felt like stepping into the middle of that. His sister had returned home unexpectedly a week before, without her new husband. When Hiroshi's mother had tried to ask her why, she'd shrugged and said, "I just needed a break from marriage." She'd been married seven months at the time.

From that moment to this, she and their mother had been fighting, though Hiroshi was far too self-absorbed to understand the significance of the conflict.

He fell back to sleep and had a terribly strange dream, one that he still remembered to this day, something about universal love. It was as if everyone in the world were part of one enormous interconnected body, and so they all loved each other as much as any one of us loves our own thumb or arm, and wouldn't think of cutting it off or killing it. So it was a very comforting dream, except that Hiroshi didn't see this huge body from the outside, but from the inside, as if he were lost inside of it. There were all these twisting blood vessels and sliding tubes, and he couldn't find his way out of the mouth and he started gagging and all of a sudden he woke up with vomit welling up at the back of his throat.

He swallowed hard. He was shivering violently. The night had turned very cold. His whole body felt unbearably stiff, he was having trouble breathing, and his chest hurt terribly, as if he were having a heart attack. But none of this was what had awakened him; it was, instead, the sound of his sister crying. Not so much crying, actually, as crying out, though she formed no words.

For the first time in his life – the Guillain-Barré attack was the second – Hiroshi found himself unable to move. He questioned whether he really was, in fact, awake. His eyes were open, and he could see the stars and hear the strange cries of his sister, but neither that nor anything else around him seemed quite real.

For some reason, what Hiroshi feared most at that moment was that if an attacker were to have come across him, he would have been unable to defend himself. He was completely still, except for the shivering. It was more awful than being buried alive, because the walls of the grave were perfectly clear, so that he could see and hear what he could not touch.

When Hiroshi's sister was younger, she and her friend Emi both had believed in something called "kanashibari" – being tied down by a ghost. A ghost came to you in the middle of the night and lay on top of you, pressing you to the bed so that you could not move at all. It wasn't clear if it was something sexual, but it seemed that way from the girls' vague descriptions. Hiroshi didn't believe the ghost part, but had heard enough tales of midnight immobility to know without a doubt that something was happening. He wondered if his sister was being held down like he was, right now, and if that was why she was crying.

But after a period of time that could have been several seconds or several minutes, Hiroshi glimpsed a white shape run past him. It must have been either his sister or his mother, though he was certain that his mother, who was turning to stone from her disease, could not move that fast. Hiroshi rocked himself to his side and slowly and painfully drew his knees up to his chest. Then he rolled to his hands and knees and slowly pulled himself to his feet. And then, though the sun was beginning to rise, he walked back into his house and lay down on the futon and once again went to sleep.

It occurred to him when he woke up later that morning to check on his sister, but her room was empty. His mother was up, working on the garden.

He decided to walk over to Emi's house near the train station. Emi, who still lived at home with her family, had been his sister's only real friend growing up. But as he walked away, his mother called out to him, "If you find your sister, tell her she's not welcome to stay here any more."

"I won't tell her that," Hiroshi had said.

His mother had shrugged, leaning on a rake. "Well, in any case, she's not welcome here. I'll tell her that myself."

Hiroshi walked back slowly toward his mother. "Do you mind telling me what the matter is?"

"You won't deliver my message; I'll ignore that defiance. But if you're so close to your sister that you feel the need to protect her from my decision and that of your father, then I suppose you're close enough to ask her yourself."

So Hiroshi went off to the train station. Toshi was a well-known reprobate who'd gotten into trouble that spring for exposing himself to some female classmates. And he'd bragged about having sex already, the first of his group to have done so, even though he was a bit younger than Hiroshi and his other friends. Could he have sneaked into Hiroshi's house and fondled his sleeping sister, tied her up, even raped her? But the thought of his fifteen-year-old pal raping a twenty-two-year-old woman like Shizuka, delicate as she was, seemed utterly inconceivable.

When Hiroshi got to Emi's house near the train station, he found it dark. He walked into the station across the way and bought a can of iced coffee to help him wake up. As he drank it, he remembered that his mother's argument with his sister must have been related to her abandonment of her marriage, and that this was why she had cried out, and fled; he felt stupid for not having made this obvious connection earlier, for having indulged in fantasies of ghost bondage and rape. Feeling inexplicably relieved, he drank the rest of his coffee and returned home. He spent the remainder of that day practicing his clarinet and, when he grew tired, reading a part of his huge backlog of manga – he had two teetering stacks of the comic books in his room, each taller than he was.

He and his mother had a very quiet dinner of beef curry and pickles. Neither spoke of his sister. Her bags and her clothes were still in her room, but as far as Hiroshi was concerned, having determined it was just a garden-variety domestic dispute, he assumed it would be settled domestically. After dinner, feeling restless, he decided to take a walk. He decided to walk over to a video-game parlor but found himself, instead, wandering into the Forbidden Pathway. He took only a few steps down the familiar path before he knew, with absolute certainty, that he would find his sister waiting for him at the end of the path.

* * *

THE DAY after the disturbing conversation with his father, near the end of his shift at the Nature Company, Hiroshi unlocked the wooden case holding the polished stones and removed an especially beautiful slice of tourmaline crystal, about the size of his hand and with green and pink colors that resembled the flesh and rind of a watermelon. He pushed the polished stone with the heel of his hand into his pants pocket. Then he informed his boss that he would need to take the day off tomorrow.

As he walked back to the hotel, he slid the fingers of his free hand up and down the cool surface of the rock until it warmed and became sticky with his sweat. He had never stolen anything before.

When he got back to his room, he called St. Vincent Hospital and asked for Vince. The operator said he wasn't in, so Hiroshi asked the operator to leave a message. Hiroshi's message for Vince was, in its entirety, "Thank you for the kindness you showed me when I was ill." If he couldn't read it himself, Hiroshi figured, someone could read it to him.

Not long after he hung up, Maureen called, apologizing profusely for what she'd said to him at her apartment and inviting him to an impromptu party that night. She'd planned the party just for him, to cheer him up, and had invited some of her classmates, and Grady and some other members of his band, who'd promised to come after their show, and other friends of hers who wanted to meet Hiroshi. Her roommate would not be there. He promised Maureen he'd come.

Then Hiroshi laboriously punched in all the numbers he needed to reach Hitomi in Japan. He had been expecting to get her answering machine, so he was surprised to hear her voice. It was nine-fifteen a.m. in Tokyo, the start of a new day; he'd forgotten that Hitomi had lost her job.

"Hiroshi, I was just about to call you. You sound kind of down. Everything okay?"

"Everything is fine. I just stole something from the Nature Company."

"Stole? Are you that hard up for money?"

"No. I just sold my good clarinet and made plenty of money. It's just a rock. I liked it."

Hitomi laughed uneasily. "Wow, that's a first for you, Mr. Straight, stealing something. Are you calling me to brag about it?"

"No, I'm calling to say goodbye."

"Good-bye? Where are you going?"

"I'm not going anywhere, actually. It's just clear to me we'll never see each other again."

"Hiroshi, did you somehow hear my news?"

"What news?"

"Are you serious? 'What news?' Why would you call me today of all days unless you knew I was going to call you?"

"I guess I'm just a genius. Why don't you just make it official and tell me?"

"Ruud has asked me to go to the Netherlands with him. I'm going."

"You sound very excited."

"Hiroshi, I'm sorry. But wasn't your call to me to officially break up with me?"

He said, "Yes." A long silence transpired.

"Hiroshi, is everything okay there? Besides your illness. I mean, selling your clarinet? I don't like the sound of that."

"Everything is fine. I just had no use for it anymore. I sincerely wish you and Ruud a wonderful time together."

"Thank you."

"I guess you went to the noodle shop with him after all, huh?"

"Noodle shop? What are you talking about?"

"Nothing. I'm fine. Everything is fine."

"So I have no reason to worry about you, do I, Hiroshi?"

"None whatsoever. I'm sure our paths will cross again some time when we're both back in Japan."

He was profoundly irritated when he hung up the phone. Why had he said that business about their paths crossing in Japan when there was no chance whatsoever he would ever see her again? Partly he was irritated because that stupid and insincere statement had distracted him from his enormous depression and the determination that stemmed from it.

He should have known he'd never see her again after that last night in Tokyo. They'd both gotten very drunk, and she'd argued bitterly against his trip to America, even though the plans had been made months before. "I can't promise you what'll happen if you make that trip," was what she had said, and he understood perfectly now what she was getting at. Despite the argument, they'd made love one last time, or tried to, but Hiroshi was impotent for the first time in his life. It wasn't a big deal, she hadn't cared – it bothered him, in fact, that she hadn't cared – but now he wondered if it had been the first symptom of his illness. Or the first symptom of their dissolution; either theory made perfect sense. They'd argued some more, later in the evening, and then he'd left. Now, he was physically capable again, but it didn't matter at all, because nothing else mattered at all.

He opened the top drawer of his dresser, where he kept his socks, and pulled out a flask of Canadian Club blended whiskey. It was the right brand, he figured, for all the blending he was about to do. Then he went to his bedside table and emptied the contents of his Xanax bottle into his hand. There were only five pills left, but considering how sleepy even one pill made him feel, he didn't think that would be a problem. He also planned to swallow a handful of Advil, just in case.

He swallowed the five Xanax pills with a slug of whiskey. Then he picked up the phone to call his father, the only other good-bye call he planned to make. But he immediately felt queasy, so he rushed to the bathroom and swallowed a handful of Advil – there must have been fifteen of the little reddish-brown pills – to make sure he'd finished the job off.

His only regret was that Hitomi might actually believe that he had killed himself because she was running off with a Dutch guy. On the other hand, he felt just right about his father's likely reaction. Hiroshi's sister might still be alive today if Hiroshi hadn't gotten drunk with his buddy, hadn't allowed her to run past him that night, hadn't slept until midmorning and stayed around the house reading manga all day instead of searching for her in the one place he knew she'd be. Hiroshi's death would be a way of evening that score. Plus, there'd be no more disappointments for his father; from now on, he could concentrate on the two little ones, who had their whole lives ahead of them, when his own career disappointed him.

No, there was no need to call his father; the message would be clear enough. But he was a little embarrassed about the paramedics coming a second time to find him on the floor of the Gramercy West Hotel and, come to think of it, didn't want to inconvenience Carmelita. She might be angry to be confronted with a dead body.

So Hiroshi picked up his cane and staggered out of the room. He was feeling very dizzy and nauseated, not pleasantly sleepy as he had hoped. He made his way with great difficulty into the elevator, across the lobby, and into Gramercy Park. It was interesting, in a way; this must be what an old man would feel like. Not that he'd ever know. Then he lowered himself onto a bench and waited to die.

He was having a very involved dream about trying to board a bus with the wrong ticket while the bus driver was screaming at him, in English, that he was a bony-assed, gimpy fuck.

Hiroshi's eyes fluttered open. He had no idea where he was, or what he had just been doing. A familiar-looking man was bent over, staring into Hiroshi's face, and screaming at him.

"Wake up, you ugly fuck, and talk to me!"

Hiroshi opened his mouth to speak and vomited Canadian Club blended whiskey, Xanax, Advil, two root beers and two slices of sausage pizza with red pepper flakes over the screaming man's legs.

The man jumped backward. It made Hiroshi think of a kitten Shizuka had once adopted, who would jump backward exactly like that when startled. That made Hiroshi think of his sister, and that made him cry.

The man was standing there, staring at his dripping pants. "You fucking moron! You pinhead! You dimwit!" He pulled a gun out of his jacket pocket and pointed it at Hiroshi. That was when Hiroshi recognized him as Trudi's husband. He felt very dizzy, and wanted to lie down on the bench. But the gun kept him upright.

"Sorry about your pants."

"Fuck the pants."

"If you're trying to kill me, I'm trying to do the same thing."

"Kill me?"

"No, kill me. So you can shoot me if you want, I don't mind. But you'll probably go to jail, so why not just help me back to my room so I can take more pills?"

"You took pills? What kind of pills?"

"Xanax and Advil."

"Advil? God, you really are a fucking dimwit. You can't kill yourself with Advil." He grabbed the barrel of the gun and swung the grip at Hiroshi's head, but it was a half-hearted blow. It stung, but it also woke Hiroshi up. It felt like the kind of swipe a mother bear would take at a misbehaving cub.

Hiroshi said, "So what do you think about the Xanax? Won't that kill me?"

"Fuck if I know. Man, I can't stand this fucking stink. You know how much these pants cost?"

Hiroshi shook his head. "Will you help me to my room?"

"No, I will not help you to your room. I can't even walk in these things. I'm gonna get the fuck out of here and you can do whatever the fuck you want."

"I'm sorry about Trudi. She didn't tell me you were still married."

The man shrugged. "What's done is done. Is that why you're killing yourself?"

Hiroshi laughed. "Of course not." The man looked nettled, so Hiroshi quickly said, "I mean, she's a beautiful woman. But I didn't want to get into the middle of something, so I didn't call her again. I'm doing it because of this." Hiroshi indicated the cane at his feet.

Trudi's husband said, "Listen, if I help you up to your room, can I borrow a pair of clean pants?"

When they got back to the room, Trudi's husband peeled off his pants and tossed them onto the fire escape. Then he pulled on a pair of Hiroshi's pants; they looked like Capri pants on him. Hiroshi was still feeling dizzy, so, with the help of Trudi's husband, he stepped into the shower and stood under the hot water for about ten minutes.

When he got out, Trudi's husband said, "I've gotta get out of here. I've called Trudi to take care of you. You need anything before I go?"

"Yes, please fill the bathtub for me. Maybe I'll feel better if I soak."

Trudi's husband regarded him for a moment. "Man, what is it with you Japanese and suicide?" He disappeared into the bathroom and turned on the water. After a few minutes he turned off the faucets with a loud skreek and re-emerged. He patted Hiroshi on the shoulder. "Okay, man, you're all set. Take care of yourself." Then he walked out the door.

Hiroshi slowly undressed and settled into the bathtub. He was feeling very weak and very depressed. He thought of the clock radio in the other room. Maybe he could get out of the bathtub, unplug the clock radio, plug it in here in the bathroom, get back into the bathtub and pull the clock radio by its cord in after him. But he could barely even pull himself out of the bathtub to begin with, much less accomplish all of those other steps. In fact, he'd have to keep on soaking until Trudi arrived. Besides, what if the clock radio only partially electrocuted him? It would be horrible to live with severe burns. Then he thought of Maureen saying, "Oh, Jesus, 'electrocuted' is an absolute. No half measures, Hiroshi." Hiroshi laughed weakly and sank back down into the tub. There was a shooting pain in his stomach when he laughed. He remembered the first time he'd heard the English expression, "shooting pain"; he'd thought it meant the kind of pain you experience from being shot. He didn't feel like laughing anymore; the dizziness was getting worse and he felt like vomiting again.

The room was so silent that he could hear the buzzing in his own ears. He said to himself, "This miserable patch of nothing." He repeated it several times, and each time his voice, and the words, sounded stranger.

Trudi arrived after about a half an hour. The door had been left open, so she walked in and found him still lying in the bathtub.

"Hiroshi, how are you feeling?"

"It seems like we're always having interesting meetings in bathrooms. I tried to kill myself today."

"I know. I'm so sorry. At least you did it in kind of a half-assed way."

"I don't know. I may still be dying."

"If you're conscious and talking to me, I wouldn't think so."

"I should be dying of embarrassment, talking to you now. But I don't care. I just feel so awful."

Trudi leaned over the tub, bracing her arms against the edge, her flat-soled shoes sliding backwards on the wet floor. She was like a baby giraffe trying to drink from a watering hole.

She looked at his eyes closely. "Seems okay."

"I'm really dizzy and I'm having bad stomach pains. Maybe we should call the ambulance."

She sat down on the edge of the bathtub and stroked his wet hair. "*An* ambulance? That's not a good idea."

"Why?"

"Because, Hiroshi, I know a few EMTs. So I know how the system works. Every time in New York an ambulance is called, for whatever reason, a police car is dispatched to the same address. That's the law. Okay? Then they take you to the emergency room where, if you've ingested something, they pump your stomach..."

"But I already threw up."

"Doesn't matter. It's by law. Have you ever had your stomach pumped, Hiroshi? Didn't think so, or you wouldn't think of calling for an ambulance. It's a really nasty, low-tech procedure with a black rubber hose down your throat. Then, again by law, a psychologist is dispatched to the emergency room, and he determines if you're an EDP."

"What's an EDP?"

"Emotionally disturbed person. A threat to yourself and others. Is that you, Hiroshi? I'd say so. Marcus would say so."

"Who's Marcus?"

"My husband. The guy you barfed on. What, you two didn't introduce yourselves?"

"So what happens if I'm an EMT?"

"You mean EDP. If you're an EDP, then you're an AMS."

"AMS?"

"Altered mental status. Actually, I'm not sure which comes first, AMS or EDP, but one way or another, unless you're DOA, if you're EDP/AMS you're basically branded a nut butt, pumped full of drugs, and shipped off to Manhattan State Hospital, which is where the street people go, and that'll be the last anyone'll hear from you for a year or so, and you'll regret you didn't just use a rope. So let me ask you again, Hiroshi, are you dizzy?"

"I'm not sure. Maybe a little bit."

"Once again, Hiroshi, are you dizzy?"

"No, I'm not dizzy at all."

"How do you feel?"

"I feel absolutely peaches and cream."

"You probably mean 'peachy keen.' You look like shit. Here, let me help you out of the tub."

She helped pull Hiroshi up from a sitting position, helped him step slowly out of the tub, and hugged his wet body to hers.

"My God, you've got a skinny butt."

"Trudi, I really am dizzy."

"I know, I know, sweetie. It'll pass. Nobody ever died from taking a few Xanax and Advil. Let's just get you dried off."

"Trudi, how come you didn't tell me you were married?"

She stopped drying him. "Is that what this is all about?"

"My girlfriend in Tokyo will think it's because she's found a new boyfriend."

"Wait a minute. You have a girlfriend in Tokyo?"

"Had."

"Have. Had. I have a husband. Soon it'll be 'had.' Far as I'm concerned, it all cancels out."

"Anyway, no, it's not about you. It's about an accumulation of things. I'm not really sure."

Trudi finished drying him off. "Do you want me to dress you?"

"No. I can dress myself."

"Well, listen, I have to get going. Marcus is in a taxi."

"He was in a taxi downstairs this whole time?"

"Sure. He feels bad he hit you."

"The first hit or the second hit?"

"He hit you a second time?"

"Yeah. Here." Hiroshi pointed to his temple.

"Oh, shit. I didn't even see that mark. He is such a jerk. Do you want to press charges?"

"No."

"That's good. Because then we'd have to tell the whole story, and the police would take you to the emergency room, and you'd be evaluated."

"I know, to see if I'm an EDP or an EMT or a GDP, or whatever."

She got a small bandage from the medicine cabinet and put it over the little wound. She used her thumb to stroke his interrupted eyebrow. "Hiroshi, anything else I can do for you now?"

"Two things. Bring me a Coca-Cola from the refrigerator. And hand me the phone."

After she accomplished these tasks, Trudi kissed him on the forehead and said good-bye.

As soon as he heard the door slam, Hiroshi drank the Coke, which cleared his head considerably.

Sitting naked on the bed, he dialed Maureen's number.

She was rather angry. "Hiroshi, where the hell are you?"

"Why?"

"Why? *Why?* Because I've got the only friends you have in New York over at my place waiting for your skinny ass to show up."

"You're the third person today to comment that I have a skinny ass."

"That's very interesting. Are you planning to show up at your own damn party?"

"I'm sorry, Maureen. Please enjoy yourself. I forgot about it, and in any event I'm just not at all able to come."

"Are you sick?"

"Yes. Just some aftereffects of my illness."

Maureen paused, seemed about to say something, then caught herself. "You sure you can't come? You want me to come and get you?"

"No, I'm really not up to it. I'm very sorry. I guess I really owe you now, don't I?"

"It's okay. Stay in touch, will you?"

"Of course, Maureen."

He hung up the phone and crushed the Coke can, which crumpled a little bit more than the beer can had. Then he flopped down on his bed, still naked, and stared at the ceiling. The dizziness had almost disappeared. After a while, he picked himself up and found the Brazilian CD Maureen had brought him after he'd been jumped by Trudi's husband. He was feeling very bad about missing his party, and thought maybe listening to her gift was the least he could do.

The CD was maddeningly difficult to pull apart with his scrabbling fingers. But when he finally got it open and into his Walkman, he was captivated, particularly by a clarinet track called "*Chorando Baixinho*," or "Crying Low," a sinuous chorino played by a musician he'd never heard of before, Abel Ferreira. The song had a sort of distant, jaunty melancholy that seemed to be more about the Lower East Side of New York than Brazil. Hiroshi had to play it four times in order to stop thinking about it, though he could have played it by ear, assuming he could play it at all, after the second time through. It made him feel much better to know that someone, even someone as far away as Brazil and forty years in the past, had once played a song like that.

He went to his little refrigerator to get another Coke, but he was all out. So he put on a robe and padded down the hallway to the soda machine. On his way back, he saw Carmelita, who greeted him with a hug.

Hiroshi asked, "Don't you work during the daytime?"

"My shift is just over. I haven't seen you for a long, long time, Mr. Mori. You look nice."

"Do I? Do I look happy?"

"You look nice and happy, yes. I hope you enjoy yourself more now and I'm glad you feel better from your sickness."

Hiroshi thanked her and went back to his room. She hadn't, apparently, guessed at what had just happened to him. On the other hand, she had given him a big hug, and eyed the bandage on his forehead critically. But maybe she thought, if he seemed a bit woozy, that it was just the result of the minor scalp injury and that, whatever it was, the bandage signified a much more minor mishap than the illness that had paralyzed him. And, if you discounted what was going on inside his head, she was right; he was in much better shape.

He went into the bathroom and looked at himself in the mirror. It was only then that he fully understood that he had just tried to kill himself and that, if he had approached the task more diligently, he would now be gone forever. Instead, he felt well enough to contemplate going for a walk.

Going to work the next day seemed unimaginable, however. So he called in sick – describing the actual symptoms he was at that moment experiencing, dizziness and a slight headache – and instead of going for a walk spent all day in his room, watching television the entire morning and eating several bowls of ramen. He clicked obsessively, exercising both forefingers, shuttling back and forth among *Clifford the Big Red Dog, Oprah, I Dream of Jeannie, Jennie Jones, The View, One Life to Live, Maury, Access Hollywood, Introduction to Entrepreneurship, Divorce Court, Rosie, Sally*, and *Judge Mathis*. The only show he knew by name was *Clifford the Big Red Dog*. All of them looked interesting, and it made him feel a bit the way he did when he first opened up a bento box, his chopsticks hovering over all of the delicious choices, not sure where to go first. But after several hours of watching he began to feel literally nauseated and laid the remote control aside.

Chapter 12

THE FOLLOWING DAY, as soon as he returned to the Nature Company, he pulled the watermelon crystal out of a paper bag and slipped it into the drawer where he had found it. His manager walked up behind him and Hiroshi swiveled awkwardly, his legs turning to water, expecting to be fired or arrested for theft. The dizziness that had faded away the previous evening began to return. But his manager, it turned out, was only concerned about his apparent unhappiness and offered him a $1.25-an-hour raise as an inducement to stay on the job.

He went out that evening to celebrate getting a raise and not getting caught, though the latter made him feel ashamed and the former like a fool. Maybe he was also celebrating the fact that he hadn't died, but he didn't want to think about that at all. But he was feeling relatively strong physically, that was a better thing to celebrate, so he walked over to Second Avenue and paced back and forth in front of a couple of bars jammed with young people, trying to decide which, if any, to enter.

One bar had a long window facing the street out of which

a very pretty brunette watched Hiroshi hobble back and forth. After watching his indecision for several minutes, she beckoned him in by unpeeling one long finger from her gin and tonic and crooking it at him with a faux-seductive, pleasantly mocking smile.

Hiroshi, electrified, walked into the bar to find this vision, but the bar was so crowded, he couldn't make it much past the entrance, and ended up sitting down at one of the few open tables, across from two other brunettes — somewhat less young and beautiful than the first, and a good deal less hip-looking, in overly tight dresses that showed a lot of cleavage. One of them offered Hiroshi a cigarette.

"Sorry," he said, craning his neck around them to look for the woman who had first beckoned him into the bar, "I don't smoke."

"We don't smoke either," said the more attractive of the two, a woman who looked even more out of place here than her companion. But there was in her eyes a glittering avidity that Hiroshi liked, though it seemed to indicate no more than the desire to have a few drinks and a bit of banter. Interestingly, even her makeup had bits of glitter in it; this was clearly their big night out.

Hiroshi beckoned a waitress over and ordered himself a Maker's Mark. "So if you don't smoke, why are you smoking?"

"Oh, we're just being naughty. We're playing hooky from our husbands."

"And where are they?"

"Back at the hotel watching our babies. I'm Molly," the glittery one said, "and she's Adrienne. We're first cousins. Mine's two and hers is seventeen months. This is our big fun weekend away from home, but we couldn't leave our babies."

"You'd miss them too much?"

"No. We're both still breast feeding."

"So is it okay for you to drink?"

Molly said, "Ginger ale and cranberry juice. So cigarettes is the only fun we can have. Hey, what's your name, anyway?"

The waitress came over, and Hiroshi carefully lifted his bourbon off the tray. "Ichiro Suzuki. Do you know me?"

"Why should we know you?" Molly said, but Adrienne clapped her hand on her cousin's forearm. "You know, the baseball player. Oh my God, you're incredible! Are you really Ichiro Suzuki, or are you putting us on?"

Hiroshi lifted his drink carefully with one hand. "Do I look like I'm putting you on? Look at this strength. I can lift my drink with one hand." His hand trembled a bit with the weight of the glass.

Adrienne looked concerned, but Molly laughed. "Hey, I like this guy. He's funny."

Her cousin said, "So you're really not this Itchy guy?"

Molly said, "No, he's just kidding."

"I thought you looked a little skinny," Adrienne said. "So what is it you really do?"

"I'm a famous jazz musician from Japan," Hiroshi said. "So what do you two do?"

"Do? We nurse," Adrienne said. "We told you that."

"Well, I mean, what do your husbands do? I was just trying to be, you know, American, by assuming you had careers."

"Well, actually, I'm a real estate agent. I'm just taking a break," Adrienne said. "Are you really a famous jazz musician?"

Her cousin said, "No, of course not, he's just joking again. Wait a minute, if you're a jazz musician, you'd know who Boney James is, right?"

"I keep on hearing that name, but I have no idea who it is." He drained his glass of Maker's Mark and signaled for another one.

"Okay," Adrienne said. "So you're not a baseball player and you're not a jazz musician. What are you?"

"I have no idea," Hiroshi said. His second drink arrived and he took a long pull at it. He started to put it down, but then he drained it.

"Man, you're making us thirsty," Adrienne said. "I'd love to start drinking again, but I don't want to stop nursing."

"Yeah, because you'd lose the big boobs," Molly said. "That's the best thing about having a baby." She pointed at her own deep cleavage. "I used to be really flat, now look at me. My little one and my husband fight over these babies."

Adrienne said, "I don't think he gets it. Japanese men are into feet or the backs of necks or something."

Hiroshi made a little motion with his forefinger as if he were about to plunge it into Molly's smooth cleavage. "Are you kidding? 'Necks?' 'Feet?' Not where I come from. What do you like when you eat chicken? The feet? The neck? Or the juicy breasts?" The women both seemed to think this was hilarious. He drained his drink and ordered a new one. "Listen, I feel guilty that you have to watch me enjoy myself drinking. Can I buy you some dinner?"

"Are you trying to pick us up?" Molly said, with an eager smile.

"Two married ladies such as you? No, I'm just celebrating tonight."

"Celebrating what? Your sixtieth homer or the release of your new album?"

"Actually, to tell you the truth, my job is, I'm a famous custodian."

Adrienne said, "A what?"

He said, "No, seriously, I'm a clerk in the Nature Company and I just got a $1.25 per hour raise." He raised his voice to a shout. "So I'd like to celebrate by buying everybody in this bar a drink!"

Adrienne said, "I think you're a little drunk."

Hiroshi staggered to his feet. "Yes, I'm especially drunk. I'm *particularly* drunk." He did a joyful little pirouette, almost bumping into a couple passing behind him. "Particularly drunk and happy and crazy." He grabbed the hand of Molly, his favorite, and tried to pull her to her feet, but her hand pulled right out of his soft grip. "Sorry, we don't shake hands much, so we don't develop much of a grip." But Molly, getting the idea, got to her feet and Hiroshi encircled her waist with one arm, doing a sloppy, soulful little dance to the music, barely audible in the crowd's din. He buried his head in her chest and tried to execute a dip, but Molly almost stumbled and fell. "Alright, that's enough," she said, but she clearly was delighted. She helped Hiroshi back into his seat and sat down herself. Her cousin excused herself to go to the washroom. As soon as she left, Molly said, "Are you really a clerk? Why would a Japanese person leave Japan – you are from Japan, right? – just to become a clerk?"

"No good reason. Some things happened."

"Shit happens. I hear you."

"Shit happens. Yes. I like that expression. It suggests the randomness of fate. Like what happened to me."

Molly looked closely at Hiroshi. "What *did* happen to you?"

"Well," he said soberly, "I got drunk."

* * *

IF HE HADN'T BEEN drunk, he would have slept on his own futon and gone into his sister's room to see what the matter was. If he hadn't drunk those four beers with his reprobate buddy, he might have been quick enough to grab his sister's ankle as she ran right past him, or followed her down the Forbidden Pathway or tracked her there soon after she had run out of the house, instead of waiting nearly a full day to do so. By the time he finally had gone after her, he took the most direct route to the old store instead of following the intricate turns that his sister had laid out and that constituted the official Forbidden Pathway. Maybe that was the right thing to do, but maybe he would have arrived at a happier conclusion if he had done it her way. And maybe his sister still existed, waiting, suspended in time, in some other shack that could only be reached by the proper combination of steps that only the two of them knew.

* * *

THE NEXT MORNING, he lay in his bed at the Gramercy West Hotel and thought about Molly and Adrienne. He had continued to drink with them until about one a.m. He'd even told them about the suicide attempt, which made him feel much better. Now he had a clattering, clamorous headache. He thought about the view down Molly's dress for a while, which cheered him up.

Then he dozed, and when he woke up again, his headache was a little better, but instead of Molly, he was thinking again of his sister. He went into the bathroom and ran some cold water over his wrists. The cold penetrated all the way to his bones; it felt thrillingly good.

The odd thing was, he didn't even miss Shizuka all that much. He just felt badly for his father, who missed her far more, and for his mother, who'd died not long after, never having reconciled with her only daughter. He wanted to make it up to his father by not disappointing him as his sister had. That's why he wanted to reach back into the past and refuse the last two of those four beers and reach out with his strong hand and grab his sister's ankle like an iron band and not let go.

The thing about being dead was, you really missed out. Shizuka had missed out on his success, such as it was, and never had gotten a chance to write another story or get one of her stories published. He'd never even read a word she'd written. The good thing, though, the good thing about being dead was you didn't worry about all of the stuff you missed out on. If he really had lost his wallet in the hospital, it wouldn't have mattered as long as he'd died. Having had a taste of Europe and America, having stuffed himself with croissants and calzones, he knew he'd never get another chance to see Europe and little chance to see the rest of the U.S. His CD list was at nearly seven hundred items, and there was a backlog of hundreds of things he'd never do, movies he'd never see, places he'd never go. He'd certainly never record another CD of his own. It was better, maybe, not to think about them, not to desire them, and the only way not to desire was to die.

* * *

IF HE DIED, he wouldn't have to think about how he hadn't grabbed his sister's ankle.

Or think about how he wouldn't even be *able* to grab it if she appeared in his room today.

He wouldn't have to think about his father, either. Not that his father blamed him, not exactly. When she became frozen at that restaurant a few years before, everyone in the family must have known something was wrong.

Everybody else in the family was a doctor.

And yet, what had they done for her? Hiroshi's uncle with his expensive silver MG, and his sons, and Hiroshi's mother's father and his brothers, all of them doctors. They had done nothing. They weren't specialists in psychological disorders, true, but they could have evaluated her, at least. They could have grabbed her ankles too, gotten her some kind of treatment, forced her not to enter the Pathway.

He had no memory of Shizuka ever being inside the walls of his uncle's clinic and that bothered him more than anything. He himself had rarely gone inside, except for his regular check-ups and the occasional judo injury or bicycle mishap, because of the smell – but why had it bothered him? Because that sterile, sour, bandagy odor smelled like apathy.

The clinic was always cool, though, even in the summer, and Hiroshi could remember as a little boy opening the clinic's mail slot so he could feel the cold metal on the inside of the slot against the tips of his fingers, an action that, at the same time, released a sterile gust of scent. He'd let the flap drop with a little *tink*, and run away.

But why, if everyone but his father had wanted him to be a doctor, hadn't he been pushed to go inside the clinic more often, just as he had been pushed to play with his toy stethoscope? But that wasn't the right question, that wasn't even an interesting question. The real question was, why hadn't his sister been forced to go to the clinic, or some other clinic, to get help?

Hiroshi closed his eyes and saw an image of a long line of patients waiting to get into the Mori Iin. He was there, as an adult, with a bandage on his forehead and a cane. So was his mother, with a stone-like expression from her scleroderma, and so was the woman with the huge port-wine stain. Everyone in the neighborhood was there except for his big sister, who was already dead.

When you were dead, you missed out on the bad stuff. You didn't have to squeeze rubber balls every day just so you could hang on with your fingers to a life that was bound to be disappointing anyway.

Just so you could click through a whole morning and afternoon of talk shows, courtroom confrontations, and soap operas. In the old days, the ticket takers at the train stations in Tokyo would click their little metal ticket-punchers all day long, hundreds or perhaps thousands of times an hour – during rush hour and even during the slack periods when there were no commuters coming through the wickets, the little clickers nipping at the air. It was easier, apparently, to keep on clicking continuously than to start and stop over and over again.

Hiroshi rolled over in bed and a cluster of hot ball bearings thudded against the side of his skull. He decided to try to lift himself out of bed to get a couple of Advils. If he were able to roll out of bed, he decided, he'd go on. If not, he'd just lie there and never get up again.

He pawed for a moment at the side of the bed with his hands. Both hands slid off the edge of the mattress simultaneously. He thought of his hands on that hot bumper, slippery with sweat, colliding with Shizuka's hands and the hands of those other two people whose car they'd helped push out of a ditch and who could barely be bothered to thank them afterwards.

As heavy as it was, it had only been a car, with no feelings in the matter, and there were four people back then and two little girls who'd looked on, laughing. Now he had no one to help.

He wished for a moment that his father were back again, reeking of brandy and Ballantyne's, wedged in behind him to push him out of bed. But why would he wish this, he thought, if he didn't think he wanted to get out of bed? Did he in fact want to get out of bed, or did he not?

He considered this question for a moment, but it was at once too momentous and too banal to resolve. *Either way, the dog will attack.* Then, because he wanted to distract himself from this slavering vision, he lowered his legs to the floor and found himself, almost without volition, standing on the floor.

Of course, he suddenly knew, his little bargain was absurd. He couldn't just lie there and never get up again. He'd starve to death, and that was a terrible way to go. Better to smack that miserable, misbegotten cur on the snout and see what happens next.

He padded to the bathroom and grabbed a fresh bottle of Advil but noticed, to his irritation, that unlike the other bottle, this one had a childproof cap.

He looked at the unopened bottle. How could he put these pills in his mouth after he'd used them to try to kill himself? Of course, for all the effect they'd had, he might as well have taken M&Ms.

He suddenly felt overwhelmed with resentment. Why hadn't Trudi called an ambulance? He understood what she'd said about the legal complications, but he'd clearly needed help. Why hadn't she at least recommended a doctor he could see? Sure, he didn't want to get caught up in the medical bureaucracy in New York City, but she could have done something more for him than just slap a bandage on one side of his forehead and kiss him on the other.

Maybe she was trying to get back at him for not calling a doctor when he discovered her injuries. But if she had wanted to get back at him, why had she shown up so quickly after her husband had called?

Hiroshi had lined up the arrow on the cap with the mark on the bottle. He didn't expect to be able to open it. But he pushed with both thumbs and the lid popped open with surprising ease. Hiroshi flexed his hands a few times, swallowed three Advil with a glass of water and, lacking anything better to do with the rest of the day, went out for a matinee so he could eliminate one of the movies on his list. Maybe, he decided, he could devote the rest of his life to seeing every movie ever made.

* * *

OVER THE NEXT FEW WEEKS, he established a regular schedule of work, movie-going and long walks up Fifth Avenue and in Central Park. He spoke on the phone with his father and Maureen, though he'd told neither about the suicide attempt, and even met with Grady a few times for drinks. He didn't drink otherwise.

* * *

THERE WAS AN EARLY, very wet snow in the second week of November, and Manhattan was blanketed. The snow fell all day Friday, and by the afternoon, as the temperature rose again to the low fifties, it had already begun to melt. At about eight-thirty a.m. on Saturday, Maureen called and invited Hiroshi for breakfast at Barney Greengrass on Amsterdam Avenue on the Upper West Side.

Hiroshi took a taxi there and found Maureen waiting outside. The day was sparkling. "Hey, Hero," she shouted as he approached. "Let's take a walk first. It's a little crowded in there."

She took his arm in hers – he'd decided to go without the cane today – and they walked down 86th Street to Central Park. Hiroshi felt as if they were a married couple. After they'd walked a while, in fact, he turned to her and said, "Why don't we get married, Maureen?"

She laughed. "Just what you need, marry a lez. Really, what're you going to do with yourself?"

"I don't know, Maureen, I can't move forward and I can't move backward. I'm stuck."

Maureen smiled. "I know."

A long silence ensued. Hiroshi, still with his arm in hers, broke it. "Now I think I would have preferred not to have been becoming then what I probably will have become a year from now until I had at least become what I had wanted to be at that time before then."

Maureen smiled again and said, again, "I know."

Hiroshi broke free from her grasp and bent over to make a snowball. "Look, my hands have really become strong." In fact, the icy and partly melted snow was so cold it drained the strength from his bare hands, but he still managed to make a chunky snowball.

Maureen pointed to a metal garbage can, an old oil drum, in the middle of the patchy grass. It was at least sixty yards away, in a part of the grass where all the snow had melted.

"Hey, Hero, see if you can get that snowball into that can."

"I don't think that's possible." Hiroshi had been a decent baseball player in high school, a shortstop, and his arm had been pretty good before the illness. But the oil drum was so far away, it looked to be the size of the nail on his little finger.

Nonetheless, he wound up to throw, but could tell immediately that he didn't have the strength to get the snowball anywhere near the oil drum. The icy ball was burning his hand, but rather than drop it, he'd decided to try an under-hand throw.

He spread his legs to brace himself and pulled his arm back as far as it would go. Then he flung the snowball into the air, hopping a bit, and then stumbling with the effort.

Maureen looked up at the sky, then down at the oil drum in the distance. "I think I lost it," she said.

"Forget it. I don't think it went anywhere near the garbage can."

She grabbed his arm. "C'mon, let's look anyway. There's no snow around it, so it should be easy to see where it landed."

They walked across the grass. There wasn't a splotch of snow anywhere around the can. Hiroshi was beginning to think the snowball had merely disintegrated in the air but nonetheless, with growing excitement, approached the can.

He and Maureen peered over the edge. There, along the inside wall, was a streak of icy snow and, at the bottom, which was otherwise empty, a half-smashed snowball.

It had hit almost dead center. Hiroshi stood there, unwilling to move, as Maureen shrieked with delight.

It was the greatest single moment of his life.

* * *

THAT EVENING, he lay in bed, thinking about nothing in particular. He was getting sick of being in the Gramercy West Hotel, sick of being in bed.

His sister had lain there for twelve, thirteen hours before Hiroshi had found her. She was still alive when he came across her on the floor of the abandoned store. She was lying on her back. Her lips were cracked and swollen, and there was a dry white substance on her upper lip.

She was breathing shallowly and her eyes were glassy.

She had taken a bottleful of pills.

She had done what Hiroshi had wanted to do.

She had succeeded where Hiroshi had failed, and failed where he'd succeeded.

It was an incredible thing to witness, to hear, to smell, to feel against the back of your hand, a person's last breath. She had taken in and expelled millions of breaths in her life, and her heart had beaten without interruption, without failure, millions of times. Of all of these times, there was only one first time, and then there was only one last time.

Hiroshi had run as fast as he could to the house nearest the Pathway and called the police. Then he'd run back and found her still breathing.

It was almost as if she'd been waiting for him. Waiting all

day – for someone, he assumed, if not necessarily for him – since early in the morning when she'd flown past him.

Waiting for him to get back to her after sprinting to the neighbor's house to call the police.

He'd missed her first breath but he didn't miss the last; she died before the police arrived. She said almost nothing in the time she had left except for "gomenasai" – "I'm sorry" – and "akichatta no yo."

"Akichatta no yo" meant "I'm bored." But it was rather odd. It was the kind of thing you'd say if you were bored by a movie, or by an idle afternoon at home, not when you were very near death.

He'd thought about it from time to time afterwards. It filled him with horror to think that she'd been referring to the long day she'd spent in the shack, drifting in and out of consciousness, while she waited for Hiroshi or someone else to find her.

But the alternative meaning was even worse.

Hiroshi fell asleep very late that evening. He slept late on Monday morning, right through his alarm, and woke up in a panic. He was due at the Nature Company in less than an hour. He quickly got dressed and then, before leaving, picked up his original clarinet case. It felt surprisingly light, a sign, he assumed, of his growing strength.

He walked to the Nature Company and arrived a few minutes early. He didn't feel quite like going in, so he leaned against the wall of the shop next door, and opened the case. A very hard chocolate éclair fell out and tumbled into the gutter.

He had grabbed the wrong case.

He stared at the petrified éclair in the gutter for a moment. Then he hailed a taxi, took it back to the hotel, and asked the driver to wait. He picked up the correct case containing the regular Regent clarinet, the only one he had left, scrambled back into the taxi, and went back to the Nature Company.

Now he was quite late. His manager and several other employees all stood at the window and stared at Hiroshi as he took out his Regent, laid the case on the sidewalk, and worked his fingers across the stops. He thanked himself silently for his foresight in not having disassembled it, because he probably wouldn't be able to put it back together now. The reed was probably no good, but he didn't care.

A passerby dropped a couple of quarters in the case. Hiroshi stooped down, picked them out of the case, and returned them to the man.

Everything was trembling — his lips, his fingers, his legs. He nodded once at the people gathered at the window, ran through *"Chorando Baixinho"* in his mind for a moment, and, seeing in an instant the composition whole and complete, began to play.

Afterword

WHIPPED BUT NOT BEATEN

"There's a lot of things swimming within every human being, so many things swimming that we don't see." — David Lynch

During the entirety of the two-and-a-half years I lived in Japan, I was convinced that one day I would write a novel about my experience of that land. Not a novel of Japan itself, because I was hardly qualified to write about that country, being a gaijin — literally, "outside person" — and, even at the end of my stay, speaking the Japanese language at barely the level of a kindergartener. (Indeed, my wife and I had a conversation with two kindergarteners who lived next door to us, and one of them said, in Japanese, "Why do you guys talk so funny?")

Nor was I qualified to write about the Japanese "people," whatever that means, because I strongly dislike tribalism and gross racial or ethnic generalizations, and prefer to consider people first and foremost as individuals, *sui generis* and irreplicable.

Nor did I want to write a self-deprecating comic novel about the fumblings of a gaijin like myself in a strange land, not that I didn't have an abundance of such embarrassments to choose from.

But it was, I thought, a tired genre.

We lived at first in Toyokawa, a small town near Nagoya in central Japan, and, more specifically, in a tiny neighborhood in that town called Ushikubo, which means "cow in a hole," named in honor of a long-ago cow that, well, fell in a hole and broke its leg. The residents supposedly had a barbecue feast on the spot, and the name stuck.

Later on, we moved to the western part of Japan, and lived in an apartment complex on the outskirts of Okayama with rice fields on either side of us. We'd often find tiny frogs gathered at our front door, chirruping as if they wished to be let in. They were almost identical in color to the young rice shoots they lived among, a lovely pale green, though the frogs were jittery and loud and the stalks were silent in the moonlight.

I wanted to write about both of these places, and the little-known Japan they both represented, and yet I wanted to write about something universal as well, something that wouldn't require a reader to have any special interest in, or knowledge of, Japan.

It took me ten years to figure out what I wanted to write.

Those ten years were well-spent because, all along, the little wheels were spinning in the background. As a long-time book reviewer and literary critic, I have encountered far too many novels over the years that didn't seem to know what they were about, and that were written not because the author wanted to write a novel, but rather because they wanted to have written one.

A subtle distinction, but a crucial one.

I was willing to wait as long as it took until I had something I had to write about. During that ten-year period, two revelatory incidents occurred, one seemingly insignificant and the other deeply upsetting.

The insignificant one first. We had invited a newly married young Japanese couple we had befriended in Okayama to visit us in Chicago and took them to see all the sights. It was their honeymoon. The husband was physically slight, but during the visit he had an enormous appetite, something that struck us as unusual, because we had often gone out to dinner with them in Japan, and his appetite had been normal.

We went out to a nice Italian restaurant on their last night in the U.S., and he ordered two appetizers, an entree, and a dessert. When we were done and waiting for the check, he asked to see the menu again, found a kind of Italian sausage he'd never had, and looked stricken that he hadn't noticed it before. Very apologetically, he ordered that as well, and, while the rest of us sipped our coffees, consumed it slowly with a grim determination mingled with ecstatic satisfaction.

He was neither greedy nor gluttonous. He was just afraid of missing out on something. He clearly had a hole inside of him that he was trying to fill, and that would, I surmised, never be filled. This was obvious throughout his and his wife's trip to Chicago, where he displayed a nervous irritability and guileless excitement about everything he saw, and equally great disappointment about everything he missed.

I did not know him well enough to speculate on what might have created that hole, but I knew that he must have one, for I had one too, and had often behaved, in different contexts, much as he did.

Not long after that, my wife and I took a trip to the Galápagos Islands, and on the very day of our return, we received an urgent message that my father, who had been painting landscapes, portraits and nudes for every day of his retirement, had just been stricken with a rare neurological disorder called Guillain Barré Syndrome (GBS) and was temporarily paralyzed from the neck down.

Nearly instantaneously, within minutes after departing from my first visit to my father's bedside, the theme I had long searched for hit me like a clap of thunder: What happens when a person who is driven to experience everything suddenly cannot experience anything?

Does the hole inside of him grow steadily larger?

Yes.

Or does he find himself forced, for the first time in his life, to confront the traumatic cause of that gaping, gnawing hole and attempt, at last, to repair it?

Also yes.

This is the situation facing the protagonist of Cherry Whip, an exceptionally talented young jazz musician named Hiroshi, visiting New York on his first tour of the U.S., who is obsessed with new sensations and new experiences. (The title, a reference to a cherry-flavored chocolate bar, symbolizes his insatiable, childlike avidity.) He is an almost alarmingly alive young man; early on in the novel, confronted with an ambiguous sexual situation, he experiences no fewer than seventeen different emotions simultaneously.

But then, just as my father was, Hiroshi is stricken with Guillain Barré Syndrome. In the barren stillness of a New York hospital bed, thousands of miles away from home, with little else to occupy his mind, he is forced to come to terms with something terrible that happened many years before to his physically and emotionally fragile older sister at the end of a tangled, only half-real passage through the countryside she called her "Secret Pathway," in the little town where they lived.

That town, of course, is an amalgam of Ushikubo and Okayama.

And the hole, of course — which, crucially, he has no idea even exists — was created by his long-buried guilt about not following his sister down her secret pathway and doing more to help her in her moment of extremity, as well as by his refusal to follow another, more conventional path dictated by the rest of his family, nearly all of whom are in the medical profession.

Hiroshi is no innocent — he lives the high life in Tokyo, is not unacquainted with drug culture, is on the road to achieving greatness as a jazz musician, and his father is a famous Zen poet — but the very last thing many of us learn about in this lifetime is ourselves, who we are and what motivates us. Brilliantly talented musician that he is, alive to sensation as he is, Hiroshi nonetheless focuses less on his art or on its genesis in the limitless human soul than on distractions and irrelevancies, overthinking trivial occurrences to a comical degree while stumbling blindly past anything that actually matters.

He was asleep all of the time he was awake, and becomes awake only when, by dint of painful circumstance, he is forced into a kind of long-term sleep.

Hiroshi's journey to self knowledge takes place primarily in New York, a city I know well from countless business and personal trips I have taken there over the years. Though Hiroshi revisits small-town Japan in his memory, it is New York that brings him down, baffles him, and defeats him, and yet at the same time fascinates him, energizes him, and brings him back to life, so that his blood feels "carbonated." Thus, I ended up writing a novel not about Japan or "the Japanese people," but about one very particular Japanese person, and the highly specific versions of New York and Japan he sees through his acute and intensely curious eyes.

One of my literary agents years ago expressed concern that my books were too focused on psychology, on my protagonists' struggles with their own psyches, pasts, and subjective perceptions. I suppose he wanted me to write a detective story, or a fantasy about a medieval world. It is true that my characters slay no dragons, only their own demons. But then dragons don't actually exist, whereas inner demons are as common as lungs and guts and hearts.

Nonetheless, my agent was correct. In my literarily perverse fashion, I had written a novel that seemingly had everything going against it — no bad guys, no shoot-outs, no grand romances or bloody conflicts. I won't pretend that, back then, it sold a great many copies.

But something in Cherry Whip must have struck an emotional chord in its readers, perhaps because it's the story of one young person's belated discovery of who he is, and the reason he was put on earth. And that is a story every one of us has lived, or — perhaps more to the point — needs to live but as yet has not.

The story behind this novel is, for me, a gratifying one. My father lived long enough to read it. (He also was able to go back to painting after his recovery.) After a near-miss with Random House — it was accepted for publication by one editor, who later was overruled by her boss — it found a congenial home with a small boutique publisher called ENC Press, and stayed in print for nearly 20 years before ENC closed its doors.

But then, by some miracle, Cherry Whip was discovered by a new publisher called Donovan Street Press. It is difficult enough to write a novel, and — as nearly every novelist will attest — still harder to promote it and keep it alive and breathing through the years. So I consider it an astonishing gift that it is being republished in this 20th Anniversary edition. I hope that as new readers discover it, it will help some among them to discover themselves as well — just as poor Hiroshi, whipped but not beaten, manages to do, and I myself, nearly too late but not too late, and after a lifetime of trial and error, have also done.

There is no greater joy in art, I believe, than in attempting to inhabit, understand and recreate the mental processes of a fellow human being, and to then have still other human beings read your work and gain a greater understanding of one of their fellow inhabitants of this planet. That — well, plus a cracking good story, of course — is the very purpose of writing fiction, and of reading it.

I am deeply grateful to my fellow novelist Mark Rayner for championing Cherry Whip, and for Joe Mahoney from Donovan Street Press for bringing Cherry Whip back for a new generation of readers. There were others along the way who have helped me or offered insight and encouragement, and I list them in the acknowledgments. My Italian sausage-loving friend from Okayama? I have long since forgotten his name, but I hope that, wherever he is, he has found whatever it was that he might have been missing.